Meryl McQueen is a novelist, poet, sociolinguist, nonprofit program developer, and citizen scientist who loves astronomy, ecology, and evolutionary biology. She has lived on four continents and is currently a tree-hugging Seattleite. Several of her other novels including *A Stranger's Map*, *Only Salt Remains*, *Velvet Corner Blue*, *A Close Approximation of an Ordinary Life*, and *The Slavery of Flight* are also available on Amazon.

I0543636

Meryl McQueen

The Solitude of Broken Glass

Indigo Falls Press

ISBN 978-0-9806670-7-3

For all of us with miles to go

Cape Cod (September 2018)

Either someone drowned, or they didn't. There was a 'someone,' or wasn't. Either there were arms rigid with surprise above the white froth, mouth sucking air, water, air again, or there weren't. It was a man or a boy, a girl or woman, or it wasn't. Either there were unsummoned tears of absence, near or distant, or there weren't. Yes or no, over and over like the march of conscripts' boots on a field turned to mines and to mud.

Diane Howard rolled up her loose, paint-smeared corduroys and kicked off her leather sandals. She stretched toothpick-thin arms above her head, knuckles cracking as she flexed her hands. Pausing, her mouth half-open to catch the scents of the ocean in early fall on Cape Cod's northeastern shore, the middle-aged woman half-closed her eyes against the swirl of gathering wind. The air tasted like fresh dirt and seaweed, dark and sweet before the thunderstorm that sulked on the horizon.

From her vantage point at the top of the steep dunes, Diane scanned the scene. She moved side-to-side from the waist, her body fluid except for a tug-and-hitch on her left side as she swept across. Her feet planted in a circle of sand ringed by waves of brown and yellow grass, Diane held her position thirty feet above the sea and a hundred feet from the rising tide. She murmured the inventory of the beach she claimed as home to her unreconstructed heart.

"Shipwreck, rowboat. Scalloped shellfish fringe at the high tide line." Without another step toward the weathered boardwalk and planks that led down to the sand, Diane swallowed the sea, taking in each ripple in the water and every foaming crest of the uneasy Atlantic surf.

Out of long habit, she fingered the small sketch pad that lined up straight with a soft lead pencil in her back pocket. Her blunt-cut nails tapped the reassuring paper, drumming a riff as her eyes narrowed. The curve of the promontory sloped away to the left, dunes sliding into the uneasy water like abandoned cities under the weight of erosion and decay.

Diane curled her hand around the notebook and gripped the pencil with her left hand. Without taking her eyes off the sea, she held up her palm-sized canvas until it was level with the bridge of her nose.

This week, it was waves. Diane's hard-fought artistry was in the elementals, miniature landscapes of earth and ocean. Without a natural artist's intention or point of view, with everything about her creations culled and carved in exhausting increments of improvement, the process dictated the product in a way that mimicked all the structure of where she had been instead of reflecting where she found herself in the moment.

Everything smaller than life. Contained, controlled. Beneath the constrained view, beyond the two dozen she sold every summer through a local souvenir shop, lay two decades of relentless discovery and discipline. The flow of natural talent was not hers to follow; Diane had to analyze angles and assess mental grids across the rough welcome of the paper. Her color sense relied on other people's wheels and piles of books, rather than any internal plumb line. There had been a compass, once, and the promise of more. But now the promise lay in the rhythm, in the routine of sight to sketch. Diane could not see beyond the horizon, because her horizons in this watery confinement were short, marked, and meaningless.

This was her ritual, her self-imposed meditation. Diane was not seeking enlightenment. She knew the dark better than she knew the curve of her own elbow or the incongruous flecks of black in her light blue eyes. Nonetheless, the sun rose, the days followed one another with ridiculous regularity. She sculpted a life from the inane repetition. A week of waves, a week of grass, a week of sky. For practice, a week of boats and birds, though neither ever featured in her completed projects. This week, it was waves.

The trick was never to look down. Diane stared over the page through the top third of her frameless progressives, willing her sight to focus on the wet mass below. Her fingers held the pencil like a calligraphy brush, stroking the blank sheet. Color might come later, water or ink or oil—texture too, with gel medium's layered impasto or sand's inviting grit—but in the beginning the pictures were always black.

Two hundred yards offshore, the crest of a three-foot wave collided with another racing whitecap, sending spray fifteen feet into the air. As the water splashed back to the surface, Diane's eyes traced the arc. Her gaze flickered, and she blinked hard, jutting her chin forward in concentration. As the water crashed down, the wind picked up, blowing sand along the beach towards the dune. Diane squinted, her hand moving faster as she followed the motion of the water.

Within two minutes, the early fall breeze became a hint of ragged winter, tugging at Diane's careless ponytail and reminding her to leave an extra sweater in the car. She turned away to shield her face from the invisible debris. Her eyes moved from their fixed point of reference on the horizon and Diane's head jerked back.

Nothing. Nothing to see, nothing to save. Stiff-legged, she took three steps down and scurry-hopped up to regain the higher ground of her vantage point. The waves smashed together like scattering atoms, but all was water and air. *No flash of orange shirt against the slate sea, no pumping fists.* The insides of Diane's ears tingled as she strained for sound. *A seagull screeching. Wind in the grass.* The air gathered force around her. Diane coughed and covered her mouth her sleeve, angling away from the water. *Something.*

She had left her phone in the glove compartment of the battered hatchback in the parking lot a few dunes over. Shoving her feet back into her shoes, she headed down the hill in a determined, hobbling sprint. Diane wrenched open the car door and dialed 9-1-1.

"What is the nature of your emergency?" The voice

on the other end sounded calm to the point of bored.

"I'm at Morgan Crescent, out by the beach. I think I saw—" Diane paused, trying to parse the motes of incongruent shape and flash into a suitable offering of urgent need.

"Ma'am, is someone injured?" The woman's voice settled into brusque efficiency. "Are you hurt?"

"There was a person—" Diane trailed off, her eyes half-closed but still trained on the restless ocean. She felt the vertigo of ambiguity and reached for her pencil, rubbing the tip with a nail. "No," she said, more to herself than to the voice on the other end.

"Someone in trouble?" The leading questions ticked down the page until they landed on a likely scene. "Accident? Fall? Someone in the water."

The temperature had dropped at least fifteen degrees since Diane's arrival an hour before. The thunderstorm that had crowded the edges of the sky at first light gathered its breath and rumbled low enough for Diane to feel instead of to hear the sound. She shivered, nodding twice before remembering that the ghost in the receiver could not see her. "Someone," she says softly.

The operator has already made her decision. "I'll have a squad car out there in under five minutes. Wait with your vehicle, Ms.—"

"Howard," said the middle-aged artist with little enough hesitation to surprise herself. Maybe she was finally becoming that stranger whose clothes she wore, whose wispy hair she tucked into flyaway ponytails, and whose tiny pictures she sold to summer tourists from Boston or New York. "Diane Howard."

Diane timed him with her steady heart. It was three and half minutes. The cop was Brendan Calloway, of the Trisham Calloways. Diane had known him since he and his older three brothers got caught stealing pumpkins off her porch while they were supposed to be trick-or-treating with the other elementary school kids. Every year, it was something: trees swathed in toilet paper, uneven circles of fire in the grass out by her shed. Living alone in that four-bedroom Tudor on First and Ashworth, what could she expect? She never appeared in a pew, never showed up at the firehouse pancake breakfast, never waved a flag on the sidewalk at the Fourth of July parade, never answered the door to the Girl Scouts. Everyone knew who she was, sure enough, but even most of the adults hissed under their breath and shook their heads after she walked past them on the street.

When she saw Brendan uncurl his six-foot six frame from the driver's seat, Diane knew that every word out of her mouth would be a pebble in the slingshot of town gossip.

"Ms. Howard," said the young man, flicking the brim of his hat. Brendan chewed his cheek and studied her.

Diane said the words fast, too fast to take them back. "In the water. Waving. Drowning. There, past the wreck."

"Diver, maybe." Brendan worked his jaw side to

side, raising one eyebrow. Everyone in Broadwell knew Diane Howard was a wash-ashore nut job, with her empty house and her weekly food deliveries and the fact that she somehow sold those ridiculous four-by-four-inch squares of painted cardboard. Common wisdom in town was that only the idiots who swanned in for the flicker of warmth, June through September, were dumb enough to hand over cash for something you could hardly see. Twenty-four-year-old Brendan had never seen a reason to doubt his community's assessment of the limping, sloppy woman standing in front of him with her hands held out like church on Sunday. He saw no reason now.

"Probably couldn't see the boat for the swell, but it'd be there waiting to pick up whoever it was you think was in the water." Brendan ground the sand with the rubber heel of his left shoe and fought the urge to spit on the ground. "Always a few dipshit tourists thinking they can outrun a storm come summer's end."

Trying to rewind the few seconds of footage in her head, Diane caught glimpses again of arms overhead, of orange too bright to be anything that belonged on the swarming surface. "I thought Doc's was the last dive shop to close for the season last week. Could be someone who doesn't know the currents."

Risking a glance at the barely-grown boy's stubbled face, Diane knew she had lost him. Knew it before she made the phone call, even, that there would be no one to ask the right questions or listen to the half-answers she could give.

Happening again. He doesn't believe me. They never do.

"Thought you said he was wearing a shirt." Brendan's heel-tapping got louder, more insistent.

"Might have been a wetsuit with safety stripes." Diane struggled to hold the mental image still. "Water's cold enough for it already this year, especially for a long swim."

"Sure, Ms. Howard." Brendan drawled out the acquiescence like a sympathetic passerby patting a stray dog on the head. "But let's try to think logically, okay? No car, miles from town, nothing on the beach down there that says a person went in the ocean."

Pressing her thumb into the ache of her left hip, Diane sighed and stared beyond his elbow to the sea below. Brendan shrugged, relenting. "I'll check it out. Keep an ear open. Who knows, maybe they swam out of sight around the rocks. It's been called in, anyhow."

She wanted to acknowledge his attempt at a facsimile of kindness. Brendan had never been a bad kid. None of them had been, despite their pranks and their persistence, their long-resisted attempts to find out who she was beyond the shuttered house. She wanted him to be right, with his youthful self-assurance. She wanted him to know what he was talking about, with his borderline smug frown and his fresh uniform and his over-shined shoes. She wanted a lot of things, but all she could hear was a mouth wide open, and all she could see were the waves.

Diane watched his concern evaporate. *The hell with this, he's not even listening.* "Leave it with us, Ms. Howard. We'll see if something—someone—rolls up onto the beach in the next day or two."

He glanced at the waves. "Whatever or whoever it was, too late now." Brendan pressed his point. "You thought there was someone out there, you should have called us sooner."

Diane propped herself against the railing for two hours after the cop pulled away. Her fingers twisted around the pencil. She scratched her notepad with agitated insistence. The page threw up waves: waves, and nothing more.

Brooklyn (April 1990)

The gallery had been a chop shop in another life. Surrounded by the rapid gentrification of a neighborhood more used to car chases than vodka chasers, the display space was comfortably flanked by coffee houses with open mic poetry nights and vintage clothing boutiques. A zigzagged neon yellow arrow and flashing 'OPEN' sign had been hoisted on a temporary flagpole on the sidewalk, along with a hand-inked sign with 'This Way Up Fine Art & Community' written in bubble script. The polished cement floor and fluorescent spotlights made the storefront twice as bright as any other on the block, and in the approaching twilight the gallery glowed. Chattering already spilled into the street.

Lydia McCray climbed the stairs from the subway, turning left away from the crowd for her four-block stroll home (always through the park, for the trees and the green and the relative quiet) to her apartment. She walked fast, a tall woman with long strides, her narrow tailored dark suit accented with spiky purple hair, dangling silver Celtic knot earrings, and a polka-dotted lavender pocket square. The noise behind her swelled, laughter indistinct from the traffic that slowed as rubberneckers took their time trying to get a glimpse of who might already be inside the gallery's premiere.

Art galleries were not her thing. Movies—new, fast,

and loud—and motorcycles—old, fast, and loud—were her thing. Engines and structural teams and troubleshooting mechanical engineering systems were her thing. Large groups of people were not her thing. In fact, social occasions of any sort apart from increasingly rare, inevitably half-hearted one-night stands were not her thing.

She had planned another night in. Popcorn, cup-o-soup, strawberry creamsicle. *Happy 30th birthday. Another year, another promotion, another four projects up and running.*

Lydia didn't believe in self-pity—she believed in getting on with it. Her early twenties had come and gone with a brief marriage to a man and enough one-night stands with men and women to last a lifetime, combined with a self-propelled career path that found her already near the top in her large firm. Business travel and long hours were part of the game, but Lydia found herself anticipating to the celebratory solitude.

Nonetheless, in the next quarter block, her steps slowed. *What the hell.* She ran a sweaty hand through her hair, paused under a lamppost to swipe on another coat of carmine lipstick, and wound up at the back of the throng. It was an odd mix. Curious locals in a rainbow of style and flair huddled with a pack of recent college grads who had to be in advertising or graphic design. Off to the side, a group of older women dressed for a charity auction muttered into their scarves.

At five-ten, Lydia McCray could see over enough heads into the gallery. She stretched her neck, wondering what all the commotion might be condemning or condoning. The space was small and carried about a dozen huge pictures hung frameless on starched white walls. Although the dripping original glass on the roll-up entrance distorted the scene, Lydia was left with images of bright curves and unexpected projections, abstracts that would have reminded her of Delaunay if she knew anything of epoch or art.

As Lydia stood waiting, she tuned in to the conversations around her. The cadences were distinct, but the effect of the words was a river of anticipation and excitement. Lydia picked up half-conversations that sped up as the minutes crept by.

"...there's no poster, shouldn't there be a poster? Are you sure it's her, sure it's tonight?"

"...read about in the paper, everyone's saying that she..."

"...Stella told Dave to meet us here, did you know he picked up one of her sketches last year for next to nothing? Must be worth something now, I tell you that. Lucky son of a..."

"...left work early for this? We'll never get in, can't you see they're checking a list at the door, why can't we ever..."

"...what time is this even on? Ed will be home by eight, I told him I would..."

"...disgusting, I'm telling you. You only have to see one or two, how she..."

If Lydia had passed by the gallery that morning—if

her route had carried her along that patch of commercial activity, she might have glanced over and seen the announcement:

> By Invitation Only:
> Gallery Opening 7-10 p.m.
> Amanda Marquez
> 'Collective Conscience: A Prospective"
> Inquire within for details

As it was, some unthinking soul had pasted it to the outside of the window, and that announcement was folded in half and tucked under the saddle brown cashmere coat of a grandmother of six who ran the largest medical foundation in New York City and baked enviable lemon bars for her monthly book club. That woman was not in the crowd any longer; she had come for treasure, and torn it from the window, and was content to lie about how much of the art she had seen while waving around proof in the poster.

Lydia had not seen the advertisement, and if she had, she would have forgotten it at the next crosswalk. But she was here now, drawn by the noise and the coincidence of her birthday, and she had nowhere to be in a hurry. She stood around, watching the crowd, stepping further back toward the street as the numbers grew and the clock edged onwards.

She was standing directly in front of the doorway, twelve back from the glass, when a car honked, and two black-clad curators scurried out of the gallery. The older one tried to hold up her hands as if to quiet the crowd, but all eyes jumped to the woman who got out of the cab. She was short—barely five-two—and Lydia's first impression left her wondering how someone so small could pile such a stacked deck of straight ginger hair in a pyramidal extravaganza on top of her head. From her height, Lydia could see dozens of bronze bobby pins, sticking up at angles like a postmodern birthday cake. Despite the stubborn chill of an early April evening, the artist wore a short denim romper with lightning bolt tights and an ornately embroidered sleeveless vest. The turquoise brocade competed with the hair for precedence, and costume jewelry crowded every finger on both hands.

The new arrival slammed the door behind her and planted both feet on the sidewalk. Lydia had turned one hundred eighty degrees to see and was only a few steps away from the taxi as the mob pressed against her, splitting the difference between them until the space disappeared.

She was close enough touch this unknown celebrity, this mysterious artist who took up so many people's words and so much of their attention. Close enough to feel the unexpected *whoosh!* of air and hear the hinges squeak as the car door closed with force.

Reacting to the thud, Lydia blinked and jumped. At the same instant, the woman glanced upward at the statuesque sentry with an expensive suit and critical stare. The artist recognized how the woman cringed at the jostling mass and felt a shared rush of rising anxiety.

"She's with me!" The stranger took Lydia's hand and pulled her through the shoal of people. Lydia was not sure whether she wanted to let go or hang on; in the end, she figured that her life had suddenly become a game of 'Anywhere But Here,' and she was willing to trade whatever lay beyond the glass roller door for the insistent press of the people outside.

The bouncers stepped aside and held the door as they trotted through. Inside, Lydia retrieved her hand and stopped.

"Come on!" The instigator of their escape beckoned her to the far corner of the gallery, where three bamboo room dividers concealed two trestle tables with a plugged-in warming tray and a makeshift bar.

Out of sight, out of mind. Lydia recalibrated her thoughts. *Out of my mind, more like. Strangest. Birthday. Ever.*

"Won't be long now." The stranger was panting, but after a minute she recovered enough to introduce herself. "Amanda. Thanks for that. I'm guessing we've got about six or seven minutes to hide out here before the muscle at the door starts checking names off and the gallery intern starts scribbling name tags. After that I'm on for about two hours until we can sneak out the back."

Strangest, sure. But not worst, not by a long shot. The tall woman blinked twice before remembering her own name. "Lydia. So tell me, Amanda, do you always take hostages on your way to an event starring…you?"

Amanda peeked around the side of the partition and gave Lydia a rapid-fire grin that shifted into a good-natured smirk. "You are free to walk out of here anytime you like, Lydia. In fact, I insist. The minute you're not having the time of your life, cut me loose, okay? I couldn't stand to see you bored or disappointed."

They watched either other carefully. Lydia already knew this was not a typical date. From the look on Amanda's face, she did too.

"Wine." Amanda shimmied the cork from an open bottle of red and turned over two glasses. "Wine, food, good company: what else do you need?"

Lydia realized she had begun to enjoy herself, and she ventured her own version of their first toast. "To mob mentality, which brought us together."

Amanda picked it up and carried it further. "Cheers to that, babe. May it never tear us apart." They both smiled into their drinks and found the sentiments of each wish both more accurate and less unnerving than they should have been.

The kitchenette off the back of the gallery was as crowded as the streetscape. It seemed that way to Lydia, until she realized that there were only three servers, and it was the cramped hutch that made the air feel tight. She craned her neck, grateful for the height, and concentrated on the snacks. Trays of bite-sized morsels—olives, baguette rounds spread with what Lydia assumed to be caviar, spring rolls, samosas, deviled eggs—disguised the appliances, clogged the sink, and lined the floor.

Amanda mistook Lydia's bewilderment for hunger. Tearing the plastic wrap, she grabbed three spring rolls off the tray that was balanced on the mini-fridge and dipped them chunky orange sauce.

"Mango chutney," Amanda swallowed and considered another bite. "Delicious." She dipped the second spring roll and held it up to Lydia's mouth. "Mind-blowing."

As a rule, with the exception of pre-sliced birthday cake and ice cream straight from the tub, Lydia did not share food. She was never one to reach across with an empty fork and an open request, and she would rarely offer a dinner companion access to her plate across the table. Although she did not know why, Lydia felt Amanda's offer fell into a different category altogether; it spoke of intimacy candidly established, of shared routines and mutual agreement. Lucy took that bite from Amanda, and another.

"I need a decoy."

Lydia gawked. "Don't think I could pass for you at the circus, let alone in this crowd. And I saw at least two of your fan club who were not on the invitation list standing out there with binoculars. Besides, I'm not thrilled with the idea of being your duck and cover."

Amanda squeezed Lydia's hand and dragged her out of sight behind one of the hung panels that separated the single gallery space into giants' office cubicles. "It's not about anyone thinking you're me. It's about everyone watching the gorgeous, purple-spangled goddess walk by while I slip out the back. They'll be so busy wondering who you are, they'll completely forget about me. My new girlfriend, guaranteed to be water cooler gossip at the hottest creative agencies and the country club by noon tomorrow. Misdirection, diversion. Get it?"

Lydia glanced at her. "So I'm your ersatz girlfriend?"

Amanda twisted her mouth. "That word, ersatz? I do not think it means what you think it means. How about we go with girlfriend and see where that takes us?"

"I'm the next young thing, don't you know?" Amanda stroked Lydia's palm without glancing down. "All the rage at tea parties on the Upper West Side. I hear my art makes the old ladies blush and buy."

Leaving her hand where it was, Lydia said, "Sounds like a winning combination."

"My agent reads the reviews that say I have 'broad appeal.' That's code for 'doesn't matter how the hell old you are, a Marquez on the wall means you've made it. He says the art works because I am, and I quote, 'both revolutionary and collectible.'"

Amanda's derision floated across her face in wriggling eyebrows and a toothy, apologetic grin. "But he's earning ten percent commission on everything that's got a red dot on it tonight, so my guess is that he slept with someone at the paper and he writes the reviews himself."

Lydia scanned the rom. At least two-thirds of the pieces already had small red dots on the lower right corner, and both curators were in earnest conversation with more likely buyers.

"Okay, new plan." Amanda shrugged. "You don't want to be me, we'll both make a run for it."

Laughing, Lydia drew an imaginary horizontal line

from the crown of her head into the air above Amanda's mountain of hair. "What's that they say? If a lion's in hot pursuit, all you need to be able to do is run faster than the next guy? I'm dead sure I've got it all over you in that department."

"Low. Height jokes? You gotta do better than that." Amanda mocked-stabbed herself in the heart. "Besides, babe, listen to yourself. 'Hot pursuit?' 'All over you?' We both want to end up in exactly the same place tonight, and now it's a question of how long it takes us to get there."

Lydia covered her mouth as her nervous laugh turned to a shared giggle. They doubled over, holding on to each other for support and waving away concerned offers of water from both curators and three nearby guests.

Amanda straightened up first and frowned. "Sorry babe, got to mingle. Give me ten minutes to do the smile-and-nod-like-a-puppet with the critics my agent told me I had to talk to? You can huddle in the kitchen with the cheese puffs and mimosas."

Lydia nodded. "It's work, I get it."

"Work?" Amanda twirled like an excited child, her arms outstretched, fingers brushing Lydia's hips as she turned. "This is sheer joy."

After Amanda left, Lydia stared at one of the canvasses until the shapes moved across her mind's eye like oil spills on rough ocean. She turned away, suddenly seasick from the lights and the laughter and the woman across the room who talked with her hands. *Soft, warm hands.*

Ten minutes eased into fifteen. Twenty. Amanda swiveled her head, knowing Lydia would be watching. Lydia grinned back, snagged three more cheese puffs from a roving tray, and swigged champagne.

Grumbling, Amanda finally peeled herself away from her agent and the next round of interviews before skipping across the brushed concrete floor and leaning theatrically against the wall, lax fingers draped across her forehead. "Celebrity's exhausting!"

She winked and held one of Lydia's hands in both of hers. "Miss me?"

"I have to ask." Lydia avoided the question and instead tried to see her next sentence in her mind, a long ribbon of words that fit together more awkwardly the longer they took to get out. "I'm standing here trying to see it, but I have to ask."

A moment passed. Amanda held Lydia's hand tighter. "As long as it's not 'what is it?' you can ask me anything you like."

Her voice was warm, and her grin did not waver. "Too soon in our relationship for ground rules? Or is my fuzzy art already a deal breaker?"

Lydia felt how much Amanda wanted her approval, but she did not want to offer a forced whisper when everything else about this woman made her want to shout out loud. As they stood side-by-side, Lydia scrabbled to think of something worthwhile to say about the blotches of blue and green. *Aliens on speed.* Before her mind could prevent her mouth, she blurted, "You know, it's my birthday."

Amanda spun on one heel and slapped her on the arm. "Bullshit!"

"Nope. True as true." She raised her glass. "Thirty." The number sounded more like a question than a confirmation; Lydia swigged the rest of the champagne and tried again. "Technically since five-fifteen this morning. My mother always said I kept her up all night."

The last disclosure came with an apologetic step backwards and downcast eyes. Lydia had not intended to bring her parents into this, whatever this was. Even dead and gone, her mother and father were too close to misery to bring to any party, let alone one where the woman of the hour had chosen to take Lydia along for the ride.

Amanda felt the mood shift, but she held them in the space meant for light by one-upping whatever Lydia's story pasted over. Rolling her eyes, she said, "Please. Half of Arizona knows the story of me arriving in the hospital parking lot two weeks late, after my mom had four months on bedrest. To hear her tell it, she spent forty years in the wilderness giving birth to me."

The story was not funny enough to make Lydia laugh out loud, but Amanda's attempt elicited a slashed smile.

Whispering into her drink, Amanda held Lydia's gaze. "They're people."

"What?" Lydia rubbernecked. "Of course they're people—though with people that guy over there in the half-zipped gold tone parachute suit your security might need to start checking *homo sapiens* credentials at the door."

As the evening had gone on and Amanda had fielded scores of well-wishes and requests for photos, the number of attendees had dwindled to no more than a dozen. Even though the gallery was not huge, there was a least twenty feet between them and the next couple over, who were making out in front of a painting that reminded Lydia of a moldy orange.

The two women stood side by side. Amanda dropped Lydia's hand. They stood and stared at the canvas, not touching but fastened together by the zipped-up inch of air between them. As if in reply to an inaudible dog whistle, the clumps of stragglers pointed and tagged their final purchases, shoved their hands into the pockets, and filed out the door. There was no sound now except for the gurgle of excitement from the exhibition's curators, the thrum of the open ventilation system slung across the high ceiling, and the slow, synchronized breath of two strangers who were now anything but.

"I haven't said this out loud. Not to my agent, not to my teachers. Not once." Amanda grabbed Lydia's drink and placed both glasses on a nearby table. She stood face to face with the other woman, and gripped Lydia's hands. "But I'm telling you now. All of my paintings, they're people. It's how I see them—naked, gutsy, primed."

Lydia knew that on any other night, with any other man or woman, the next comment would have sprouted wings as an off-color joke and led to complete capitulation to innuendo. Not tonight. She saw how Amanda's lip trembled with the secret.

Speaking slowly, fearless because she knew that every word she said would be the right one, Lydia said, "I think maybe you paint that because that's how you'd like to be. Seen for who you are."

Amanda's hazel eyes shone. She reached toward the nearest painting, tracing the coils and surges of her creation an inch from the canvas.

Lydia smiled again. "You don't need permission. You created this." She swept her free arm around the room, which was empty now except for the blackbird curators, who were crouched in a corner with a phoenix tail of red dots in each hand. "All of it."

"All of it." Amanda's voice came from a long way inside, but when her eyes caught Lydia's their cozy defense of the glowing space between them made her grin.

They walked to Amanda's place in silence, holding hands. At the open front door, Amanda paused. "There is one thing. I need to say it before I chicken out, but I don't know what's going to happen to us when you hear it. I don't want you to think I don't know what you're thinking. What everyone thinks when they walk in the door."

Lydia crossed her arms. She gathered her serious face and snapped her teeth. "Wasn't going to say anything, but damn, Amanda!"

The three-bedroom hugged the corner of a double-fronted Park Slope brownstone. The building had a preservation district plaque out front that had been there since 1968, and its original front sandstone steps were worn with a hundred years of residents and visitors. Although the slow, squeaky elevator ride up had focused Lydia's mind on capacity constraints, maximum force, and winding counterweights, she had to admire the unknown engineer. Anyone who had managed to retrofit a hundred-year-old building with this narrow simulacrum of an early residential lift disguising at least some modern technology garnered instant (if anonymous) professional respect.

They stepped off the elevator onto the cramped landing on the second floor and Amanda slid free a series of vertical and horizontal rod locks with a single unassuming key. Trying not to wonder what she might be locking out (or locking in) with the overlapping mortise and rim device, Lydia blinked herself past her mechanical reverie.

Even though she did not know much about interior reconstruction, Lydia could see that the four original rooms on this level had been scooped out to the wall studs before being reassembled. Wide-plank hardwood flowed into floor to ceiling windows, with translucent balloon blinds clinging to the top rail. One whole wall was a built-in bookcase. Solid shades of white and gray argued with scattered bursts of color. The couch was overstuffed leather, mottled like molasses; the throw pillows cornflower and teal. The fixtures—light, door, window hardware—reflected polished bronze, and the crystal chandelier over their heads tossed shards of rainbow light into every corner.

With a lemon-yellow bathroom sitting off the foyer, a huge open kitchen took up the rest of the space. From her position at the front door, Lydia glanced at sleek, featureless cabinets and an eight-burner range. She only had a moment to wonder where the Murphy bed was hiding before Amanda came in behind her and shut the door.

"Yes. Family money." She dropped her tasseled purse on the floor and threw up her hands. "Lots of it. No apologies forthcoming, if you're wondering. So."

She scrutinized the other woman's face, daring her to reply.

Lydia had more money than anyone she knew from back home. None of her remaining relatives knew it, but she had come a long way from her childhood spent sleeping on a sofa bed in the living room in her parents' one-bedroom rental. At sixteen, a committed teacher offered her free tutoring on weekends until she aced the SAT and secured a full undergraduate ride on the opposite coast. Once the days of supporting her parents were over, Lydia squirreled away every paycheck. *What the hell was I doing, saving for a rainy day? This woman's my future, all sunshine and rainbows.*

Lydia heard the words repeat in her head and she let out a strangled bark. *Ridiculous. Just met her. Even worse, she just met me.*

Amanda was still staring. "Problem?" The redhead wanted an answer.

Lydia returned the shrug, surprised to find that she felt both casual and calm about the revelation. "Not a one."

She grinned so widely that it cracked her lipstick. "Only question is what you do when you're cooped up here in this cramped little box and you want to spread out?"

Amanda kicked off her boots and pulled Lydia to the open Perspex stairs that wound into a narrow opening in the ceiling. She smiled with more eyes than teeth, laughed at Lydia's astonishment, and ventured their first kiss on the third step. "We go up."

The next morning, Lydia slept through Amanda's quick breakfast and long shower. As Amanda emerged fully clothed from the bathroom, Lydia rolled over still half-wrapped in a sheet and glanced at the clock.

"That's your work outfit?" Lydia laughed at Amanda's prim, calf-length taupe pencil skirt, buttoned white blouse and matching dull blazer. The redhead had pinned her hair into a high bun, and was carrying a pair of sensible, two-inch pumps.

Amanda bent down for a deep kiss. "Guess in all the commotion, maybe you forgot to ask me about my day job, huh?"

"Please, please tell me you've got Supergirl spandex under all that!" Lydia held her wrist. "And that you don't have to go quite yet."

"Downtown. Corporate law. Four, maybe five years out from partner." She nodded, mock serious. Every freckle danced. "You?"

"Mechanical engineer. PhD from Caltech. Moved

back here to the after. Too loud and not enough nature and too many people, but this is where the job is. I manage teams out of a company in Manhattan, but I spend a lot of time running projects out in the field."

Serious now, Amanda frowned. "Engineering? Must have been tough." She tipped an index finger towards Lydia's hair and androgynous suit. "I mean, you're not exactly middle of the road."

Amanda stopped. "Unless—but that's exactly who you *are*, right? Bisexual, I mean. Last night you mentioned a husband, but I'm far from the first woman you've been with."

"Is this a takes one to know—"

"True north, Ms. McCray." Amanda nodded. "Passed for straight through most of high school with a conveyor belt of suitable boys. Mom figured she'd marry me off to one of the sons of the Methodist's chosen few, but no such luck for her on that front."

Amanda paused, shifting her eyes away from Lydia's face. "Serious girlfriend in college, the real thing, until she decided that it wasn't worth the risk. That I wasn't worth the risk."

As she finished, Amanda's voice dipped and scattered, as though she had meant to say more. Lydia held out a hand, palm up, and waited until the other woman pressed her palm in a tight seal. Lydia laced her fingers through Amanda's.

"Come right on up and sit with me, babe." Holding

tight, Lydia made light of the unspoken epithet that still hurt both of them enough to prevent direct exposition. "Plenty of room on the fence for the two of us. And I'm not going anywhere."

They sat together on the bed, hands and foreheads touching, for a minute or two. Amanda broke it up with another question. "Seriously though, engineering management? How'd you shove your head through that ceiling?"

There were things—an abusive college boyfriend-briefly-turned-husband, infertility at nineteen—Lydia didn't want Amanda to know. *Not never.* The thought made Lydia shake her head. *But not yet.*

There were other stories, stories that Lydia carried around like Kleenex for first dates, that she was content to pull from her sleeve and throw away. Stories that could be anyone's stories, of a lost passport on trip to Mexico or the embarrassing slip into an oil slick in the parking lot.

Lydia had other stories. Stories she told herself to commiserate or commend, because there had never been anyone around long enough or deeply enough to do either. The story of how she gunned for the 'Senior Project Manager' title on her business card, scrambled past the rest of her cohort, deposited a bigger monthly salary check than either of her parents would have in six months in their lifelong customer service jobs, and enjoyed every inch of her corner office on the forty-first floor of one of the boldest skyscrapers in Manhattan. A story that Lydia had been telling herself for five years: first as inspiration, and later as self-satisfaction for the launch stage of a brilliant career carefully executed and successfully achieved.

Amanda sat still as a lizard, waiting. She watched Lydia's thoughts tick-tack between trust and disbelief, and she risked a brushed kiss on Lydia's cheek when the silence threatened to kill the conversation. Lydia found her decision waiting in Amanda's gentle generosity.

"L.A. McCray."

Amanda cocked her head in confusion. Lydia laughed. "Misdirection. I applied with a written application and took the aptitude test with three hundred other wannabes in an auditorium on campus. Best firm around, everyone wanted in."

"Don't get it. How'd that—"

Lydia held up her index finger. "Reply came in the mail four days later, with a standard check to cover travel and accommodation costs for the interviews here. Family was in Queens, so I saved two thirds of that."

Still confused but happy to share Lydia's obvious relish at unreeling the narrative one click at a time, Amanda held her questions.

"See, before I walked in, I never told them my first name, never spoke to a single person on the phone. No photo with my resume, no gender slot on the aptitude test."

Amanda laughed with her whole body, her shoulders round and her belly soft. She hugged Lydia and held her at arm's length. "Smart. Devious, but smart."

Lydia picked up the pace, her hands tapping out gestures as she carried Amanda with her on a journey she had already enjoyed in her own head dozens of times since she first got the job. "Believe me, I went all in. No make-up, no splash of color, triple-layered, high-impact sports bras. Navy suit, narrow tie, polished oxfords and matching leather belt. I even managed to scrounge up my old Tau Beta Pi tie pin because I'd read somewhere that their CEO was an engineering honor society member from way back."

"Jesus H., Lydia. You could find a whisper in a whirlwind!"

Seeing the other woman's question, Amanda added, "Means you know what you're doing. My dad's a Texan. It's contagious. I'd say you'll get used to it, but you won't. Years go by, you'll stop noticing it all together."

Lydia was having too much fun with her story to digest Amanda's assumption. She noticed it five weeks later, after they had spent every free waking and most sleeping moments together and decided that the only thing that made sense was to share Amanda's swanky apartment and dump most of Lydia's furniture at Goodwill.

Sitting on the bed together, Lydia picked up the last baton of her unlikely tale of disguise. "By the time they realized I was a woman, we'd already been split into numbered teams to work on case studies. The assessments were blind, and I kicked ass, hauling my team across the line first and identifying a problem in the original scenario that no one else anticipated. CEO handed out the envelopes to all forty of us in the boardroom at the end of the week. He started with the rejects, who disappeared one by one, and hired the six of us left standing with champagne and crab cakes after everyone else had gone. My offer was printed on weighty paper in a sloping cursive font: ten-thousand-dollar contract bonus, conditional pre-approval for promotion after six months, and a five-year non-competition clause. I asked to borrow his Montblanc pen to sign it on the spot."

There were more things that Lydia did not say. She did not say that she had hibernated in an underheated studio apartment over a chemical-leaking dry cleaner so more than half the money could be wired to her parents' account. She omitted any mention that she trekked out to Queens every weekend to offer respite to her bitter mother, who was caring for an abusive man she had hardly ever loved but could not leave, a man who had been struck with early-onset Alzheimer's years after any hope for repentance or redemption.

Lydia considered these facts as irrelevant as the long-faded emotional bruises from the woman she had worshipped in college or the long-buried fallout from a four-month marriage. She left home, she graduated from college, she worked, her father died, her mother followed. With nothing else to hold her back, Lydia took every subsequent paycheck, divided it carefully, kept expenses lean, and saved the rest for herself.

For us, now. The thought stung her like a wasp. For a moment, Lydia was somewhere else, but the sound of

Amanda's clapping returned her to the warmth of the bedroom.

Amanda applauded slowly and whistled with her teeth scraping her bottom lip. "I'd say impressive, but I'm guessing that's redundant. You know exactly how awesome you are, and I already kind of love that about you, Dr. L.A. McCray."

The word slid as easily into their conversation as though it had always been there. Months later, when the glow of first impressions subsided and they groped their way through fights always bracketed with the shared intention to stay and work it out not matter what, Lydia would wonder when she knew she loved Amanda. Her mind would return to that moment, and even in the midst of feeling slow and stupid for not seeing the size of what was growing between them, Lydia would be overwhelmed with gratitude that the extraordinary woman she loved had been wise enough to see it—and to say it— first.

"Details." Amanda's questions bounced around the room. "What are you working on now?"

With anyone else, Lydia would have demurred, leaning on the 'don't want to bore you' excuse and pivoting the question. With Amanda, she found herself wanting the attention. "The big ones are turbines—hydroelectric mostly—and logistics projects around automated conveyor systems and inventory management. But I'm mostly interested in water. Hoping to take over that portfolio completely in a year or two when that guy finally buys his condo in Florida and trades in a hard hat for golf shorts and tee shirt tan."

Giggling, Amanda pushed Lydia back onto the bed and kissed her before squirming out of reach and adjusting her skirt. "Jesus, Mary and Joseph. Lord love an engineer. My dad's in civil back in Tucson—geohydrology, urban watershed—and he is going to fall for you. Big time. He built viaducts and bridges in our backyard when I was a kid. Never quite got over the fact that I went to law school instead."

Lydia smiled at Amanda's childhood without bothering to compare it to her own. There was no reason; everyone did the best they could given the situation. *Some situations suck.*

"Bagels and cream cheese in the fridge," Amanda said. "Coffee's made, but fair warning: if you're going to ruin it by diluting it you're going to have to do it with water or the last of the 2%, not cream." She pretended to gag. "Ugh."

Lydia nodded her approval. "Black, three sugars. Lebanese restaurant near my place makes coffee so thick you have to chisel out the spoon."

Faking a glower, Amanda replied with her standard beverage of choice. "Black, none. But bonus points for mentioning a place that makes the good stuff that I didn't know about, and double bonus for not drinking herbal tea."

"We'd be over before we began, sweetheart." Lydia showcased her best Humphrey Bogart drawl.

"Say it ain't so," Amanda retorted, shuffling backwards with waving jazz hands into the bathroom. She left the door open.

Before she left, Amanda ran her fingers along the extended outline of Lydia's body under the covers. "Not much of mine going to fit, but you're welcome to try if you don't feel like slinking home before work."

"It's too early," Lydia complained lightly. "Come back to bed. I only start at nine."

"I'm burning daylight, babe. Got a meeting at 7:15, and I charge in six-minute increments, so in my life the phrase 'time is money' is literal." She laughed and tilted over for another kiss. "Besides, it'll give you a few extra hours to miss me."

After Amanda was gone, with the promise of dinner after work, Lydia stared at the key in her hand. The small gold emblem reflected oval patches light across the high ceiling of the master bedroom in the three-bedroom penthouse of the best renovation in Brooklyn. For a moment, she wondered why Amanda had handed it to her without explanation. She smiled to herself, borrowed a bathrobe from a hook on the door, poured herself a mug of coffee, and realized she would never need to ask. All of the important questions had already been answered.

Brooklyn (April 1990)

"You weren't kidding about this coffee." Amanda sipped approvingly and pointed to box that held their leftovers. "And I'm never going to see zucchini the same way. What's that called again?"

Lydia smiled until her teeth hurt. *"Kousa mahshi."* She was surprised by how much Amanda's opinion it mattered to her. Letting the thought slosh around inside her head, she self-corrected. *How much she matters to me.*

"No." Amanda's normally warm voice sounded cold. She muttered to herself. "Don't panic, don't panic."

"Everything okay?" Lydia knew that it was not, but the words spilled out before she could think of something more useful to say.

Amanda's eyes jerked over Lydia's head and jabbed back, the eye contact so fierce that Lydia flinched. "Too soon, too soon!"

Her confusion swilled into annoyance. "Amanda? Tell me what's wrong!" Lydia's catastrophizing found its groove. "God, you're not allergic to anything, are you? Do I need to call—"

"No." Amanda answered both questions in a monotone. She found Lydia's gaze again, and Amanda's eyes were wet. "But something is about to happen, right here and right now, and I need you to promise me you won't freak out."

The tally of possible explanations flickered in Lydia's mind. She allowed the improbable to seep into the impossible before giving in to the likely. *Epilepsy? Premonition? Apocalypse? Break-up?*

Sagging in her seat, Lydia tried to head off the inevitable by pretending it would hurt less if she said it first. "Amanda, I've been thinking, about us, and the way I see it we'd be better off—"

"He's here. How is he here?" Amanda ignored Lydia and chattered to herself.

"Mandy!" A ringing voice interrupted them both. Lydia clenched her hands and sat still. The voice swept around her and attached itself to a man: a short, wiry, gray-haired man in his mid-fifties, dressed in a green paisley waistcoat and balloon pants.

Amanda stood. The man stepped into her space, held her face in two manicured hands, and kissed her for longer than Lydia cared to stare. *She's not kissing him back. She's purposely not kissing him back. Like she has kissed him a lot. Like she wants to.*

"Gotcha." The man pulled away and cocked his head down to Lydia. "Not quite out of the closet with this one?"

Shaking her head, Amanda squeezed his hand. "Not quite yet. Wasn't sure how she'd take it, David. Early days."

Lydia was confused, and now she was angry at being talked about as though she was not there. She stood up, enjoying the height advantage. "For your information, David, Amanda's already told me she's bisexual. One thing among a lot of things we happen to have in common, by the way."

She snarled and pressed on, unaware of Amanda's horror and misinterpreting David's amusement for chagrin. "So you're the ex?" Her hand jutted out, fingers rigid. "Lydia."

"Lydia." Amanda's voice was guttural and strained. "There's something—"

David clicked the heels of his ankle boots and waved. "And that's my cue. Call me later, Mandy? It has been too long."

He trotted away. Lydia took a deep breath and watched until he disappeared around the corner. She sat down and gulped the last of her water, waiting until Amanda collapsed into her chair. "Who in the hell?"

Amanda scraped the remnants of her coffee sludge, the edge of the metallic spoon making the cup rattle in the saucer. "That's...David." She gathered her courage for more of the truth. "That's my David."

Lydia's imagination summoned a new possibility and she grinned. "Not an ex? Your brother?" She replayed the kiss. "Although jeez, excuse my saying, but does everyone in your family kiss on the lips like that? Don't know how comfortable I'm going to be able to get with that. Ever."

"Not brother. Not ex." Amanda wondered for a moment how she had not had a conversation like this in a decade and smiled as her circle of friends with benefits spooled itself like shadow puppets in her head.

"Okay." Amanda was not ashamed of her life. She simply was not prepared to share that with Lydia after two dates. She put down the spoon and reached across the table to take Lydia's unresisting hand. "Thing is, I'm not monogamous. Not now, not since high school. I didn't have a name for it for a long time, but I'm bisexual and I'm poly."

The word sat between them. Lydia nodded, realization slipping from relief to jealousy before landing square on the need for more information. She risked a comment. "Okay. Heard of it. Vaguely. And?"

"And." Amanda stopped, unsure of how to carve a path forward that honored who she had been her whole life and create boundaries of respect with the woman with whom she had already fallen in love.

Lydia had a question she refused to ask. It was the bane of every conversation she had ever had with anyone she had dated, the *reductio ad absurdum* of anyone who conflated a bisexual identity with the fear that one gender would never be enough, that somehow the label required both for fulfillment. This was clearly a completely different conversation.

Amanda took responsibility for answering the other questions Lydia could not find words to say aloud. "And David is my lover. We've been friends for years, lovers off and on for most of that time. Currently on. I usually see him once every few weeks. He's been in Montreal visiting family."

Lydia grabbed the crutch of every new relationship:

ignorance in the face of intense infatuation. "I get it. It's too soon to talk exclusivity, I get it." She stopped abruptly, not trusting the anxiety in her voice to subside in time for her words to run out.

Shaking her head, Amanda sighed. "Kind of missing the point, Lydia." She tapped her chest. "Poly."

"Okay," Lydia said flatly.

Risking a small smile, Amanda reached for the olive branch. "Okay?"

"Are you kidding me?" Lydia's monotone gave way to a half-shout. "No, it's not okay, how in the hell do you expect to dump something like this on me and ask me if it's okay?"

Retreating, Amanda sighed again. "If you're thinking exclusive, sooner or later, this isn't going to work. And David? He's—" she played with five or six options before finishing her sentence. "—uncomplicated."

"Uncomplicated, sure. I can see that." Wearing the chainmail of unfettered sarcasm, Lydia sniffed. "His tongue down your throat makes things real simple, Mandy." She curled her lip at the name.

"That's not what I meant." Amanda whispered. Furious at David that the disclosure had come as a surprise and much too soon. Furious at herself that she had not said anything to Lydia in the first moments in the gallery. *Something flippant, something that would have put her right off. Avoided all this mess.*

Amanda wiped her eyes and risked a scan upward at

Lydia's closed fists and flaming eyes. *All this beautiful mess.*

Lydia slid a twenty under her water glass. Without a word, she picked up her satchel and stalked away, blinking uselessly at the tears that forced themselves out of her eyes.

For the next three days, Amanda let it sit. But when the landline rang, Lydia unplugged it and shoved the answering machine into her closet. The shrill doorbell rang at four o'clock the following Sunday afternoon. Lydia ignored it. She slurped ramen noodles in the dark, scraped out a carton of ice cream with the TV fluttering in the background, and drank half a bottle of cheap, tangy red wine. She had to go out of town for work, to a project upstate. She was gone a week.

Checking her mail when she got home the following Friday afternoon, Lydia picked up the light blue square envelope with scalloped edges and no return address. *Probably some stupid wedding invitation to a cousin I don't even know.* She opened it at her kitchen counter while scanning the junk mail for coupons. A single sheet of paper fell out. On one side, someone had scratched out items on a shopping list: lip balm, coffee, toilet brush, matches. Before she turned it over, Lydia found herself drawn in to the strange intimacy of someone else's quotidian needs, and her mind threaded itself through the list as she re-read it.

The other side of the paper was written in lime green crayon in uneven capital letters: IS THERE MORE TO US?

Lydia stumbled as though she had missed a stair and

caught herself with one hand behind her back. The paper drifted to the floor. Lydia watch it float down. Time stretched like a lazy yoga pose, holding still before the page landed. Lydia had a lifetime of disconnection to wonder what she wanted. *Heads or tails?* When the question landed, face up, Lydia was still not sure. She picked it up in a pincer grip and set it up against the toaster, staring at the words until it was too dark to see.

Saturday morning at eight a.m., Lydia stood at the intercom of Amanda's swanky building, daring herself to ring the bell. Her mind ticked-tocked the pendulum of her opposite and equal fears: *What if she doesn't answer? What if she does?* Some shred of self-protection evaded the third option, that Amanda was not alone upstairs. Lydia held her ground and jabbed the ringer like a faulty robot, stiff and ceaseless.

"Who is it?" Amanda's voice sounded hollow.

"Yes." Lydia coughed and said it louder. "Yes."

"Heard you...the first time." The answer stuttered down through the wire.

The buzzer invited Lydia to take the next step. She held the door open, one foot wedged inside, willing herself to make the right choice.

Lydia had been standing there for three minutes when Amanda jumped out of the elevator and ran up to her. She stopped when she saw Lydia's sagging face and bloodshot eyes.

Pointing to the clear evidence of her own sleeplessness, Amanda pasted on a tired smile. "Me, too."

"Walk?" Lydia released a long breath as she turned around and wondered if Amanda would follow.

"Beginning? Or end?" Still a few steps behind, Amanda kicked a shard of loose concrete into the gutter and matched Lydia's pace.

Lydia offered her the truth as she turned her head. "Not sure."

She stopped at the next corner and gave Amanda more. "Honestly, I'm not even sure how I start thinking this."

"There's a book." Amanda's face was serious, the streaks of her mascara still smudged halfway down her cheeks. Her hair hung in long braids down either side of her peasant blouse, a crestfallen Pippi Longstocking.

Taking in the vision of this woman who had become more to her in a blink than anyone she had ever met, Lydia allowed her eyes to wander from the crown of Amanda's head to her polka-dotted pink clogs. Amanda's three words echoed in her head, until none of them meant anything, until all sense had precipitated out of what she had been trying to say.

Lydia felt the laughter rise from deep in her hips. It sang up her spine, stopping to send pulses of hilarity through her arms and legs that stung and fizzed. She stomped her feet and shook her hands, doubling over silently, before the sound found its way out of her mouth. "A...a...book? A book? A book?"

Woodpecker words tapped out until Lydia put her

hand over her mouth, but her body shook and jittered. It was New York City—no one paid attention to the loopy lady jiving on the sidewalk, or to her silent, stricken companion.

Amanda watched her with growing concern. She risked a hand on Lydia's shoulder, and leapt back in shock as the snicker turned to a guffaw and a howl.

"I can't." Lydia tried to reclaim her breath, but another fracture flared up and she abandoned herself to the laughter. "You have no idea." She finally coughed up the words, even as the giggles returned to interrupt what finally became a conversation.

Amanda pointed to the park across the street. They walked over, crossing at the light, neither shocked nor sorry to find that their hands were entwined by the time they reached the wrought iron bench under the dormant trees.

"Ask my anything." Amanda tried on an open invitation, refusing to back down from her fear of what Lydia might pursue.

Sometimes, when the whos and whats and hows have answers, the whys or why nots dwindle like dripping wax from an old candle. Amanda picked them both up and carried them through her story, the false starts and the falsehoods, and by the time she was done Lydia did not need a promise that her girlfriend could not and would not give. She needed time and information and words and fights and power and reassurance. She needed agreements and history and open-endedness and exploration and opportunity. Which there would be.

Later that night, after more yesses and ice cream and tears, Amanda held Lydia in her arms and stroked her hair. "No matter what happens with David, it will never mean I love you any less."

She tried out the language they had been discussing all afternoon. "No question that you're my primary relationship, Lydia. As long a future as I can imagine right now, you and I will come first, and we'll work out the details together."

In her head, eyes closed, Lydia ran through the one-night stands that had played stunt doubles in place of any real relationship for her since she had left the man she married after four months too many.

Amanda tried the words again. "I thought I'd been in love before. This—us—is something else."

Lydia opened her eyes and sat up, putting an arm's length between them. "There's something—someone—I need to tell you about."

Amanda crossed her arms, suddenly vulnerable. Her eyes flicked around the room, trying to find somewhere to land. She settled on the doorknob, trying to find her reflection in the brushed brass. She had rehearsed this conversation, but Lydia wasn't playing to the script.

"I was married." Three words. *Maybe three words too many*.

Taking note of the tense, Amanda's mouth spat out snark before she could reel it in. "How'd that work out for you?"

Lydia's eyes stung and she retreated. "Forget it." She glanced at her watch. "I should go."

Communication is its own worst enemy. It relies on frequently false and always unsteady assumptions of shared perspective. The foundation is faulty, and cracks are the inevitable result of parallel thought where the intention is intersection. Not noticing the structural insecurity until it is too late is fuel for every epic poem of lost love and every country song chorus. Instead of building crossbeams to locate and bolster the possibility of junctions and communion, words cause catastrophic failure at the weakest points of any relationship: the points at which the connection is either winched into place and bolted together or wrenched apart and carted to the junkyard.

The mechanical engineer knew a lot about failure, technical and personal. Technical was sometimes easy, even when it was not simple. Find the overflow or the tripped circuit or the design error in the surge tank and work the problem from the source. Understand the process, reverse engineer the build, identify the components down to serial number and manufacturer. Take it from there.

Personal was trickier. The source was an undifferentiated mass of thoughts, feelings and experiences, a bulbous conglomeration that flowed over boundaries like an amoeba, picking up misunderstanding and misdirection along the way.

Halfway to the door, Lydia paused. She could hear Amanda breathing behind her, air rasping in and out. She matched the rate, counting them two by two. *If it's something else, my chance to be someone else. For both of us.*

Lydia sat back down on the couch, pried Amanda's fingers loose from her defensive posture, and kissed the palm of her hand. She rewound the conversation, hoping to find a crossroads. "You're right."

Amanda's stiff hand softened and wound around Lydia's like a tendril, but her voice was dark and tense. "Why does it matter?"

"About this. About us." Lydia waltzed with the word in her head, watching herself stutter-step and twirl in its grip. "Love."

It was not enough. Amanda pulled away again, sitting on her hands like a chastised child. Her mouth fish-tailed, jaw wagging, but no sound came out. There was nothing to say.

Feeling dizzy with the pressure of the moment—a nauseating mix of newfangled fear of perfection near enough to taste and old-fashioned terror at losing a chance that might never come again—Lydia kneeled next to the couch, placed her hands on either side of Amanda's legs, and whispered everything she was afraid to say aloud. "I love you, Amanda. It's too soon and too crazy and too impossible and maybe even too late. But it's the least you should know, and the most I can say."

She touched Amanda's face before rising to her feet with a hollow sigh. Even when the diagnosis is correct, the cure sometimes comes too late. She picked her satchel off the floor and slipped on her shoes.

"I didn't say the words all in the right order." Amanda's sentence was an arrow targeted at her own missed opportunity. Lydia leaned against the front door. It was her turn to cross her arms. She stared at the woman on the sofa, watching as Amanda got up and half-ran the width the room. Amanda halted as though she had hit a mime wall three feet away.

For the first time in what felt like forever, they risked eye contact.

"I do." Amanda rubbed her nails with the pad of her thumb. "Lydia, whatever comes next. Whatever you decide. I love you."

Without touching, the two women moved closer. Lydia reached out first.

Afterwards, over late-night scrambled eggs with Monterrey Jack cheese and hot sauce, Amanda cracked the topic. "Husband?"

Lydia swallowed a bite, sloshed down half a glass of orange juice, and put down her fork. "Lucas."

The word tasted like sulfur and she shuddered. Amanda reached over the counter and held her hand. "Another time?"

Frowning, Lydia shook her head. She held the image of the punch and her stomach clenched against the memory. "Golden boy. Everyone said so. Second date. Frat party. Pregnant at nineteen."

Biting her lip, Lydia continued. "Stupidity. Told me

he'd do the right thing. My skewed frame of reference thought it was the right thing, too. Courthouse. Papers. Rings."

She swallowed. "Only let him hit me once." She heard the bloody splinter of pride in her confession and flared with shame. "Turns out, once too many."

The memories crested over all of her achievements, drowning all the days since that single day when she was four months in, blotting out any sense of balance. Lydia rocked on her stool, thoughts swimming in a direction she could only hope was up toward the light.

"Lost the baby at seventeen weeks. Eleven days in hospital. Placental abruption with—" Lydia heard the words in her head and spat them out with the devastating detachment the doctor had used while she lay curled around a warming blanket in the ICU—"rare secondary complication of obstetric hemorrhage, leading to hypovolemic shock and subsequent renal failure."

Amanda's eyes welled. Lydia refused to cry. A macabre smile teased itself across her face, because she already knew the rest of the story. Amanda had no idea.

"They couldn't stop the bleeding." She patted her lower abdomen to feel what wasn't there. "Partial hysterectomy after they gave me drugs to deliver the—"

Lydia ran out of words.

Amanda had met other women and a few men who had found themselves on the receiving end of a slap or a gripped blow. Despite the compassion she expressed, despite the material support she had been quick to offer, her internal voice had always been more sympathetic than empathetic. But pity by its nature inoculates against respect because it implies underlying weakness. Amanda felt no pity now—only deep humiliation at the moments she had allowed understanding to be clouded with a sense of 'how could someone let that happen.' She cringed at how easily she had caved to the propaganda, protecting herself with the fiction that it could not happen to someone independent or strong.

Nothing in her own experience of this extraordinary human being sitting in her kitchen prepared her for the impotence and fevered confusion that rose up in her chest. The febrile rush sparked through her veins like magma seeking a place to rise up and rip everything apart. She stood up, cocooned Lydia in a rigid embrace, and grunted a few inchoate expressions of what they both recognized as barely lidded fury.

Despite her girlfriend's planked arms and snarling breath, Lydia relaxed. In all the storytelling scenarios she had spooled out over the years, the imagined response of an anonymous listener was the disappointment of mercy fueled by unspoken contempt. Lydia settled in to Amanda's paralytic wrath as though sinking into a bubble bath, allowing all of the other woman's stress to fill and overflow and overwhelm her with a mirror image of the anger Lydia had crushed inside herself far too long. They held on until daylight snuck in through the living room's wall of glass.

Brooklyn (May 1990)

Five weeks after they met at the gallery, Lydia moved in. They both felt the change was less a decision and more a return to what felt right.

She arrived on Amanda's doorstep with two college students she had hired to move the eight boxes that constituted her entire adult life. The furniture in her tiny apartment she left for the tenant she sub-leased to, a foul-mouthed, twenty-something aspiring actor who smelled like hash and sweat.

Amanda met them at the elevator. "I can't believe I never even saw your place."

Lydia laughed and pointed the movers up the stairs and across to the bookcase. "First pile up there and heavier three in here, thanks."

Turning to Amanda, she said, "This is it. Last chance to uninvite me."

"Unless you're a vampire." Amanda grinned and pulled Lydia inside. "Once you've been invited in, I'm doomed." They kissed hard, and Amanda pushed Lydia up against the antique hat stand.

Pulling away as the guys clattered down the stairs for the second load of boxes, Lydia feigned despair. "Indeed, that's you all over, helpless damsel in distress. Why didn't I see that before?"

"That's it, ma'am." The men stood uncomfortably across the living room. The taller one leered.

Lydia shot him a death ray and spoke to the other one. "All good, thanks." She dug in her pocket for an extra twenty on top of the hundred she had paid up front. "That's for the stairs, I know they're tricky."

Alone in what was now their apartment, Lydia and Amanda found themselves walking off in split directions. Like pinballs, they bounced around the shared space, unsure of what came next. Finally, the new arrival wandered up to the bedroom and stood over the boxes of clothes. After a moment, she found Amanda behind her. "Unpacking can wait."

Lydia swiveled her head. "Only take a few minutes, get this out of your way."

Amanda pulled Lydia's whole body around and held her by the shoulder. "Nothing about you is in my way, Lydia McCray. And I don't want to wait."

Her heart pounding, Lydia felt the memory of her dingy studio vanishing over a horizon she had only begun to explore. She wrapped herself around her lover, everything else forgotten.

Brooklyn (December 1997)

"Of course it feels ridiculous." Amanda rolled her eyes at Lydia and reached over for the folder that sat between them on the couch. "The whole thing is a crapshoot, babe. All of it. A to Z, birth to death."

Lydia scowled. "What's the point? If we're not going to know much more than when we started, if there are no guarantees, why not..."

Amanda set down the folder on the coffee table and pressed Lydia's hands between hers. "I didn't say there weren't any choices. I meant no matter what choices we make, some things we can't even imagine right now are going to be defining features of our lives in the future. Good and bad."

Lydia shrugged off her partner's hand and crossed her arms. "You do it. My input's irrelevant, anyway, you're going to be the one carrying..."

"Lyds, don't." Amanda closed her eyes, allowing her shoulders to relax into the other woman's pain. "None of that was ever your fault. None of it. And there'd be no us without you, remember? It's never been only me in this room."

Amanda's gaze held hers longer than Lydia could have imagined possible. Lydia's thoughts rolled over one another, gathering momentum, as her body pressed closer to the woman she loved. *Not an angry stare, not impatient or arrogant or power hungry. Not through or at or to. She's with me. This second, this amazing woman, she's with me. And she knows, all of it, all of those impossible years, and still we're here, about to change everything. Everything.*

"So many reasons not to..." Lydia's expression shifted, unwinding all of the months of questions and likely answers and final choices that they had constructed together like a glass house, one brittle pane slotted into another, until the light shone on their shared dream. She had followed Amanda into the rabbit warren the first time the topic surfaced, trusting this time would be different. Trusting that the woman she had fallen in love with at a local art gallery opening would hear all the words she wasn't saying. "Do you think we should maybe rethink...?"

Amanda laughed again, a gentle chortle that belied her frustration. She understood Lydia's fear. Sometimes she even shared it. But this moment needed someone to fall forward into the future, and Amanda Marquez had been doing that her whole life. "Pros and cons, right? Too expensive, too much time, career killer."

Lydia's past elbowed its way through. She shook her head and hugged herself tighter, not meeting Amanda's eyes. "We've worked hard, both of us."

"Babe, that's my point." Amanda's voice found a softer tone, matching warmth with resolve and a flush of mischief. "Forget planning those trips to Croatia and

Vietnam for ten years, or ever. Forget Sunday brunch with Brit and Aiko or any more pre-work rides with Miranda and Jo. Which I know you love."

Lydia met Amanda's wry grin with a more resigned smile of her own. She had always been a reluctant cycling partner. "Okay, some stuff won't be a big deal. But another human being's impact on the environment? College fund, school drama, puberty." She winced. "You might not mind a second go-around of that, but adolescence was a nightmare for me the first time."

As Amanda watched, Lydia's focus shifted. "If you could ask my mother, she'd tell you."

"You're not her." Amanda didn't move, but her words slid over and under the other woman's story. "Never going to be her. Or my mother, for that matter."

Without a breath between, Amanda added, "Never going to be your dad, either. You're going to be...magnificent."

"I didn't mean that," Lydia said. They both knew she had. "There are so many good reasons not to go through this. Not to try."

"Exactly." Amanda slid over to share the sofa cushion, curling her legs around Lydia and kissing her on the cheek. She cradled her hands in front of their bellies. "A thousand reasons to say no, and on the other side..."

Lydia finally exhaled, a laugh creaking up through her fear to come snorting out of her nose. "A baby." She held on to Amanda and nodded her head. "Our baby."

"Besides," Amanda said, "If my cousins pop out one more sprout before you and I get this show on the road, my dad will run out of ways to spoil the kid and my mom will run out of ways to criticize. Time we got in on the bandwagon."

Returned to herself and to her love, Lydia wrinkled her nose. "Diaper rash, colic, co-sleeping, doctor's check-ups?"

"Our lives will never be our own again, babe." Amanda scribbled soft lines on the inside of Lydia's elbow. "I think that's the whole damn point. Of all of it."

The folder was nothing special on the outside—a white three-ring binder, yellow tabs sticking out the side. It was two inches thick, with a nondescript 'Files Pending: January-March' printed label and a phone number. No company name, no address. No mention of Amanda Marquez or Lydia McCray, two people whose identities of daughter, cousin and friend, corporate lawyer and mechanical engineer, were moving on to becoming something more than one to another. Pushing towards becoming someone—some tiny someone's—whole universe. Two people who had come to a singular decision over early coffee and late movies, over bright arguments and unexpected congruent lines of thinking and feeling their way towards to the improbable.

Inside this bundle of unfulfilled wishes were stories, written and unwritten, paths traveled and paths yet to be discovered. Waiting.

"And before you ask, yes. I've examined at the

contract, twice. If we were my clients I couldn't dream up anything better. Clause, line and sinker. Plenty of protection for both sides. There's the 'confidential with openness to a meeting' bit in there, like we wanted."

Lydia reached for the comfort of logic. Science made sense. "Great. Modern approach to this, the science and the story."

Amanda smiled again, as they opened the folder into their laps and scanned the first profile. "No secrets. No lies."

They found the donor on page four. Amanda read faster. She spoke first. "Older. Graphic designer, loves animals."

Lydia nodded, mouthing the words to herself. "Math club in college. Builds Legos with his kids and rebuilds vintage engines in his garage." She skipped a few sections and read more aloud. "Heart disease and stroke on both sides, but not much cancer. German, French, Dutch."

Amanda pointed to another line at the bottom of the page. "Says his reason for donating is that his best friend struggled with infertility. Got the whole 'What would Jesus do?' sort of vibe to it, don't you think?"

She saw Lydia's slight frown. "Not in a bad way, love—in a 'love and let love' way."

Lydia's expression deepened. "At least Beth screened out the crazies who'd rather send us straight to hell than let two women have kids together."

"Not about them, babe." Amanda snuggled closer. "It's about us. From now on, it's always going to be about us.

The three of us."

Placated, Lydia kissed her and returned to the profile. "Only three? Don't you mean seven, or nine?"

Laughing, Amanda said, "Don't tempt me. You know being an only child means I want a clutch—I'm thinking eight little munchkins at least."

Glancing around at their angular living room, the late afternoon sun pouring through Art Deco windows and a hint of green from the park across the way, Lydia held her hands up in mock surrender. "You want a parade of kids, you got a parade. We'll line the walls with triple bunkbeds and call it a day."

At their request, the agency had paperclipped the photos of potential donors behind the profiles, so that Lydia and Amanda's first impressions were of personality and preference, not height or eye color. The two women held hands as they turned the page.

"Great smile," Amanda said, squeezing Lydia's hand. "Someone our kid could talk to about all this, someday. Fifteen, twenty years from now?"

Sucking air through her front teeth, Lydia hesitated. Her adult life had taught her that a plan two days out was asking for trouble. After the stilted, invisible bubble of her parents' house, all of what came after, and before Amanda, she had lived her life in short horizons: the next exam, the next promotion, the next project.

Her memories never spanned longer than a day or two at a time, either. When Lydia revisited the events in her life, she chopped them into bits like dicing onions on a cutting board: an unlikely invitation to a sorority party, her freshman roommate's inexplicable taste for ska music, the second day of her engineering internship and that first-class flight to the power plant project in Dubai. These neatly tagged and easily accessed memories helped scrape away the others that she had tried hard to forget.

Lydia McCray's two decades between leaving home and sitting on the couch in a fancy apartment picking out DNA were parsed into the remembered and the discarded, the necessary and the never-agains. Her career toe-heel-toed upwards, each platform preparation for the next promotion, and the next. Her closet swapped out consignment store suits for tailored three-piece pantsuits with matching heels, her costume jewelry traded for forgettable pieces of silver and gold that marked what felt like inevitable professional success. The rest of her life floated along, a raw undercurrent of misdirection and missed opportunities. The little stuff, she forgot. The big stuff, she ignored. Lydia had wallpapered over enough of her past to be able to pretend it did not belong to her at all.

Amanda made her different. Amanda's presence was an arrow in motion, dragging each moment into the next with precision and speed. Lydia's life with Amanda was not discrete intervals—it was a continuous curve that propelled her along from the inside out, a straight-and-narrow path of self-discovery.

Even so, thinking twenty years ahead pressed against

her chest. Lydia resisted the urge to turn away. "Yes," she said, knowing she was saying yes to Amanda and everything that came afterwards. "Someone who might listen."

Brooklyn (February 1998)

"Marquez/McCray?" The nurse called out from the open internal door in the clinic. Amanda and Lydia stood together. The nurse smiled and pointed them down the hall. "Dr. Crenshaw will be right in."

Amanda gripped Lydia's hand. Lydia squeezed tighter and led the way. They sat side-by-side on low leather chairs. The nurse closed the office door behind her with a soft click.

Fifteen minutes later, their doctor knocked and swished through, her long cotton skirt brushing the floor. She clicked her front teeth. "Big day."

Amanda cringed. "Not soon enough. Not a fan of needles."

Dr. Crenshaw nodded with practiced sympathy. "I know this has been a long road." She pulled Lydia in to the circle. "For both of you."

Lydia dragged her thoughts away from her center, from the space between her body's history and her heart's future. She sat straighter in the slinging chair and grounded her feet to the floor. Not trusting her voice, she focused on her breath. Amanda felt Lydia's mood shift and turned to face her. "But we're here now. Together."

As she had done every day for their eight years

together, Amanda found the light scattered through the dark and tapped it. "Besides, if it weren't for you, I'd still be standing naked in our bathroom on Day 1, damn syringe half-inch from my skin, trying to get the guts to poke myself in the stomach. Pun intended. Ugh."

Laughing, Lydia nodded. "You can count on me, love." Back to business, she asked Dr. Crenshaw, "One or two?"

Dr. Crenshaw narrowed her eyes. "Here's the thing. I was hoping we'd have better news this morning, but seven of the nine that fertilized didn't make it through the weekend."

Lydia chewed the inside of her mouth. Her thoughts fluttered, ins and outs of missed opportunity colliding with another expected disappointment. Amanda held the balance, anticipating a brighter second half of the story. "And?"

"And, we've got two five-day blastocysts that are pretty good. On balance, I'd say this is an excellent result at this point in the process."

There's a but. There's always a but. Lydia's calcified pessimism threatened to spill from her mouth, but she glanced at Amanda's bravado and swallowed the words. Dr. Crenshaw filled in the space. "Amanda, given the aggressive protocol you've been on, and with yesterday's endometrium ultrasound results, I'm going to say let's go with two."

It wasn't the answer Amanda wanted to hear. Her buoyancy dipped. "No backup? None left on ice? And what about all the additional risks with multiples?" She let go of

Lydia's hand and tugged at imaginary lint on her sleeve.

Dr. Crenshaw was quiet. Lydia saw her chance to swap roles. "We're not going to need it, Amanda. This is it. This is us."

Amanda nodded, biting her lip. "This is us. Come on, doc, let's go grow a baby." As she stood to follow the doctor out of the room, Amanda turned and winked at Lydia. "Or two. Now wouldn't that be something?"

Brooklyn (December 1998)

"What time's our flight?" Amanda called down from her perch on the ladder in the nursery. Lydia took the stairs two at a time and stood in the doorway, a broad smile swimming across her face. "Are you kidding me? First it's, 'oh-sweetheart-you-know-I-like-to-get-to-the-airport-early' and instead of packing you're hanging off a ladder painting ladybugs and leaves around the crown molding?"

Amanda grinned in return, shook her loose ginger pixie cut out of her eyes, and dipped her brush into the bright red canister balanced on the top step. "You're the one who wanted it done before the New Year. Besides, Dr. Crenshaw said I need to keep moving. Only six weeks to go when we get back from Arizona."

Lydia tugged her partner one step down the ladder, so that they were eye to eye, and kissed her nose. "Pretty sure she said yes to yoga, stretching, and walks in the park, love. Not scaling tall, wobbly structures armed and dangerous with art supplies."

"Come on!" Amanda grabbed another brush from the drop cloth and handed it to Lydia. "You know you're dying to help! What are you going to say to our son when he asks which insects are yours?"

Lydia laughed. "Right. Because I know the minute I

dab paint on the wall it's going to be mutant insects and the forest from hell." She tapped the narrow brush into a can of bold green and shrugged. "But hey, you asked for it. Don't say I didn't warn you. There's only one artist in the family, and that's…"

Amanda interrupted her with a hip-to-hip hug. "Only one artist so far, babe." She rubbed her belly, round and full under a paint-speckled smock. "Besides, I've still got that whole corporate attorney day job thing going, at least for now."

Snorting, Lydia dipped her paintbrush and returned to painting. "Right. Because four sold-out gallery shows and six commissions in the last twelve months is you as a starving artist, babe. Face it—your days of arguing over contracts and staring down the opposition over a conference table or in court are pretty much over. No matter how good that money is."

With a wink, Amanda parried the compliment. "Easy come, easy go, love. Remember me in that first month we met, all the rage at old girl sorority auctions? Hot one day, frozen out of the market the next."

Lydia chided her. "Not that you're bitter, babe. But don't worry, I'll still love you, starving artist or cutthroat attorney or…"

"Mom," they said in unison. Amanda's smile joined Lydia's grin and they held the silence, guarding the best of what was yet to come like hidden treasure.

The moment passed. Amanda switched paints to a

small pot of black, swirling circles and antennas on the drying ladybugs lower on the wall. "Yep. My days of everything except breastfeeding and napping when he naps will be over soon. Anyway, this little guy? Creative genius, I can tell."

She climbed up the three steps and returned to freehand drawing red ovals along the edge of the ceiling. Amanda's arm moved confidently, her fingers holding the paintbrush as though it were glass, her whole body flowing with soft, delicate strokes.

Lydia leaned down and began to tap out feathery splotches at regular intervals on the room's baseboard. "I'll do the grass. Measured it this morning. Should have sixty-seven tufts spaced four inches apart. Give or take."

Amanda's eyes scrunched up as she laughed, her round face wobbling. "Or an engineer. I can see him in there now, testing out the distances inside my uterus with his thumb and one eye closed, mapping out the shortest route, figuring out how it all works. For all I know he's measuring our heartrates, calculating nutrient flow and energy expenditure, and charting his own course through the birth canal."

Holding the ruler up to the wall, Lydia counted under her breath. "Should be about right."

She stopped suddenly, her eyes on Amanda's stomach. "Some things take a little more engineering than others, right? But we got there in the end." Lydia concentrated on her decorating.

Hearing the controlled tightness in Lydia's voice,

Amanda stepped off the ladder again and kneeled awkwardly. "This isn't the end, babe. It's the beginning. You, me, and..."—she tucked Lydia's hand under her belly and covered it with her own open palm—"Nathan Theodore Marquez-McCray."

Lydia smiled with effort and put her arms around Amanda as they stood up together. "Thank God we settled on Theo for short. That's a big name for a baby to carry around."

"Great expectations. Pun intended." Amanda pointed to the paint lids. "Probably time to call it quits for now. Help a pregnant woman out with the clean-up?"

"Sure," Lydia said. "We'll pick it up right when we get home."

The frothy paint dried on the walls as the sun set on a gray New York City afternoon. Sleet gathered on the windowsill, night fell, and the half-finished ladybugs glowed in the light from the streetlamp below. Inside the nursery, a matching walnut wood crib, changing table, rocking chair, and dresser sat empty. Waiting. In one corner, piles of to-be-washed, hand-me-down baby clothes wrestled with an unopened diaper bag and a six-pack of unscented, hypoallergenic wipes. Waiting. Spread out across the floor away from the paint lay a yellow-bordered, hand-quilted blanket of storybook rabbits in waistcoats and monocles. Waiting. Unboxed but unassembled, an infant's car seat huddled next to the open closet with vacant shelves and tiny padded hangers. Waiting.

The occupants of the three-bedroom apartment packed a week's worth of warm weather clothes, watered the houseplants that swarmed across the kitchen cabinets, triple-locked their front door, and headed west for their last extended family Christmas as a nucleus of two.

Tucson (December 1998)

Although she could not hear a thing, Lydia knew that she was screaming. Her hand was trapped against her throat, knuckles pressed into her skin, and the vibration of a guttural, arching vowel made her palm itch. She tried to pull away, to stop the noise, but her arm would not budge.

Broken. Kaleidoscopic, the word settled into woman's as she stretched one leg to wedge it against the door. Her ankle sent lances of bright pain up through her hip, distracting her for a few seconds from the surge of blood across her lap. *Leg, too.*

All Lydia could see was piercing, slanted sunlight out the smashed windshield and unbroken window. The glare sliced into strips of orange and white, pinning her like a blind beetle, but her eyes couldn't focus on metal or glass. Her brain insisted on asking impossibly small questions: *What time is it? Should I have booked a later flight home on Tuesday? Did I pack my toothbrush?*

Under the screaming, other sounds competed for Lydia's attention. There was the wind, blowing harder than it had been all week, rattling through the thorny, low brush along the roadside. She could hear the engine muttering to itself, inexplicably still alive, and the noise laid a cool hand on her thoughts. She reached for the habitual and closed her eyes as the words returned to her, words reeled out so often to eager students on the first day of class. *Equilibrium conditions of structural elements. System of forces. Geometric parameters. Equivalent transformations.*

As Lydia fought to steady her thoughts into sequential coherence, equations and variables, the comforting whir of the engine abandoned her. Her life returned to the expanding ring of pain and confusion in the wreck, past and present compressed into acute awareness of snapped bone, impossible angles, and short horizons.

She tried to crane her twisted neck at other sounds, grunts and thuds. The screaming stopped, and she wondered it if had all been in her head. Lydia flapped her lips and tried to inhale, but the crackle of misplaced ribs kept her silent. *Wait.*

"Going for help," mumbled a rough voice through the smashed window in the back. "Saw a building behind us across the scrub, probably a house. Quarter mile, maybe."

The voice wheezed, filling the space inside the car with the smell of clove cigarettes and alcohol. "Twenty minutes tops." As if in reply to itself, the voice from the back surrendered to staccato breath, a soft groan, and stumbling, receding steps.

Lydia swallowed more air. *Wait. I didn't see you, I…*

Her pain folded over itself, body stiff, hand still at her throat, eyes racing under twitching eyelids. Her spiky, purple-tipped hair flashed red where the blood congealed at her ear. The airbag sagged, and her lower body slid forward towards the dashboard. Something in her hip swiveled and stuck. Memories and plans hung in twisted ribbons in Lydia's mind. Her thoughts scurried and dug: an hour ago, week, a month, a year.

How long? Eyes wide against the darkness, trying to move her neck against the locked seatbelt that had wedged itself against her collarbone, Lydia searched for a clue to up, down, sideways. The middle of the night Arizona sky in December gave nothing away save a rash of dispassionate stars out the passenger side window. *Hours at least.*

To her left, another soft sound. This time, warm words and warmer voice. "I think I need to pee again. Let's stop at the next gas station, get some snacks. They'll have those protein bars I like out here, butterscotch pecan. Can't get those on the East Coast, no matter what people say about New York."

A half-laugh gurgled, banal chatter sloshing up against something sinister and unstoppable. "And yeah, love, no matter what *you* say, caramel cashew isn't the same."

Lydia blinked in the darkness, her half-aware mind splicing casual conversation with the smell of antifreeze and burned rubber. The smell of something else, too—dense and sweet. *Blood. Whose?* She fish-snapped her mouth, trying to fill the gaps with air.

The other voice, that voice, again. A little lower pitched this time, like dying batteries in a talking doll. "What happened to the music? You know he loves it when we sing…"

Ignoring the flash of pain through her leg, Lydia tried to leverage her body against the seat to turn to the subsiding voice. Her throat constricted as she pushed, trying to use her one good arm to reach across and touch Amanda. The seatbelt pinned her neck against the headrest. She could not move, could not see, could not say a thing.

More words from her love, half-whispered in what sounded like a smile. "I'm rethinking all those ladybugs, babe. Dragons on the ceiling, maybe? Silver and purple, or maybe green and gold?"

Lydia tried again, and this time her hand brushed the fabric of Amanda's loose shirt. Pushing harder, her good knee leveraged under the dashboard, Lydia followed the seam down to a familiar wrist. She gripped Amanda's fingers, tight enough it should have hurt them both. It did not. The pain traveled out from digits to limbs, resting at the base of their skulls. More neurons fired, or misfired, up into junction of the cerebral cortex that cradled the intersection of the parietal, temporal, and frontal lobes. The amygdala's wrenching attempt at pain modulation bowed into the background, and their anguish registered exactly for what it was: shared experience, certainty, and commitment. The moment bent into itself, searching for the scatter of meaning, that pressing attempt to impose order on the impossible colliding with irreconcilable facts. Facts which, at the boundary of short twilight on a rusty stretch of Southwestern desert, lent themselves to a single interpretation.

Amanda's voice, again. Less sure, breathier.

"Dragons? Fierce but friendly? I think he'd love…"

"Sh-sh-sh." Until she heard the susurration, Lydia didn't even realize her voice had returned, as the noose of the seatbelt slackened jerkily with her straining. She risked another breath. "We're fine, we're all going to be…"

Afterwards, when Lydia replayed what happened next, her mind did not have to fill in the gaps. For her, there were no mercies, large or small, in the gifts of traumatic amnesia or willful suppression. As a student, she had remembered everything there was to know about the effects of supersaturation, or the rate of change of momentum being directly proportional to the impressed force. Each separate detail of a machine—the parts and the piecemeal of it, the calculus of components and whole—tapped itself into her mind on the first or second read. Though Lydia had worked hard on some aspects of her career, she knew she owed her considerable professional success as a headhunted-three-times-over mechanical engineer to this neurological quirk. Until the car crash, her memory had always been a faithful companion, rewarded with gratitude if she thought about it, and simply ignored when she did not.

But that night, like it had every study session in graduate school, her Rubik's cube memory clamped down on facts and figures, formulas and mechanisms. Lydia's subsequent relentless rehashing of the inputs of visual, auditory, tactile, taste and olfactory stimuli while she sprawled across the seat after the accident spared her absolutely nothing. The fishy tang of leaking brake fluid. The scrape of residual gravel on the floormat from their morning hike along the ridge of the mesa to watch the sunrise. The threat of patient tears at the back of her throat. And blanketed over all that, Amanda's voice: quieter than she had ever heard it, but clearer.

"Doesn't matter, love. None of it matters except…"

Lydia heard the surrender, and she fought it. Harder than she wished she had fought off fists in another life, harder than she had fended off cruelty and condescension in another life beyond that. She pressed their fingers closer, trying to write a different ending to their story. "We need dragons, Amanda! Fire-breathing, ground-stomping, crystal-smashing, death-defying—"

And under that, with the sound of her heart ricocheting along cracked ribs, Lydia's unspoken words. *Here, love. I'm here.*

The breath beside her stuttered but did not stop. The voice crept out this time, calm and slow. "I guess the ladybugs will have to do for now, hon. Until you learn to draw…"

The final syllables disappeared in a raspy exhalation. Lydia completed her lover's thought. *Dragons.*

Amanda's fingers, which had at first clung as hard, went abruptly limp in Lydia's rigid fist. Lydia gripped tighter, knowing there was nothing she could do that would hurt Amanda.

Lifting their bound hands upwards, Lydia found the outline of Amanda's chin and cheek. Expecting the intimate, recognizable map of Amanda's raised freckles, Lydia recoiled when her fingers found a sticky, gritty sheen. *The last word. Always had to have the last word.*

Without compassion or generosity, in a time all of its own, the biology of the impact interceded in Lydia's reactive despair. All the patterns of connectivity, all the strands of understanding between the two people in the car dissipated with Lydia's unwelcome descent into unconsciousness. Her mind retreated into the protective shield of shock. Her temperature dropped with the desert's own rhythm, as gray darkness gave way to blue and black. Although her tensed hand resisted until her cramped muscles threatened to overtake the agony of her fractured bones and shattered heart, at last even her frozen fingers succumbed to withdrawal. The final sound Lydia heard as her eyes shut was the thud of Amanda's slack fist against the steering wheel.

Time looped. A journey begun in the wash of an expansive Arizona sunset ended in a ditch on the side of a road. Hours collided with the season of stubborn night and reluctant dawn, and physics took a holiday to keep the stars cold and bright long past when they should have given way to the day's rebirth. Amanda's stillness cradled a fractal of itself. Against the improbable, beyond the impossible, Lydia's heartbeat kept their life moving forward, her dreams of dragons painted across the high arc of an imaginary sky.

Time began again. Headlights of a vehicle coming towards them glanced off Lydia's closed eyes. She forced her eyes open and followed the white beacons as they veered to the side of the road. *Help here.* In the momentary daylight, all she could make out was a thin tube of metal that didn't belong in the car, stretched from the windshield above her head to the driver's side through the seat. *Missed me. Through Amanda. Through them both.*

Tucson (December 1998)

The state trooper's uniform was at least two sizes too big. Everything about the man who stood at attention at the end of Lydia's hospital bed was shrunken except his clothes, which gathered and folded as though they were reluctant to cover him at all. He was in his mid-sixties, with an armadillo shell face and a drab mustache clipped too short on the left side and not short enough on the right. What was left of his shriveled hair clung around his desiccated ears and sprouted in a half crown. The tendons on his neck and his Adam's apple were so close to the surface of his skin that Lydia could count the ridges of collagen and cartilage. She did, over and over again, even after he caught her staring.

Propped against four pillows, Lydia found herself at eye level with the strange envoy of knowledge and power. He coughed twice, a sound that was more hairball than virus. Lydia ground her nails into the sheets, willing herself not to laugh, wondering how much of her gulped giggle was this absurd vision and how much was her mind trying to sequester itself from everything outside that small room.

Her mind failed her as she stifled that impulse, and the laugh spewed out sideways, twisting like an acrobat in mid-air, to collide with a swallowed sob.

Ignoring her, the cop dug in his clown pockets for a

pen and palm-shaped pad of paper. "Thing is," the he said, consulting his notes as though reading them for the first time, "Says here in the initial officer's report that you indicated there was a third occupant of the vehicle."

Lydia blinked, reached for the pain medication dispenser button, and shook her head. Her throat was raspy, her mind was ruffled, and she tried three times before the soundwaves found enough air to travel. When she spoke, none of the words that mattered most came out. *Are they alright? The baby? Where's Amanda? How?* Instead, Lydia's thoughts caught her in midstream agony and redirected her gently, in a direction that seemed safe and simple. "She went for help."

The state trooper's confusion found his eyes, which squinted in the awkward over-and under-lighting of the hospital room. He coughed again, open-mouthed, and retreated to the basics. "Miss McCray? Lydia Ann McCray, says on your driver's license. I'm Officer Perez. One of my men was the first on the scene, after—"

Lydia's automatic reply startled her, as her brain fought again to divert and protect. "Ms. It's Ms. McCray."

Sighing with rising impatience, the officer put one foot up on the chair tucked next to Lydia's bed. "Miz." He buzzed the last sound, adding an eyeroll and a single-shoulder shrug. "Lydia, this is serious. Who's this person you keep talking about, in the car with you?"

The morphine had slipped out from the metered pump, feathering its way through the IV in Lydia's right hand. The drug did exactly what it was supposed to do to the neurons that fed pain messages up and down Lydia's spinal column from her leg, hip, and arm. It blunted and corralled, rerouted and returned. It also slathered damp nausea that tasted bitter at the back of her throat, and Lydia tried to lift herself higher on the bed to ease her discomfort.

"Let me do that." The voice from the doorway reprimanded her like a wayward puppy. A young woman stepped inside and retrieved another blanket from the closet near the bathroom. She was dressed in turquoise scrubs and purple clogs, her ears a riot of studs, a forest tattoo sleeve swirling around one arm, and a simple, one-word name tag. Lydia read it and repeated it in her, over and over. *Nikki. Nikki. Nikki.* "You don't want to hurt yourself."

Turning to go, the night nurse scowled at Officer Perez's leg until he reddened and placed both feet on the floor. "Fifteen minutes," she said, leaving no room for discussion. "Visiting hours are over at nine. No exceptions."

"Here's the thing, Lydia." Officer Perez took out his aggression at the nurse's dismissive attitude towards him on the woman in the bed. "You keep talking about 'they' and 'them,' but there was only one other person in the car. This woman,—" he spat the next words—"this friend of yours, what was her name?"

Lydia could see he had only feigned forgetting. She refused him the satisfaction of filling in her lover's identity. Under the warming blanket of morphine, Lydia brushed away the past tense and wondered why they hadn't put Amanda in the room with her. *Maybe still stitching her up. Checking them out. Making sure everything's al—"*

He snorted, interrupting her reverie. "Amanda. The driver, who caused the accident in the first place."

"A hitchhiker, someone on the side of the road." Lydia ground her teeth and took another breath. "Over the ridge, impossible to see with the sun in our eyes. Not on the road, not the cause of the accident. Unexpected. That's why Amanda swerved. But she was fine. She went for help."

She followed the narrow furrow of thought, ignoring the spliced images that threatened her story. "Amanda was conscious, and I'm sure he was okay. Seatbelts and driver's side airbag, right? He was protected from the force of it.

Officer Perez loomed over the bed, until Lydia could smell burned coffee and cherry lozenges. "She was found deceased on the scene."

Lydia's mind flicked images and sounds back and forth like a slideshow. Her mouth turned down. "What happened? Heart attack? She seemed alright, though, said she was going to…"

Wait. Lydia's eyes fluttered and she bit her lip. *Something's not…*

In the half-breath before the cop resumed his interrogation, Lydia's brain latched onto structure, and the swirl of mis-identifying pronouns attached themselves to people. Three pronouns, two the same, a different pair named and loved, floating in the space between what should have been and what was.

The hospital room shrank, until all Lydia could feel was the scratch of over-washed sheets and the cool flush of the saline drip where it penetrated her skin. She closed her eyes and dropped her head into the pillows. Half the story of the accident faded, as Lydia packed away her two beloveds— 'he' and 'she'—into silk-sashed boxes in her head. *Not now. Not in front of this guy.*

She opened her eyes to find that Officer Perez had stepped closer, his arms folded and his sneer entrenched. When she spoke, her words marched across the air on a mission. "I didn't catch her name. Only saw her for a second on the shoulder before the crash. Didn't even know it was a woman until she told me she was going for help. Backpack, I think? Dark jacket, hood. She sounded older, sixty maybe?"

When the cop didn't move, Lydia added, "Don't you need to write this down?"

Officer Perez snorted. "Lady, you've been through a lot, I get it. But there's no damn point in making up a stranger. Jesus, who'd be hitchhiking out on that road in December? You'd have to be crazy. Desert's freezing at night."

"But…"

He stared at her and sniffed. "State trooper out on routine patrol found your car about six hours after the driver went off the road and hit the pole. Lucky break. You probably wouldn't have made it through the night."

Lydia frowned, the memory of that raspy, determined voice and fading footsteps rising to the surface.

"She was there. In the road, and through the window. You have to find…"

"Enough. You're not protecting anyone. Not anymore." Officer Perez flicked an imaginary speck of link from his sleeve, retrieved his hat from the tray table, and half-turned to the door. "Likely the result of reckless driving is all. No charges left to be filed, given the circumstances. Case closed."

Lydia tried again. Tried to save someone, even though her heart already knew that she had no chance to save the ones who mattered most. Knowing Amanda and Theo were already too far away for her to reach, Lydia pushed against his indifference. "You need to find her. Find the woman who walked away."

The last sentence echoed in Lydia's ears. She tasted the woven triple meaning of the words, which left her wondering. That night, days and nights to follow, through the details of death and geographical dislocation and another stranger's unexplained disappearance, the how and the why and the where gathered themselves around Lydia McCray's mind like fibers of a fungus. They wormed their way in and left spiral sediment in every conversation. In that moment of not knowing who might have rescued them all—and who did not—Lydia's past and present fell away from her future and swallowed it whole.

The cop took her long silence for acquiescence.

"I'm…" His weak lie tried to eat itself like a snake. "Sorry for your loss, Miz McCray. There's paperwork waiting when you're ready. Standard procedure. I'll have one of my deputies drop it at the nurse's station in the next day or two. You'll be in here awhile."

As the messenger of death disappeared out the door, Lydia gripped the glass of water in her good hand. She squeezed with everything she had left, all the exhaustion of not-quite-knowing replaced with the impossible energy of now-there's-nothing-left. Her sorrow hadn't found its way yet to her heart, but the rage arrived with bells on, jarring and bright. She shivered with fury against that hateful man with his questions, his judgments and his smug, withered frame that filled the whole room.

Lydia concentrated her desperation on the after-image of his face and the glass in her hand. The glass resisted, holding its shape, and Lydia flailed, smashing the tumbler against the metal bedrail so hard that shards skittered across the shadows of the room over the threshold onto the fluorescent-lit tiles of the bathroom.

Nikki's clogs thumped and crunched through the door. "What in holy hell?" She dodged a few of the larger chips of glass on the linoleum and squared herself at Lydia's side. Without another word, Nikki double-checked the IV line, systematically patting Lydia's exposed skin for splinters of debris. After half a minute, satisfied that there were no new wounds that required attention, Nikki held Lydia's hand in hers and found her eyes. "He's an asshole. Grade A. Doesn't like what he doesn't understand."

"Can't do this," Lydia muttered. "She was the point.

They were the point."

The next morning, over Nikki's loud protest and with only ten minutes before the occupational therapist was due to wheel her down to the gym for mobility testing, Lydia called the police department. She asked to speak to the other cop assigned to the case. "Officer Lewis?" the operator was obnoxiously cheerful for a job when the likelihood of someone making a social call was close to nil. "I'll see if she's at her desk."

Lydia's hopes rose. The next voice she heard was young and friendly. "This is Officer Maddie Lewis speaking. How can I help?"

After introducing herself, Lydia launched into a rambling explanation of what she had heard on the night. Halfway through, the cop cleared her throat. "Ms. McCray? Can I call you Lydia? Lydia, we've…"

She's already made up her mind. Lydia took another angle. "Officer, it's not for me."

After a moment, the voice returned, direct and open. "What do you—?"

"Officer Lewis—Maddie?" Lydia risked a reciprocal first name, her eyes glancing down at the pages of the police report she held in her hand. "Maddie, I am one hundred percent sure that there was another person on the scene that night, and if something has happened to her, I'd never forgive myself for not doing everything I can to find out what. She sounded older, and she may have been more seriously injured than she thought, and if she collapsed on the way to get help for my family—"

Lydia's voice broke and her eyes burned as she tried to pull Amanda and Theo back into her world. "If something happened to her while she was trying to help us, I'm the only one who knows she's out there somewhere. It's my responsibility to do whatever I can to make sure that she gets home safe."

The police officer waited until Lydia taken two full, noisy breaths before she spoke again. "Officially? Case closed. The techs have examined at the car, and there's nothing to indicate the presence of anyone else. Besides, what if you are right and it was a hitchhiker? We get a lot of people out here on the roads, people not from around here. People who don't want to be found and know how to make sure that when they're gone, they stay gone."

"I know. I know!" Lydia winced as her broken bones protested the tension. "I've read every word of the accident report summary the other guy left here three times through. But—"

The cop on the other end of the line, eighteen months out of the academy, interrupted her. She dropped her voice and slowed down, and Lydia imagined furtive glances around an open-desk police station from a young person determined to do the right thing. "I said officially, Lydia. Unofficially? Well, my shift ends at two, and I don't have to pick up my niece from daycare until five-thirty if I tell them I'm running behind."

At the unexpected and unintentionally insensitive mention of a child, Lydia bit the inside of her cheek and waited for the cop to finish. "I'll drive out there, scout the area again myself. Plenty of daylight left. I'll check with the farm up the road."

"Thank you." Another stranger's kindness threatened a storm, but a drumbeat on the door cut short Lydia's uncried tears. She nodded at the phone. "When I asked yesterday, Officer Perez said—"

Maddie scoffed. "Never mind that. Besides, nothing to thank me for yet. Promise though, Lydia. After everything that's happened, you rest and focus on one second at a time."

As the therapist steered her wheelchair into the elevator, chattering with small talk about the weather and local traffic during holidays, Lydia replayed Maddie's last sentence in her head. There was something comforting about the time frame the cop mentioned, something infinitely more possible than the one data time that Lydia seem to have heard a thousand times over since ambulance officers asked her if she was conscious on the way to the hospital.

There is always something small and unexpected, something which, before tragedy, carries less weight than a lost button or a crumpled paper cup. But after catastrophe, after the fire has been put out, the metal has been wrenched apart, after the bones have been set and the gash has been sutured and the blood has been mopped and the glass has been swept from the floor, even the idioms of time reset themselves. There is no taking it one day at a time. There is no next year, next month or even tomorrow; there is only the long now. The length of an ordinary day seems obscene, every single one of the 86,400 seconds allotted to an earthly rotation bending itself into a Mobius strip without end or beginning.

When the faceless cop gave her permission to feel her way blindly through each particle of the day, Lydia found herself counting how many times she blinked as the buttons flashed floors. In the rehab gym on the second floor, two sets of four-count knee bends and the half-dozen seated core twists fractured into stop-motion in Lydia's mind. She could count to a thousand between breaths; but as long as she kept counting, she kept breathing. And as long as she kept breathing, some part of those she had left in the car kept breathing, too. Even the disembodied voice that had promised aid and vanished into the dying day had permission to stay, with only a slim possibility of recovery and return. *Not nothing. Hope is no small thing.*

An hour after lunch the next day, everybody died. Nikki retrieved the handset for Lydia, who was recovering from sedation after a second round of surgery on an unpredictable radial head.

"It's that cop you mentioned—the other one. Thought you'd want to take it if you could." Nikki smiled encouragingly and raised the head of the bed with the handheld remote.

With a slow thumbs-up, Lydia nodded. "Maddie? Tell me you found something."

The voice on the other end sounded like a child who had lost a puppy. Treading carefully, taking refuge in police jargon, Officer Lewis read her bullet point notes. "Nothing. Completed a thorough round on foot without any indication that another person had walked through the scrub in weeks. A few owl pellets and crow carcass, but nothing beyond that. Spoke to all six occupants of the two residences in close proximity to the scene without success. All were home at the time of the incident, and all report not seeing or hearing anyone or anything unusual."

Taking a deep breath, Maddie hurried on before Lydia could respond. "They corroborate one another's stories, and there is no reason whatsoever to suspect foul play of any kind in this situation. As part of the supporting documentation that was not contained in the police report made available to you, a computer search has been conducted on all missing persons reports matching the description of an older women across three counties. I have to conclude with confirmation of the findings of the initial report, and you'd do best to consider it the final word on the matter."

Digging her way through the landslide of terminology, Lydia finally found her moment. "What about an aerial search? You might have missed something, she might still be out there, the desert gets so cold at night, she..."

"Nothing more I can do, Ms. McCray. As I've already stated, no further resources are available to be allocated to this line of inquiry. It has already gone too far."

The barrage of cop-speak continued. "In fact, protocol dictates that I inform my superiors immediately of my overstepping the boundaries of my authority in this situation and—"

The voice on the other end cut off, and when it returned she was Maddie again. "No. That's bullshit. Lydia...Lydia? I am truly sorry. By rights I shouldn't have even been out there yesterday—don't know what my bosses would do if they found out—but please believe me when I tell you that the only person who wanted this to work out as much as you was me. I didn't want you to be disappointed. Not after what's happened."

She paused again, unsuccessfully searching for a kind way to say what came next. "For what it's worth, I believe you think you saw something. That's the thing when it comes to situations like this, Lydia. Sometimes, even the questions that should have answers don't."

Tucson (December 1998)

"No one else coming?" Nikki glanced out the double doors of the hospital and pushed Lydia through into the warm January day. The taxi driver swished the brim of his baseball cap and loaded her bags into the trunk. "Sure you'll be okay to get home?"

Lydia patted the young nurse's hand and practiced her smile, feeling the creases shuffle across her cheeks. "Just one stop to make on the way to the hotel. Flight leaves on Tuesday, airport knows I'll need a wheelchair, and we've got…"

The plural snapped her mouth shut. Lydia exhaled and lied. "There will be someone on the other side. Friends."

Nikki hugged her. "Don't tell my boss, but if you need anything, call me. Number's on a Post-It in the inside pocket of your bag. I'm off Monday."

The taxi driver held the door as Lydia scuttled herself into the springy back seat. Without being asked, Nikki reached inside the car and buckled Lydia's seatbelt. "Sorry, I know the bruises are still…"

"It's nothing." Lydia shook her head and brushed off the other woman's attention. "I'm good to go."

As they pulled into traffic, the driver held up a scrap of paper. "Says here you want to go to this address in La

Madera and out to the Catalina Foothills for an hour, but
you're staying at the Hyatt by the airport. Picking up some
people on the way?"

Lydia had cried twice in the three weeks she had
spent in hospital. Once after the police officer, with rage and
helplessness, and once on the phone with Amanda's dad the
day after the accident. Roy had been the first in Amanda's
family to welcome Lydia with a bear hug when they had met,
and the first and only one of the Marquez clan who was more
than doggedly tolerant of the prospect of a baby with two
mothers joining their family. Telling Roy made it real,
because he had made her and Amanda's expectant
exhilaration as much part of his heart as theirs.

The rest of the time Lydia's face had molded itself
into somber distraction, through the parade of her lover's
local friends and family who arrived with flowers and cards
and their own grief on fresh display. Each block of visiting
hours for the first week spat out a new parade of mourners
eager to offer Lydia solace and tend to their own loss, and
Lydia had waded through them with stoic resignation. She
had talked to funeral directors, Amanda's boss and three co-
workers, and representatives from ever-distant concentric
circles of their New York tribe, each time without a hint of
distress beyond what seemed necessary to convey the news.
To every person who responded with a wail or a sob, Lydia
offered the platitudes that she had been offered herself, and
she moved on to the next phone call or e-mail or visit.
Taking care of other people's feelings was straightforward;

admitting that she had any of her own was not.

The taxi driver was different. His question was simply a transactional communicative act between strangers, meant to provide useful information to him for the task at hand. Ask, answer, do: the transparent trifecta of social congress, practiced billions of times a day in thousands of languages. When contact is minimal, when the expectations are well-known and the tableau well-rehearsed, when knowledge of the other is flat and sterile, the easy-come-and-easy-go of everyday interaction runs cold and clear. But when the first actor's lines cannot be met with cued call-and-response, when the second party is absent or unsure or ignorant, the illusion of shared understanding splinters.

Lydia's hand reached for the Kleenex in her satchel as her chin sagged, and the tears rumbled down her cheeks in fat, open defiance of her intentions to keep it all inside.

Frowning in concern in the rearview mirror, the driver tried to backtrack. "Miss, I'm so sorry, I didn't mean to…"

Lydia waved her hand without replying and slid so he could not see her. He cleared his throat and noisily opened a tin of mints. She wept silently at first, the only sound the intermittent scrape of the tissue against her cheeks. When that wasn't enough, her first inhalation was a staccato squeal. The driver reached to the dashboard without another comment and turned on the radio.

The music was a march: grandiose, gaudy, with enough percussion and brass to conceal Lydia's jarring cries.

As they drove through the city, her voice unfolded into a muted howl. Each time she got louder, so did the radio, this time directed discreetly by the driver with the flick of a finger on the steering wheel's volume controls. He crunched and chewed and watched the road. She shuddered and squirmed and closed her eyes.

With a clash that made the driver of the next car over frown disapproval at the noise, the music pounded its way through five more minutes of trumpets and timpani. Lydia rocked back and forth, her head in her hands, her sobbing unhinged.

Suddenly, nothing. The music blasted its final bar, and Lydia instinctively exhaled all that she had left into the last ringing notes of a messy harmonic.

She could not acknowledge the stranger's witness. She did not have to. As they waited their turn at a stoplight, he spoke gently, slung his arm around the passenger headrest. "My Almira was eight years old. Bone cancer, started in her leg. I ask myself every day if she'd still be here if I'd noticed sooner. With her mom already gone, I was working all the time, I didn't see anything until it was too late."

The car behind them honked at the stab of green. The taxi driver stomped the accelerator hard enough to jolt them both. When he spoke again, his voice sounded like bone and glass, and Lydia's horrific, precise memories of her recent catastrophe scraped against his from a half century past. "Twenty-three years next October."

Boundary broken. With the play come undone from

the puppet strings of a common script, two people can find themselves unimpeded by expectation. The center shifts to embrace a new path for the chance encounter. Even when the moment is small—a shared elevator that stalls before resuming its climb, a low jet engine rumbling too loudly overhead—the conversation that comes next can step outside the frame of the commonplace. That is where everything that is interesting about human action and interaction happens, in the liminal mist of not knowing what comes next.

Lydia's eyes snapped upwards, her hand on his shoulder, before she realized she had moved. She found other words, words not mean to comfort or commiserate, but only to pry open their reciprocal sadness. "Feels impossible. I'm supposed to ask all those questions about whether it gets better, or how did you make it through the first few weeks. I'm supposed to apologize for your suffering."

She sighed, leaving her hand where it rested. Her eyes found his ID tag on the window. "I'm supposed to do a lot of things. But all I can do, Mr. Abadi, all I can damn well do in this exact second is wonder when I'm going to wake up and how she'll hug me and say it's all a nightmare."

The cabbie paused the meter and pulled over. As he unclicked his seatbelt and swiveled, Lydia saw the man for the first time. His eyebrows met in the middle, an arched collision of gray hair that was indistinguishable from the tight curls that hung low on his forehead. He wore half-rim glasses that clung to his speckled ears and perched on a rounded nose. His face was slack, three chins vying for prominence, and his mouth was small, full of nicotine-stained teeth.

"Miss, I cannot say where you have been in your life until now." He lay his liver-spotted hand on hers. "Only that this place you are in…it is your new home. You will live here from that moment forward, and a part of you will always be trying to wake up."

"I'm Lydia." She declared it more loudly than intended, as invitation and recognition of where they found themselves, idling on the side of the road from one version of fresh hell to another as her future arrived whether or not she was ready or able.

He touched his heart with his other hand. "Nashwan. I would like to say I am pleased to meet you, but given how we find each other, that would be the worst sort of insult I might imagine. You are right to presume the end of formality between us, Lydia. Because you and I? We know."

She didn't have to ask what. A few straggling tears squeezed themselves down the side of her face and she clenched her jaw.

Nashwan continued, as though talking to an audience beyond the car, beyond anyone Lydia could hear or see. "Other people who don't know? Family, friends, doctors? They will try to name it, this feeling you have." He sneered. "Grief. Mourning period. What is that other one?"

His snicker drew icicles in the dry heat of the car and mocked the ridiculous sunshine of a warm Arizona winter's day. "Bereavement, yes. A favorite of the psychologists my brother sent me to in the years after. Cold, specific, direct words. But those words mean nothing, because your house now is made of death and darkness and endings."

Lydia nodded slowly, her mind warping itself as it tried to detour around the Cimmerian imperative. "People keep trying to say there will come a time for new beginnings. I can't breathe, and all they want to talk about is next steps, new life."

Nashwan put his seatbelt back on and glanced over his shoulder before merging back into the watery flow of traffic. "There is no new, and running? Running only gets you back here faster, Lydia. Some people say it's where you need to be. I say it's merely where you are."

They sat in silence for a minute. Moving slowly, and grateful for the codeine-laced Tylenol Nikki had dosed her with on the way out of the hospital, Lydia scooped up all the discarded Kleenex that had fallen in icy cascades across the back seat and onto the floor. She squeezed them in both hands and shoved the soggy sphere into her satchel before dabbing her hands with disinfectant.

There is a moment in every instance of true communication when all the right words have been sown by one voice and harvested by another, when any more air between them is either worn out or wasted. The truth hovers in the space between. Nothing—neither good will nor grunting labor—can prolong its efflorescence. Lydia felt their instant pass, but before she surrendered the unexpected and startlingly welcome intimacy, she offered one last whiff of affinity and trust. "La Madera, and Catalina Hills?"

Nashwan's returned question was in the shrug. Lydia swallowed the rising bile in her gorge, tasting acid and grit. She clung to the grim recognition that her body would get plenty of practice holding things down. "Funeral home, Nashwan. I told her dad I'd bring the ashes to their house for the memorial. My plane to New York City leaves tomorrow first thing."

They both knew that was it. There would be no exchange of numbers, no extended shared lament, no more details proffered. As happens with a glimpse of communion in the emotional soup that is the human experience from birth to the death of those around us to our own mortality, both mourned the loss of what they could not name. Nonetheless, in feeling it for what it was though they could not turn it over in their minds and study it like a stray insect or a favorite poem, they felt its transformation from added burden to unforeseen gift.

Distracted by a semi-trailer making a wide turn at the intersection ahead, Nashwan waited a beat before delicately tugging loose the threads of their unlikely connection. "No much traffic across town this time of day. Have you there ten minutes tops."

After their first stop, Lydia stared determinedly out of the car window and counted mailboxes as they wound their way north into the ritziest district of Tucson's ringed suburbs. She resolutely ignored the paper bag with sturdy twine handles and blocky lettering on one side, but she had torn off the green piece of paper with the words 'Marquez-McCray/Tuesday 22nd' stapled to the outside like Thai take-out.

She stared down endless driveways that curved into long, low swathes of earth-toned stucco, counting the bends until they finally arrived at Amanda's parents' house. The multi-winged, mocha brown mansion squatted on the hill, its ornate stone and mosaic fountain balanced by a grove of bare honey mesquite trees along one edge of the garden. The branches of the trees swirled around one another like knotted string, rough and wild. The fountain bubbled and splashed, ignoring the chaos inside and out. Flanking the driveway, red cylinders of firecracker penstemon competed with low-slung desert mallow for winter glory.

Wrenching her eyes from the vivid colors that reminded her sharply of sunsets and blood despite the idyllic pair of hummingbirds that swooped among the flowers, Lydia concentrated on the rounded archway of the front door. It was painted sage with melon green accents, to match the semi-circle bed of creosote and jojoba that cradled the entrance to her lover's childhood home.

And you know all the names of these plants, and you notice color variation, and you appreciate the carved blocks of Southwestern architecture now because...no. No. No.

With the echo of the negation in her head, Lydia slung her satchel across her body and exhaled through her nose.

"Dispatch said you'd wait," Lydia said as she carefully stretched one leg and pulled her crutches off the taxi's floor. "Flat rate for the next two hours, right?"

Nashwan moved fast, and he held the door for her as she climbed out, using both hands and a knee to steady herself before venturing onto the crushed gravel and irregular flagstones of the walkway up to the front door. "No problem," he said. "I'll be out here by three, but I can wait as long as you need." He held on to the last word, knowing Lydia would notice. She did, and she dug her fingers into the hard, molded plastic of the crutches until it hurt.

"Thank you. I'll leave my suitcase in the trunk unless it'll be in your way." Less than she could have said, though as much as she was capable in that transition between the sanctuary of the cab and the dismal prospect of people on the other side of this house's entry. With only a minute before the door opened to greet her, Lydia tried to stabilize herself against their collective grief.

She smiled to herself when Roy stepped through first, his six-foot-six-and-half-again-as-wide frame wedging through the door like a hobbit. Roy Marquez had the same ironed-straight ginger hair and embossed run of dark freckles that his only daughter had been blessed with, and his round face showed every minute of his hard-earned path to material success at the top of this Arizona hill. He talked fast, in a Texas twang that would have done his cattle auctioneer dad proud.

Roy did not smile as he strode toward her in his

loose jeans and scruffy blue t-shirt, arms open, dark eyes rimmed with exhaustion, daring her to blink. She didn't. "Holy hell, Lyds. Dammit it to Hades and back in a goddamn gold-crusted golf cart, you should have let me scoop you up out of that Christ-forsaken place."

He hugged her as though she might break again, but still managed to tug her halfway off her feet before she groaned and pulled away. "I know I'm late."

Roy laughed with his mouth. "Ha! Joke's on the rest of 'em, because I knew the doctors wouldn't get their claws out of you before noon. I told everyone this—" He searched for the word, discarding 'party,' 'gathering,' and even 'shindig' inside his head, chewing his lip before seeming to accept the implausibility of any alternative. Holding out his arm so Lydia could lean on him as she hobbled on one foot, Roy continued, "They'll be here at five, half of 'em dragging casseroles and salads and Jell-O molds filled with canned pineapple and what-not."

Nashwan headed off Lydia's apology. "How about I head to the airport for a few fares and we say eight o'clock pick-up?"

Roy frowned at the cab driver. "Pick up? Thought your flight was in the morning, Lyds."

Lydia tried to concentrate over the rising buzz of a headache. "Staying at the airport hotel tonight, Roy. Can't." She tried again, the words speeding up as Amanda's mother clip-clopped down the walkway with hooded eyes and measured steps. She was short and narrow-shouldered, pale to the point of blue translucency, and dressed in a cashmere twin set.

"Won't," Lydia said. "Not after what happened at the hospital with Evie."

Roy's loyalties split as his face clouded over. He couldn't absolve his wife for the unforgivable or explain to Lydia how far his unrelenting Catholic wife had come to make even grudging room for the truth of Amanda's love and life, but he could forgive her almost anything after the death of their only child. He gripped Lydia's arm more tightly and steered her around Evie's unspoken query.

Evie Marquez had trusted in good manners her whole life, and the absurd despair of this occasion called for nothing less. She nodded a quick greeting to Lydia, who returned the gesture, and walked around the other side of the cab.

Nashwan had retrieved the brown paper bag and was cradling it against his chest. When Evie saw how he was holding it, she winced and took it from him impatiently, gripping the handles and holding her arm out like the broken wing of an injured bird.

She pressed a wad of bills into the cab driver's hand and spoke more slowly than she needed to. Nashwan Abadi had lived in America a long time, and had endured more tapered, over-exaggerated interactions from well-meaning cretins that he cared to count. Without open rancor or even internalized dread, he filed Evie in that drawer in his head, thanked her for the generous tip, and reiterated to Lydia that he would be back to pick her up.

"Don't ask," said Roy as the car drove off and Evie frowned.

"Is what it is," Evie said, still holding the bag like a load of dirty laundry. Her upbringing reasserted herself and breached the absurd. "I trust you were able to rest in hospital, Lydia?"

Lydia McCray managed a stifled, "Well enough," before Roy put his arm around her waist and propelled her inside.

Roy and Lydia sat in the breakfast nook with a view across the valley, Lydia's leg propped up on two pillows and a wicker chair. Evie tucked the bag out of sight against the refrigerator and served coffee in china cups complete with a set of silver tongs for the sugar bowl and matching polished tray. Crystal water tumblers with rounded ice cubes sulked on square cork coasters, and wafer cookies crowded a fluted ceramic serving dish. Lydia counted her breaths and craned her neck.

She lasted five minutes and mouthed an apology to Roy. "I haven't opened it. They had it ready in reception when I got there."

None of them needed to ask. Evie took a last, lingering lap around the perimeter of the kitchen and picked up her water glass from the table before retrieving the bag.

She pulled up a stool, sitting a foot above the others, and opened it slowly, as though a bomb might go off. *Already has.* Lydia tensed every muscle she could remember how to move. *Nothing worse could...*

The thing about absolutes is that the world ebbs and flows in such a way as to ensure that every thought like Lydia's last immediately invites Fate to dance and jeer. The middle finger of fortune waits for those moments when the human heart can bear no more, when the brain can send no more neurons cascading down a rational pathway of cognition or consequence. Beyond the quantum reality of physics and probability, in human stories too old to tell, the Moirai or their equivalent can be cast as vessels of destiny or predatory opportunists. Primed for slivers of chance, which Lydia gave, and instantly (but belatedly) regretted.

What Evie pulled from the nondescript sack could be described in simple terms: two containers, rectangular, one larger than the other, both taped shut.

What Lydia saw was something else. She recoiled and swung an open palm to her mouth, retching. As her arm swept across the table, the two remaining glasses and the plate of cookies took flight, smashing into the terracotta floor and spilling crumbs and liquid in a pond of damp debris.

Roy found his voice, though it took two tries to swallow the worst of his epithets. "What in the good Lord in Heaven's name is that supposed to be, Evelyn?"

She gazed at the containers below. "One for Amanda, and one for the baby, Roy Marquez. And I'll thank you not to take His name in vain."

Lydia gulped twice before she risked speech. Her questions tumbled out like uncut diamonds: dull, tough, and unfinished. "Two urns? Two, Evie? How did they? Why did you? What were you?"

Evie's smile came from somewhere beyond reason, where her faith lulled and soothed her, where the plan (as painful as it might be) was unfolding as her chosen deity decreed, admitting neither error nor deceit.

Sitting side by side on the table, the urns seemed to occupy the entire room. They shared angles and sheen with the silver tray and tongs of the coffee service, glinting in the tumble of bright light from the looped chandelier overhead. The lid of the larger container was covered in scrolling border of tiny etched flowers; the smaller sported a finely-detailed baby rattle, complete with open looped handle to uncover the capsule of death.

Without lifting either top, Evie caressed the child's toy and pressed the tips of her fingers into the grooved floral decoration.

Lydia recoiled, and her shoulders shook. Roy reached over to give her a side-on hug; he stopped halfway when he saw she was giggling without a sound.

She slapped the table as the laughter found its way out of her nose and mouth, eyes streaming with tears, smiling cracking her face. "Jesus, Evie, what'd they do, scoop up a handful of Amanda and hope that a bit of Theo made it in there, too? Sift for bones, quarter-inch fingers and penny toes to the left please, ten-inch ribs to the right?"

Shocked at her own anarchy but unrepentant, Lydia swigged her too-hot coffee and sputtered as it scraped her throat. Her next words were a growl. "I don't care what you think about me, but if there's a chance you ever loved your daughter, that you could see beyond your own pinprick worldview, tell me how you imagined this moment was going to go?"

Amanda's mother had already retreated to a place in her head where the sound waves ricocheting between Lydia's mouth and Evie's ears could not follow. Her fingers skimmed back and forth across the urns, to a beat only she could hear.

When Evie spoke, her voice was supple, made warm and soft by a belief that could be stirred and even nudged to suit the unwelcome circumstance she found herself in the moment her daughter came out at seventeen. Stirred, but never completely shaken. "Two souls, Lydia. Two souls for Heaven."

Lydia did not reply. She could have retorted that Evie's standard version of gay people regularly had them rotting in hell, or that doctrine dictated that a child gone unbaptized and who died *in utero* might not pass angelic muster at the pearly gates. She could have rehashed both sides of the angry argument in the hospital, when Evie spewed insult over Lydia's injuries, blaming the survivor for the death of her daughter and grandson. But there is a difference between spitfire and spite, between a spontaneous gush of venom and a calculated vortex of malice. Lydia had the first in abundance; having experienced the latter as the target too often, she refused to capitulate to using it as a weapon herself.

Roy reached over the table, gathered up the coffee cups, and stepped over the puddle on the floor. Without a word to either woman, he retrieved the brush and pan and a dishtowel and began to sweep up around their feet. As soon as he placed the cloth on the floor on Lydia's side, she picked up her crutch and stumbled upright. She hobbled to the sliding kitchen door, wrestled with the latch, and stepped outside.

The xeriscape of the backyard sported rockeries full of bear grass, cholla, compass barrels and prickly pear, interspersed with large specimen trees of ironwood and acacia. Eager to share her heart's geography, Amanda had walked Lydia around this grassless expanse over and over during their infrequent visits to Arizona, until the interloper was sure she knew as much about botanical water use as she did about her life's work in mechanical engineering.

Leaning against the broken ridges of the ironwood's main trunk on that impossible afternoon, Lydia tried to catalog all she could see. She had ticked her way through most of the raised beds when her eyes landed on a domed, waist-high shrub at one end of the plunge pool. The plant was drowning in bright yellow flowers, petals arched outward and down from a darker center as if trying to escape its gravity. The leaves, gray-green and ghostly, where clustered below like a mat of algae.

Lydia muttered a few possibilities to herself. She squinted, but didn't move from her observation perch, not trusting her footing on the dry, loose soil. She breathed slowly as a round of nausea rumbled through and passed her by. A moment later, the incongruence hit her. She whispered the cautious revelation under her breath like a prayer. "Brittlebush! Winter flower, sure—but you parade like that now, you'll have nothing to show for it in February."

Closing her eyes, Lydia sighed. "Stupid, stupid plant. Peaked too soon. Nothing left to give in a month. Serve you right if Roy digs you up and roots a cockatiel or organ pipe in your place."

"A what now?" Roy stepped out next to her and closed the door behind him. He smiled gently and crossed his arms. "I get that botany isn't exactly your thing, Lyds, that you're all about machines and such, and an organ pipe cactus would be at home anywhere out here, but you know a cockatiel's a bird, right?"

Lydia returned his smile with a small, grinding one of her own. They were hip to hip, staring at the wayward plant while she spoke. "Inside joke. Amanda was always after me to learn the name of every plant we ever saw. Got that from you, I guess. She's the only one I know can—" Lydia paused as grammar caught up with reality—"Only one I know could walk through Brooklyn and name every weed bursting through cracks in the sidewalk."

Roy nodded without turning his head. He answered so softly that Lydia strained to hear. "She always saw the beautiful, y'know?"

The big man dropped his arms and shook out his

hands. "What am I saying? Of course you know. I could tell that from the first time she brought you home. Amanda was always ambitious, always focused on the next goal, the next trophy. Two years out of law school, top of her class, her mom and I figured all that ever mattered was the job."

He walked a few strides forward, pulling a branch of the ironwood toward him and daring the thorns on the young bark to draw blood. "Until she met you."

Lydia could not follow him, literally or figuratively. She remained still, dragging them both through a merciful U-turn. "I got a lot of the plant names down pretty fast but could never quite remember ocotillo. Amanda figured cockatiel was close enough."

The dead woman's father returned them to the danger zone. "That's our Amanda, alright," Roy said, his voice breaking. "Always driving herself toward perfection, and perfectly willing to grant 'good enough' to everybody else."

They stood in silence for a minute, and Roy continued as if to himself. "Gets that first part from her mother. Neither one could ever accept anything less than the best from themselves, no matter what."

Like an ice skater on the first day of winter, Lydia ventured a wobbling few paces toward him. Turning towards her, he caught Lydia's free hand and held her steady. "I'm sorry, Roy. In the kitchen, I had no idea what she'd done."

Roy squeezed the bridge of his nose and sighed. "I get it. But you don't need to apologize, not to me."

He gazed upwards as a hawk spiraled in the dying light. "When you first arrived here with Amanda six years ago, I only had a walk a few steps to meet you. Didn't take much, from where I'd been standing my whole life, letting people get on with whoever or whatever or however they were meant to be."

Taking a deep breath, Roy put his arm around Lydia. "Wasn't like that for Evie."

Lydia struggled for graciousness and settled for begrudging grace. "I know."

"No." Roy held her more securely. "You think of it as a switch, as something she could flip and forget. But after that first time in high school, when Amanda found voice to come out to us, Evie packed the information away like a winter coat. And when the years went by and we never heard a thing about it, I guess Evie figured she'd never have face the whole thing square."

"Until me." Lydia felt the anger careening in her gut, threatening to crash into Roy's explanation.

He felt her go stiff and released his arm. "She knows. Knows that you were the best thing to happen to Amanda by a long shot. Knows Amanda's truth was more important than her own ambivalence and distress."

Roy pivoted as he found himself too deep in the swamp of someone else's emotions. He pointed to the valley below. "Still miss it, sometimes. The work. Firm did it all, y'know. Flood control, erosion abatement, urban storm water management. Even managed to dip my hand into a bridge project or two over the years, but I always came back to water. Didn't always get it exact, of course. Too much or never enough, that's the trouble."

Gratefully, Lydia followed him into the minutiae. "You know as well as I do, engineering projects are only as good as the data they're based on. Civil, mechanical—yours or mine—it's all a balancing act. Using what we know, planning ahead, predicting what we can."

"Mitigating the fallout from what we can't." The words were out in the world. Lydia tried to steer the conversation to higher ground with a question about Roy's engineering top ten list. They talked shop for a few minutes more, and silence reasserted itself. There was nowhere to run.

Turning to go, Roy offered Lydia a bleak smile, "All you need to know about Evie, you should understand—she loved that baby, Lyds. Come his first breath, his first cry, Evie would have loved your baby with her whole heart."

Without knowing what he'd done, Roy put words to Lydia's elemental terror. "You're the only one left of the three, see?"

Lost in her fear, Lydia missed the rest of what Roy said as he went inside and closed the door. "The one most distant from her. We're family, Lyds. With Amanda and Theo gone, it's going to take a little more time before Evie realizes she can love you, too."

Lydia stayed in the garden another hour, sitting on a stone bench under a forty-foot madrone tree and tracing imaginary maps with her fingertips over the pinkish brown bark. She tried to count how many times she'd heard Amanda's name since the accident. How many times had she said it, or thought it? How many times had she wished someone else hadn't? It wasn't the six letters in isolation, spun in the air over rehashed conversations wondering why.

As she heard the first guests pull up in the driveway around the front of the house, Lydia thought she knew what they had all been doing. Like a witch doctor or a paramedic, they had all been trying to bring Amanda back.

Names cannot be merely names. At first pass, they label and locate, distinguish and document. But there is something untoward and desperate about repetition of a name, over and over again, the same sounds pouring into an indifferent universe. Beyond designation or symbol, names promise the alchemy of invocation made material. They are desires made possible, dreams made real. The language of nomenclature is not a placeholder; it is the sticky science of DNA, unique prints of this creature or that, this molecule or that. A person's name can be a totem or a talking point. It can be a shield or a showpiece, and the whole returned by the name alone is always much less than the sum of its parts.

She left herself on that bench at dusk, with the gathering trill of strained conversation spilling from the house's long, low windows. She put her name down into the rock and the wood and the dirt, and she left herself, and went inside, and walked, and talked, and was Lydia McCray. And was not.

Grief's power in an open forum like a memorial

service is a great migration, with each person eager for information of the dead. It is a hard press for data transfer, one to another, most abreast of details to least, in a diminishing concatenation of twisted storytelling about what happened and why. This was not the gross gawkishness of overt inquisition—the accident had been covered well enough in the paper and the back channels of Tucson's high society gossip, though mention of Lydia had been relegated (at Evie's request) to the wasted phrases 'close friend,' 'family friend,' or even 'New York associate.'

No. This was the soft, persistent scratch of the same conversation, over and over again, until Lydia could see the words rising in front of her open eyes before they spilled from the next person's mouth. She nodded, mumbled, accepted a hug or a pat or a double-fisted handshake, and moved on, around and around the room like a music box ballerina, until the twilight turned to tar and Roy marshaled out the last invited guest.

Evie tutted at the mess of paper plates and foil-trapped casserole dishes, offering a diffident wave over her shoulder as she headed for the kitchen. Lydia shook her head when Roy pointed to the urns, which had presided over the gathering from a double cake stand on the dining room table, edging out layers of cold cuts, sticky fruit punch, and filigreed petits fours. "Better here," she said, giving him a long hug. *With people who want to remember.*

He was confused, but he did not say another word as she jerked a thumb at the door. "Taxi's back. See you—" she couldn't finish the lie, not to Roy's face. "Take care, Roy. Both of you. Take care."

Back in Brooklyn by the next afternoon, half-finished ladybugs mocked her from the bedroom down the hall. Long past midnight, face down on the couch, she dreamed of alphabet dragons.

Brooklyn (December 1998)

Lydia awoke to the sound of the coffee maker that she had set the night before. She had been on automatic pilot: shades down, lights out, coffee from the freezer timed and ready for her first cup of the day. She listened to the sound of bubbling water for a moment before she remembered it was coffee for one. Lydia moaned and rolled over, wishing the light away.

An hour later, she opened her eyes and half-fell off the bed before reaching for her cane. Her crutches stood waiting for her failure, but she was damned if she was going to hobble around without a free hand to open her own doors and press her own buttons as she set about the task of finding whatever life she might have left.

The doctors had weaned her off the real medication, and she had not found a zone of détente with the tornado of pain that spiraled up her leg and into her hip. Her ribs were still tender, and her bruises mostly faded to lilac and kiwi, but her leg was clear that it would be a long time, if ever, before the storm of reconstructed bone and torn ligaments healed to the point of not noticing they were there.

She fought the nausea that arrived as she placed her leg on the floor and tested it for stability. Finding none, she stood up anyway and used her free hand to press into the wall as she made her way to the door.

The apartment glowed. The sun had found its way through a Christmas of rain and slush, and New York City had decided to go all-out angelic on Lydia's first morning home. She grabbed the remote from the coffee table and stabbed buttons through streaming eyes, until she hit the right one and the slats closed, one by one, on the white winter sunshine and the promise of someone else's new day.

Thank God someone told the post office. Without stopping to wonder which of Amanda's inner circle of absurdly considerate friends it could be, Lydia limped from the elevator past the mailboxes to the front door of brownstone.

She wedged open the door with her cane and glanced up. The sky had had the decency to cloud over a little, but the air was still fresher than it had any right to be in the middle of a big city and she could hear birds from the park across the street. Lydia took a right turn, the way she had done hundreds of times before with Amanda on their way to their favorite breakfast place. Seven days a week, six a.m. to midnight, Xeno's served olive bread drizzled with thyme-infused honey, bowls of rice pudding and thick *galotyri*, and *kaseri* cheese that Amanda had introduced Lydia to and where they had been eating at least once a week.

Xeno's was quiet on this late Tuesday morning. Lydia had taken a month from work, two weeks of that without pay, to try to reconstruct whatever might be possible from the rubble of her life. She was not used to the pattern of foot traffic that deviated into old/alone and young parents with babies, and she was confronted with more strollers than she could be expected to ignore. But she tried, and she felt the hunger pangs in her stomach, and she thought of what breakfast had been.

From the sidewalk, Lydia could see several empty tables inside as well as those occupied by the perennial crop of old men playing cards and backgammon. She was making her way so slowly that the owner's son, a short twenty-something with arms the size of logs and a broad, crooked smile, saw her and beckoned her inside. When she shrugged and began to turn away, he pushed open the door.

"Miss Lydia, no! What have you done?" He walked around her, inspecting her injuries from every angle he could see.

This cannot be happening. Lydia felt the tears hurdle her defenses and she jerked her head down. "Little accident, that's all. Soon be all as it was, Belen."

The man frowned and reached to pull open the door. "Breakfast on me. I insist."

For a moment, Lydia was tempted to surrender to his kindness. His next words broke everything as though it were not already in pieces on the floor. "Miss Amanda not up for breakfast this morning, eh? Not too long before you'll both have the little one in here, though. I remember with first one, my wife, she—"

"Can't, sorry." Lydia tacked her face into a smile. "Promised Amanda I'd stop by the market for cottage cheese and cola lollipops."

Belen nodded, laughing. "Got it in one, Miss Lydia. Whatever the pregnant lady wants, the pregnant lady gets."

Lydia limped away. She kept her eyes down, dodging cigarette wrappers and half-empty juice bottles and counting leafless trees around the block. She was back home within an hour, and she did not leave for two weeks.

The phone rang all the time. Lydia answered every fourth call. She hung up on insurance agents, pleaded illness to Amanda's friends, ranted at the telemarketers who tried to sell her electric blankets or toaster ovens, and replaced the receiver in silence when Roy called. She ate everything in the house, down to the last of the frozen blueberry pockets that Amanda loved and she hated. She spooned olives into her mouth and chased them with vodka or gin. She dug out packets of soy sauce from a near-bare refrigerator and made a puddle of the salty gunk on a plate, dipping stale crackers and stirring Apple Jacks in with a spoon. The only thing Lydia kept down those first two weeks after Arizona was the alcohol. At three nominal mealtimes every day, she methodically chewed every morsel that she and Amanda had shopped for together, and methodically (though not deliberately) vomited it back up within twenty minutes of swallowing the last bite. She started drinking at six o'clock, four o'clock, three, thimbles full at first and gradually ratcheting up the shots as sleep became increasingly elusive.

She lived in sweatpants and tube socks. She slicked her hair back with globs of rosemary-scented gel, showered, and slept with all of Amanda's clothes around her on the bed like penguins huddled together.

There was no getting warm. Lydia nudged the radiators up the same way she increased her drinking: mark by mark, until the heat never turned off and the thermostat held steady at eighty-four degrees.

Fifteen days after she came back to Brooklyn from Arizona, Lydia woke with the worst hangover she had had in years. She ran her tongue over her teeth and gagged at the thick layer of mossy grime. The sheets were steaming where she had sweated through the night, and Lydia could smell a fetid mixture of body odor, vomit, and toilet bowl cleaner as she shambled into the bathroom.

"Jesus Christ, most of that's me." She had not heard her own voice in days, not since she had stopped answering the phone or messages on the machine, and had shouted a disgusted, "Get the hell away from me, she's dead goddammit it, but I'm not!" when David had shown up sobbing at the front door.

Lydia had cried enough. She had screamed into her pillow enough. She had drunk enough booze and eaten enough junk and puked back up enough and hidden away enough and ignored the world enough.

She inhaled through her mouth. She exhaled instead of holding her breath. She showered and washed her hair (twice), did six loads of laundry, called out for groceries to be delivered, and booked a cleaning service for the following afternoon.

At the agreed-upon four-hour mark, Lydia turned

the key in the door and dragged herself inside. Her muscles were stiff from sitting in the park while the cleaners had been giving the wretched apartment the full treatment, and her injury was still screaming despite alternating painkillers all day. The house smelled like mandarin, almonds, and rubbing alcohol. *Nothing like us.* Lydia dug at a hangnail, willing it to bleed. *Nothing like her.*

With the cleaning out of the way, Lydia turned to her next project, which was to tease out her books from Amanda's on the huge built-in bookshelf in the living room. She had not had many books all those years ago when she had moved in, but the house that became a home also became a resting place for books on all of Lydia's favorite topics: engineering, geology, biography. As she inventoried them in her head, she spied a few throwaway novels that she had started but had not finished, along with Amanda's collection of everything from the obvious law and art history books to the more esoteric origami, coin collecting, volumes of sports records and more than two dozen albums of photos that Amanda had carefully curated since she was ten years old.

Lydia had not set out on a treasure hunt. She was not even sure what her intentions were, but she found it three hours in. She remembered the book: how it stood out from the others on the shelf, tall and bulky, and how she had pried it out impatiently in her own nesting stage, when it seemed the most important task in the world was organizing every single book on that wall by size and shape.

It was spiral-bound, portfolio style, with a laminated cover tattooed in blazing puddles of multi-layered color. Inside, the phases laid out like a cookbook: recipes for first sketches, ingredients that assured (with patience) an artist's way of taking on at the world. Amanda had loved this book: her father had given it to her on her twelfth birthday, and she had carried with her through law school and beyond. She had scratched cryptic notes into the margins, underlined entire pages with doubled emphasis, and drawn proto-hearts in place of every dot over each 'i' on pages seven through fourteen.

Lydia had never paged through this book, seductively (or perhaps simply mystically) titled *The Path of the Way: An Artist's True Companion*. Amanda had shown it to her when they had been sharing childhood trajectories. Lydia's story was the first night she had called the cops on her parents' arguments as a frightened six-year-old who screamed at the 9-1-1 dispatcher and had to take the harsh-but-barely-this-side of-not-technically-abusive punishment her father saw fit to mete out. Amanda's story was one of a surprise 'half-birthday' present from the man she worshipped above all others, the civil engineer who drew comics about cats and drafted tiny replicas of historical monuments on table napkins over blueberry pancakes every Saturday morning.

Lydia eased herself into the forgiving depths of the sofa, kicking her cane with her good leg. She held the book as a small child might cling to a spelling primer. Her heart knew first that the book held some of Amanda's first secrets: line, form, space, shape, texture, tone. Scanning the table of contents, the engineering training that was as much part of her as the now-chronic pain through her leg translated each chapter heading into a part of the process diagram in her mind's eye.

An idea germinated at the base of Lydia's skull. She could only catch it sideways, when she was weary, in the space between what felt like terminal sadness and dreamless sleep. The book seemed important, though Lydia could not say how. She reorganized the bookshelf—*hers and hers,* the snarl of her cruel inner voice. But that one volume stayed close, directly in her line of sight or at the rim of her peripheral vision, that day and thousands of days besides.

A clean apartment. A fastidiously systematized bookshelf. Lydia sat in every chair. She limped into Theo's room. Her eyes were dry. Two days later, her makeup flawless, her jewelry loud, and her outfit impeccable, she lied through her salon appointment and came home with perfectly normative hair, stripped of its brash stain and tucked into a new suede headband.

Lydia called her boss. He argued, he cajoled, he bribed, and he raged. Lydia was immune to his language and held her ground in a monotone she had practiced in front of the bathroom mirror.

She spent the next two days in bed, feeding dark chocolate truffles to her migraine and cursing the universe. When the aura wafted away and she could see out of both her eyes, Lydia set up the dining room table like a conveyor belt: address book, notecards, dark purple pens, stamps, phone. She made a list of all the people Amanda might have called friends, labeling people in broadening concentric circles, until Lydia had run out of names, lime seltzer, chips, and salsa. She ordered Chinese delivery and settled in for the day.

"Okay." Lydia spoke aloud, more to hear the sound of her own voice than anything else. She organized Amanda's social network like soldiers in the war against ignorance and unsolicited anything. "Family's done, they don't even get a level. Top tier we've got David, Corinne, Marcus, Debbie, Kyle, Bethany, Sarah, Marguerite, and Brad. They all know already, and Corinne being her agent would have told—" Lydia crossed off another series of names—"everyone from the gallery shows, press connections, artist co-ops."

She scribbled a note next to Kyle, Amanda's work buddy. A simple message on his voicemail after hours and he'd be the megaphone for the office as well as Amanda's extended web. One by one, Lydia assigned each name on the innermost ring a role in making sure that everyone who needed to know would know, and anyone who had been left out would never be able to say she had not tried.

After the first few attempts at phone calls, when Lydia careened off-script and had to hang up and try again, the rest went exactly to plan.

Lydia left David for last. Although she tried to convince herself that it was because she felt like a coward and a jerk for having rejected his repeated attempts to contact her since she had arrived back in Brooklyn alone, Lydia knew the deeper reason was that it would tear away the bandages of denial that she had wrapped around herself.

She dialed slowly, pressing the square buttons on the console and triple-checking the number in Amanda's address book as she went along.

David answered before the phone had rung twice. *He's got caller ID. Her name from this number.* Lydia swallowed her rising bile.

"Hey there, babe, what's—oh, God, Lydia." David went silent, but Lydia could hear him sniffling away from the handset.

Breathe. Lydia watched the blood leach from her hands as she gripped the phone, until her fingers were as white as the walls. *Grief makes stupid people stupider.* She squeezed her eyes shut, ashamed of her covert pettiness.

Over the eight years they had been together, Lydia had come to accept David's place in Amanda's life and even (on occasion) hook a glimmer of what the love of her life saw in him. After the unplanned disclosure at the café, Lydia had read the books and had the discussions and even attended one session of a support group for monogamous partners of poly folk. She had learned that essential chunks of Amanda's life were (in the glibly stated but fully true phrasing of the facilitator of a poly conference they had attended together three years in a row) 'not about her.'

She recited the mantra to herself as David blew his nose down the wire like a trombone. *Not about me. Not about me.*

"I wanted to let you know I'm hosting something at our—at my place. This Saturday, starting around three and going until whenever. Will you please sort out invitations, make sure whoever needs inviting has an invite? I'll make sure catering's covered, and Bethany already said she do the set list with her own equipment. I told her light on the death metal and heavy grunge but anything else is fair game."

"Anything for you, Lydia." David gushed, relieved to be of practical use after all his failed efforts to build reciprocal support. The sentence sounded false even to him, and he shifted the focus. "Everyone loved her. Everyone."

They chatted about nothing for a minute or two, and Lydia began her goodbyes. David interrupted her. "This is a good thing you're doing, Lydia." His voice sounded formal, as though he were the first speaker in what was billed as a rousing debate. "For you, I mean. It'll help you—help us—move—"

Lydia bit her tongue and tasted blood. She pressed her thumb against the mound of flesh inside her injured hip that still swelled to the size of a golf ball by noon and allowed the rush of pain to drown out his last obscene suggestion. *Not about me. Not about me.*

Three days after that, Lydia hosted a memorial service for a hundred people that everyone in the room tearfully proclaimed a 'fitting tribute for a beautiful soul' and 'a party Amanda could not have planned better herself.' She caught some people staring, but no one mentioned her bland hair.

David was a puppy the entire afternoon, following Lydia around and pestering her with questions about how else he could help. Lydia channeled a level of monastic graciousness she would never feel, sending him this way and that with suggestions for music and errands.

Towards the end of the gathering, when the speeches were over and everyone's tears had been cried and there were dozens of tiny scribbled Post-it notes over the back of a two-foot by three-foot blown up photo of Amanda Marquez in all of her ginger-topped, sparkle-eyed, huge-hearted glory, Lydia cornered David.

Without a word, she offered him the hug he had been waiting for all day. Without compunction, Lydia McCray expertly guided her dead lover's boyfriend into the enthusiastic arms of a flirty acquaintance who had confessed her crush on the man to Lydia over pre-Christmas drinks at Amanda's latest gallery opening.

"David, have you met Fiona May?" Lydia positioned them in front of one another. David sniffled into his handkerchief and Fiona patted his arm.

"I know you and Amanda were together a long time, David." Fiona looked at Lydia, who nodded encouragement. "She was an amazing person."

Glancing up, David nodded. He noticed Fiona's eyebrows first: she had shaved one off, and in its place sported an intricate henna tattoo that flowed down the side of her face, across her throat, and into the deep neckline of her toothpaste-tube squeezed orange sheath dress. She had long reverse mohawk braids in alternating layers of blue and white, with a tuft of new black hair sprouting in the middle.

"Fiona May. Are you an artist, too?" Despite his grief, or perhaps because of the desperation of it, David was interested.

Nodding, Fiona left her hand on his arm and smiled. "Sculpture, mainly. Right now I'm working in concrete and copper. I've got a studio in a warehouse not far from here."

"Sculpture, eh?" David kept his arm still. "Not sure I know that much about sculpture. Maybe you could tell me more."

Lydia left her hands on their backs a moment longer. When David smiled, Lydia's façade threatened a breach. *He's smiling like I bet he smiled at Amanda the day they met.* She shook it off, nodded somberly at both of them, and went to ask the bartender for a refill of her club soda. By the time she saw them again ten minutes later, David and Fiona had walled themselves off on the loveseat that had been pushed facing outwards against the windows, and Lydia was sure she heard a laugh to go with the sight of forehead-to-forehead conversation.

Settled. Lydia ticked another thing off her long mental list. Placating Amanda's long-time lover with a distraction and the gift of his choice of Amanda's unfinished pieces in the studio, Lydia knew she had done enough to ensure that he would not be back to find out how she was, or where, or who. *None of them will.*

When the last guest left, with air kisses on wet cheeks and obscene pledges to keep in touch, Lydia retreated upstairs to allow the hired team to clear everything out. Right on time, the buzzer rang with the rest of the crew.

Her plan wobbled as the movers were getting ready to leave. Sitting with her good leg under her and her gimpy leg stretched as straight as she could manage, drinking in the ladybugs and the ladder and the paint and the furniture, Lydia swore as she dragged herself to her feet.

"Wait! There's one more room!" Her rough voice stopped the last man out the door.

Trotting up the stairs, he tipped his cap. "What else can I do for you, ma'am? Boss said whatever Ms. McCray wanted Ms. McCray got."

Lydia turned her back on the room and limped out. She pointed. "Everything in there, please. Your office has the details of where it all needs to go. Might need to dismantle the—"

No. She willed away the word. Whatever the man knew about the situation, he had been around people long enough to know when they had talked as much as they were able. He filled the air with confident declarations. "Leave that all to us, Ms. McCray. I'm sending one of the youngsters out for coffee and donuts—you go down to the kitchen and I'll make sure he brings you something, too."

People had been offering to help Lydia since the accident. She was more grateful for the stranger's gift of sugar and caffeine than she thought she had ever been to anyone in her life. "I'll be sure to tell the boss how accommodating you've been, Mr.—"

The man laughed. "Theo's the name and moving's the game, ma'am. I'm not mister to nobody."

Lydia faked a sneeze and reached for a crumpled Kleenex in her pocket, ignoring the rough tear through her paper heart. "Thank you, Theo. You have no idea how much easier you've made all of this for me."

By nine o'clock that night, the apartment was ready to be shown. All the furniture (except for one of the three tall stools at the kitchen counter), kitchenware, linen (except for a sleeping bag and single towel), and art were gone. Lydia made a mental note to double check Roy and Evie's address for the paintings and photo albums.

She brushed her teeth, peeled her clothes into a jumble and stuffed them in the duffel in the hallway. She pulled on her most comfortable sweats and shuffled into the only t-shirt of Amanda's she had kept, a Pink Floyd second hand cutoff. Fumbling with one hand as she balanced with the cane on the other, Lydia dragged the sleeping bag and single pillow into the baby's room.

Easing herself on to the floor, Lydia groaned and retrieved the bottle of ibuprofen from the bag by her feet. She swallowed two pills dry, punched the pillow to fluff it up, and stayed awake all night. Lydia held Amanda's book to her chest, watched the city lights crawl across the walls with the black-spotted bugs, and counted blades of grass.

Cape Cod (September 2018)

Morning rushed in. A trail of paper stretched from the drafting surface upstairs down to the kitchen in the back of the house, interrupted by an unlikely brood of pencils, pastels, and charcoal sticks on the floor in the hall.

Diane regarded the tiny sketch on the kitchen table. The pencil lines were smudged, but the waves were over-precise, as if shredded and reassembled in a modern abstract collage of a wave drawn with a ruler and compass. The sky magnified this effect of sharp lines and narrow contours, because the clouds were drawn as overlapping, chopstick planks of alternating light and dark bands.

Between two angled crests, darker against the striped sky, something else vied for resolution: two raised bent poles, a rough circle, a sloppy rectangle. The shapes across the waves were inchoate graffiti sprayed across geometric perfection, shattering the illusion of order and symmetry. In the grayscale of the drawing, against the sure lines of the waves, the figure was only a hint of a person.

Pressing her temples, Diane forced herself to stare at the square of paper. She lifted her mug to her lips without and swore without moving when the liquid scorched her tongue.

Cape Cod (September 2018)

Diane's landline had been ringing for ten minutes by the time she reached for the receiver. She mumbled the tail-end of her nightmare before her eyes snapped open, mouth twisting.

An hour later, she sat in the hallway at the Broadwell police station, her legs curled like maypole ribbons around the frame of a metal folding chair. Cape Cod didn't have much in the way of crime over the winter, except for the drop-outs on drug benders and the odd booze-up that ended in jail. No use stealing much once the locals were the only ones left—larceny was only lucrative when the wealthy migrant birds from Florida or Arizona stashed their jewels in their summer mansions. On this midweek morning, the police station resembled a library or a small-town law practice: two desk clerks nodding over paperwork behind a counter, the hum of computers, and the mild smell of mildew from willful rising damp.

Eighteen years on the edge of the world. Diane sat on her hands to keep them warm. *Right back where I started. Missing. Missing.*

"Through the third door on your left." The clerk's voice made Diane jump.

The interview room was a box with slime green

drapes and a speckled linoleum floor. It smelled like bleach, cinnamon gum, and wet sneakers. Diane took a seat at one end of the rectangular table, trying to decipher the scribbles etched into it by thieves and junkies.

"Okay, Ms. Howard. I've got ten minutes. Dispatch said you wouldn't take no for an answer, wanted to talk to me direct. What did you see?" The question slid over Diane's head and she turned to face Broadwell's police chief. Dennis Turrell was only thirty-three, with an algal mat of dirty hair and thick fingers. He breathed noisily, like a walrus, and talked like someone used to not waiting for a reply.

Before Diane could press her palm into the table and stand to face him, Chief Turrell stepped into view. He crossed his arms and sighed indulgently. "From the top."

The story took longer the second time around. The sky was darker, the tide higher. The figure, the wraith, was the only thing that did not manifest itself as more than it was. Diane could not reach her vision to alter it; she could only report, report and wait.

Chief Turrell's upper lip twitched. "I'm only going to say this once."

Under the table, Diane jammed her knees together, wincing. She kneaded her old injury, ribcage to knee, feeling the metallic pain through her hip.

"It's been four days. No one reported missing. Told you yesterday on the phone, without a missing persons report, there is no missing person. Locals all accounted for, and believe me, if we had a drowned tourist out there in the bay, slick family lawyers from Boston or New York would already be all over my ass."

Diane tucked an escaped strand of gray hair back into her ponytail and shifted her weight. "But someone will come." Long dormant, Diane's hope stretched and tried to shake itself awake.

Chief Turrell moved his hand as if to pat her on the head. He snatched it away at the last minute. "And if they do, I'll open an investigation. In the meantime, don't you worry about a thing, Ms. Howard. I'm sure you've got some…"—his mouth curled at the word—"*art* to attend to."

The house in Broadwell had always been too big. Diane knew that before she even saw it, skimming through escape routes out of New York after Tucson, stabbing at real estate possibilities. A ridiculous shape—who built Tudor on Cape Cod?—with its double stack of windows in bands around all four sides and a workshop extension on the detached two-car garage.

Most of the rooms were empty, hallway doors perpetually shut, radiators at minimum so the pipes didn't freeze. She had left the previous owner's drapes up in every room except her bedroom and studio, which faced the bay from an obviously-added-after-initial-construction tottering single garret. She used three cabinets in the kitchen and the smallest bathroom. Her closet was not near half-full.

Diane did not fret over the closed doors and the vacant space. She had moved up here with two suitcases and someone else's Subaru, paperwork in hand, house key left by her request in the mailbox at the end of the short gravel driveway. Clean, clear, simple. Controlled.

As she had done every day, Diane single-stepped up the short brick stairs, unlocked and pushed open the front door, and headed right to the top floor without turning on a single light. Her studio was narrow, with a drafting table covered in tiny square sketches and a high stool.

Despite the rising wind, she unlatched the creaking window and wound it open as far as it would go. Diane stood there in bare feet and a secondhand sweatshirt, gripping the ledge, until the sea and salt from the air and her memory ran in twin rivers, outside and in. The house was overwhelming, but never room enough.

Cape Cod (October 2018)

Except in freezing conditions, when she knew more about the thermodynamics of water condensation than anyone else in Broadwell, Diane Howard never filled the Subaru before the amber light came on. In the big and small and in-between decisions of crafting a new existence on the margin of the Atlantic continental shelf, she allowed her bills to be paid a little late, her gas to run a little low, and her hair to frizz and disperse like disoriented bees. On the last Saturday in October, Diane climbed in to her ancient car and drive her usual three-quarters of a mile on local roads to the cheapest gas station for twenty miles.

The door squeaked as she wedged it open with her shoulder, unbuckling the seatbelt and digging in her jeans pocket for her credit card. She tugged a strand of ponytail out of her mouth and slid the card in twice before the machine beeped approval and the screen requested her zip code.

Diane huffed into her fist. "Son of a bitch, it's cold out here!"

Someone on the other side of pump number four laughed, a too-loud guffaw that ended with a gulp and what sounded like someone mumbling to themselves. Diane frowned. *Tourists. Too damn late in the season, but tourists all the same.*

As Diane watched the digital display siphon money from her bank account, a woman sidestepped around the pump. She was as tall as Diane and half again as broad-shouldered, dressed in flared, frost-blue corduroy pants, a charcoal wool sweater with a chunky silver necklace, two hoops in each ear, a huge garnet ring on her right middle finger, and makeup as smooth as newly-varnished wood. Her thick hair matched the sterling and was curled under, sitting on her collarbones.

Diane blinked, trying to match the vision with the noise that had preceded it. She glanced down. The other woman had on black strapless sandals with toenails painted tangerine. *She sees me.* Diane swatted the thought, which was replaced by an even more horrifying one. *What if she doesn't see me?*

The woman's smile was a lighthouse that began in the center of her face and spread outward. She stepped over Diane's gas pump hose, glanced at her own feet, and nodded. "Yes. Crazy lady's wearing open-toed shoes in Cape Cod when it's forty degrees out."

She laughed again, and Diane felt the vibration at the pit of her stomach. "Only pair I packed—moving van doesn't get here until next Tuesday."

To call Diane Howard out of practice would insult every couch potato in the world whose idea of gym attendance is the three-week special every January or to call Leap Day the guest who never left. Diane Howard had known how to talk to friendly strangers, once. Diane Howard had even known how to flirt and grin, in a life packed away with everything else she had owned before Broadwell. Diane Howard had no idea what to say next.

Her uninvited conversation companion saw Diane's hesitation, but not before she saw something else: a beautiful, sharp, complicated woman. She filled in both parts, hoping that at some point dialogue might supplant soliloquy.

"Helen." She held out a narrow hand with long fingers, also polished like citrus. "Helen Gilbert-Jones. Moving from Philly, semi-retired. Strategy consultant, big corporates mostly."

She stopped, watching. Diane nodded, her long hair swishing across her face, and coughed twice into a tight fist before she returned the introduction. "Diane. Howard. Twenty years."

For the third time that morning, Helen's laugh burst into the space of unknowns between them. "You make it sound like a life sentence, Diane! Surely this place can't be that bad? Or are you telling me I've made a huge mistake, selling out to come live on hell with high water?"

Diane felt the giggle. She swallowed, trying to contain it, but the high, rattling squeak exploded out of her nose and mouth at the same time. She shut her eyes against the sound of Helen's clip-clop sandals retreating to her perfectly ordinary perfect life, and opened them slowly when the only sound was Helen's roaring laugh in response.

"Normally don't laugh at my own stupid jokes,"

Helen said between rounds of asynchronous amusement. "But usually no one else laughs, either, so I guess in this case I'll make an exception."

Helen shook herself like a wet dog. "What I meant to say was, "Nice to meet you, Diane. My mouth sometimes runs off." She winked. "You'll get used to it."

"Nice to meet you doesn't cut it, Helen," Diane said as she sniffed into her sleeve and wished her rising blush could be explained away by frostbite or a fatal disease. "This is the most fun I've had in…"

The sentence tried to finish itself with truth. Diane swerved mid-sentence, klaxons blaring inside her head and internal monologue over-pronouncing every syllable as though scolding a child. *Literally. Just. Met. This. Woman. What. Are. You. Thinking?*

Helen ignored the break. "Okay, so here's the thing. I know no one." She paused, tapping her chin with a rounded nail. "Unless you count my real estate agent, a bright young man named Matthew from Worcester with too much mousse in his hair and a fake Southern accent."

She shook her head and the ends of her bob swayed gently. Diane could not disengage. Helen continued. "And in case you're wondering, Ms. Diane Howard, Matthew doesn't count."

Countless things arrive unannounced: inconsiderate cousins, the flu, surprise parties, pregnancy. Diane opened the door that morning expecting two hours of errands, a trip to the library to return and restock and an idle hour at the hardware store, bookended by a standing lunch of mild cheddar and multigrain crackers chased by a handful of seedless green grapes. The rest of her day promised little more pleasure: a bundled up walk (with the constant shadows of guilt and rage) at Morgan Crescent, a few hours staring at the sky from her studio window, a restless nap, frozen dinner, and three episodes of whichever British crime drama was next on her automatically-curated streaming queue.

Helen Gilbert-Jones arrived in Diane's life like a landmine. In the first two minutes of standing two feet from her, Diane felt all the tethers of her life break free of the anchors that grounded the whole delicate enterprise of her Broadwell existence. Later, she would wonder about before and after, but she would only remember before in static screenshots of lonely drudgery punctuated by the dark periods of perseverating depression that covered her like a second skin.

"But now I know you. Sort of." Helen double-barreled her index fingers at Diane and arched one eyebrow. "Which pretty much makes us instant—" Helen hesitated, trusting her instincts and hedging her bets. "Instant best friends, in my oh-so-empty date book."

Diane felt her world fragment, slivers of predictability trampled by the force of nature standing an arm's length away. In a half-hearted effort to fend off whatever might happen next, she crossed her arms and eased the pain on her left side by cocking her hip. The geometry of her smile stayed put, a straight line as narrow as her nose.

Helen backed off. Six months ago Cape Cod had seemed an obvious choice, to jump off the cliff and land in Massachusetts, in a setting she remembered from childhood vacations when her family had briefly lived in Maine. She retreated from her brazen desperation and turned to go. "Maybe I'll see you around, Diane. I'll be the one in a parka in July."

In Diane's mind, Helen's movement clicked frame by frame, and every inch away left her inexplicably bereft. Diane dropped her arms and reached out. She caught Helen by the elbow. "Take it from me, the locals can be hell on newcomers. It'll be five years before anyone else knows your name, so you're better off sticking with me."

Her smile returning home, Helen shrugged her shoulders, palms turned up in surrender. She stepped close enough that Diane could smell green apple shampoo and floral. *Gardenia? Frangipani?*

"Lunch?" Helen's request landed in the middle of Diane's reverie.

Helen's eyes, a startling dove color with dark rings, were deep set and widely spaced over soft cheeks. Diane stared, feeling self-conscious for the first time in more time than she allowed herself to remember.

Leaning closer, Helen spoke more softly. "*Where* will have to be up to you until I get my feet wet in this town. Got any favorites?"

You. Diane's inner voice betrayed her. For half a second, she thought she might have said the word aloud, but

Helen's face remained patient and open. Diane nodded briskly, consulted her watch, and surprised them both. "Diner on 4th. Thursday at noon? If we get there a little early we'll beat the crowd."

Helen laughed again. Diane was already used to the boom. She missed it a little when Helen stopped. "Haven't seen anything like a crowd around here."

Diane found a faintly recognizable stride. "One word for you on that little nugget of late fall transplant ignorance, Helen: July."

"Guess you'll have to hang around and help me navigate the seasons." Helen wrinkled her nose and patted Diane's hand. "Least you can do, after having been so pushy getting me to go on a date with you."

Date. Date? Date! Diane tasted the word in her head, hoping that repetition would force semantics to dovetail with her shifting reality. She waited too long to reply and Helen amended her transparency. "Lunch. I meant a lunch date. Like a power breakfast, only with burgers instead of bagels. You let me talk shop for fifteen minutes and I can write it off as a business expense. I guarantee there's a ninety percent chance you'll survive the monotony of spending an hour across the table from me."

Diane could see that Helen had an unerring internal compass for ways to nudge other people off-balance in one breath and rescue them in the next. She navigated with the social grace of someone both used to being the center of attention as a matter of sheer presence and willing to use grace and verbal agility to help other people into the light.

In the space of eight minutes, Diane Howard felt smarter, faster, and more present than she had since arriving on Cape Cod. She felt the sticky scum of a self that was dimmer, slower, and more distant slide off like a soap bubble, leaving her feeling more vulnerable and more like someone she had once known than she had dared hope would ever come again.

"It's a date, Helen." Diane nodded and turned away, her last words muffled but still audible. "A date date."

Diane pulled in to her driveway before their shared stupidity hit her. *No numbers.* For the second time that morning Diane traced the physical sensation of loss to her tingling fingers and a mouth full of dust. *And there's her excuse, when I see her at the farmer's market buying zucchini and flowers in the spring.* Diane trudged up to bed, taking two painkillers and a lavender scented heating pad and pulling the covers over her head. It was long past midnight before she fell asleep.

Helen stopped at the drycleaner one town over before returning to her mostly empty house. She kicked off her sandals and pulled on thick socks, made a cup of tea from the fragrant stash of herbs in her top kitchen drawer, and scrolled through e-mails on her phone for ten minutes before she snorted to herself. "Idiot!"

She stomped through to what she had already begun to think of as the sunroom and stared through the bay window at the lank branches of a dormant tree. The flint sky mocked her. Helen muttered another minute of self-recrimination before her buoyancy reasserted itself.

Unpacking the second of three suitcases she had flown into Logan with, Helen whistled the hook from a pop song that had been playing on heavy rotation since Labor Day. She ate three handfuls of kale chips and a shaved pastrami and radish sandwich with wasabi mayonnaise on fresh rye. Her eyes watered with the spice and dripped on the dishes as she washed up in the sink, still talking to herself. "Of course you hate first dates. Cheer up, buttercup—you only need *one* helluva good one. This one."

Diane woke up cranky, the fizz from her flirting the day before now stale and flat. She skipped breakfast and scowled out her studio window. The morning rolled on without her.

Helen woke up ready. By a quarter of eight she was already parked in the diagonal lot of the gas station, and she tried to follow the first employee through the padlocked front door.

"Open in a minute," groused the scruffy teenager, pointing to the closed sign that still hung inside the glass. "Pumps'll take a few to start up. Which one?"

Laughing, Helen wedged her foot in before he could pull the door shut. "Not here for gas, young man." She surveyed him, top to bottom, and her arched eyebrows found him insufficient. He squirmed and gave in.

Helen touched his elbow and tried on her conciliatory voice. It oozed like an alligator through tall reeds. "I was hoping you'd be able to help out an old lady." She read the name tag he held in his hand. "Chris."

Chris had worked at the gas station since not graduating from high school two years earlier. He told himself that he did not have to be courteous to this weird woman—he did not have to be anything to her—but something in her tone told him that his obedience was both requested and required. He nodded.

Reality's loss is a good story's gain. Helen spun out the narrative she'd stitched together over her third cup of tea and second piece of sprouted grain toast before the sun had come up. "See, Chris, I'm trying to dig up an old acquaintance. Worked together more years ago than it'd be polite to count, she moved up here, and I could have sworn I saw her pull out of this driveway the other day while I was driving by. Recognized her for sure, but damned if I can remember her last name. Figure she's a local now, maybe you know her?"

Chris Wallace had lived in Broadwell his whole life. His best friend was Brendan Calloway's little brother Jimmy. Chris might never scrounge up a high school diploma or a second dead-end job, but he knew everyone who was anyone in Broadwell and three towns around. He said as much to Helen with a smirk.

Ignoring his attitude, Helen continued. "Tall older woman. Long gray hair, jeans and plaid."

Chris sneered. "Half the town, lady."

Helen tried a different track, guessing correctly that Chris the gas station attendant was also Chris the frustrated motorhead who got his kicks watching spectacular Daytona crashes in his parents' basement and dreaming of what he would drive someday. "Gets around in an ancient Subaru, rust to match the rust."

The crooked smile cracked open, revealing nicotine-yellowed teeth and a half-moon chip out of one of his canines. He rocked on to his back foot and his shoulders shook with suppressed laughter.

Helen's supercilious glare intensified. She crossed her arms and tapped her foot, sole thwacking against sticky linoleum.

Caught out in mid-snort, Chris was abruptly quiet, his eyes planted at the ground.

"Well?" Helen spun out the word, leaving it between them like a drill sergeant's command.

The young man nodded, his attitude deflated by her power. "Howard. Diane, I think, or Debbie? Lives over on the other side of town, huge ugly house on the corner past the library."

"Thank you." Helen said the words through steel, daring him to add whatever insult he held close. "And for your information, it's Diane."

As Helen turned to go, Chris risked it. "Been there forever, barely ever comes out. Draws this stupid little pictures that sucker in the tourists. We call her a crazy old—"

"That will be quite enough from you, Chris." Helen interrupted him mid-insult, a ballerina pivot and lunge bringing her within a foot of his face. She was grinning on the inside, enjoying her Mary Poppins moment. *All that's missing is a fancy hat and pointy umbrella.* She pushed the door open and offered him a dismissive wave. "Quite enough indeed!"

By the time she reached the car, Helen's corked laughter had popped into uncontrollable cachinnation. She toppled into the driver's seat, dabbing at her mascara, chirping the name between outbursts. "Diane Howard, Diane Howard, Howard Diane!" *No one should be this happy.*

The thought slammed her into silence. Taking a deep breath, Helen checked her make-up again and eased the car into light traffic, counting the blocks to the library.

The house floated into her field of vision and she slowed down, intending to pull in and knock. Her foot refused to press the brake and her hand ignored frantic intentions to indicate the turn; Helen watched herself drive the car around the block for a second go-around.

"What the hell?" Helen lectured herself aloud. "Park, knock, talk. Simple."

Nope. Too late for simple.

She pulled into the parking lot and stirred the detritus in her glove compartment until she caught a large square notepad of heavy mauve paper and a leaking pen. The moment stretched. Helen grumbled to herself, staring out the window at the steady parade of parents and toddlers arriving for what was no doubt the storytelling highlight of Broadwell's literary week.

"Shouldn't be this damn hard. It's only a date. Won't

even have a chance to reject me to my face, if she meant to leave me without a way to find her. Besides, she already said yes."

Helen stumbled through her pep talk, wondering why it already mattered Diane ever called her at all. In the end, she settled for silly, adding three smiley faces and her number in scratchy, inked-in lettering circled three times: I KNOW WHERE YOU LIVE.

Helen's practiced hands folded the paper across on the diagonal and across again, smoothing it into deft creases with the edge of her thumbnail. When she was finished, she held up the message and inspected it for hesitation. Satisfied, she jogged across the road, hoped no one was watching, and propped it up inside the waiting box.

Diane accepted the cliché that the only mail she ever got was bills, but checking the mail fell into the category of 'things she did every day because that's what people do.' At four p.m. she opened her front door, still in her sweatpants, and shoved her feet into waiting boots. She limped the twenty steps to the battered mailbox, the latest reincarnation of its predecessors that inevitably succumbed to late-night local hoodlums with aluminum baseball bats and too much beer.

Diane's closed her fist around what was inside, expecting a wad of paper, and gasped as she pulled it out. The purple origami dragon unfurled its wings and kissed her palm.

Helen's phone rang at five to nine the next morning.

Diane's bravado bled through her anxiety. "You found me first. Guess that means I owe you lunch."

Cape Cod (November 2018)

She had not been on a date in more than twenty years. *Wrong. Diane's never been on a date.* She stood in front of the mirror, dragging her fingers through her too-long gray hair. She sneered at the wan lip gloss and insipid gold studs that had been her only ornamentation since this house had enveloped her all those years before. She applied them anyway, obedient to her life's dark choices, and snapped her hair into its customary floppy, flyaway ponytail before shrugging into a pair of old jeans and clean plaid shirt.

The virtue of truth for its own sake is a monument built on quicksand. For all its commanding Doric columns and imperious sentry statues, all its kaleidoscopic mosaics and cleverly concealed escape routes, the groundwork founders in the slurry of lived experience. And when the footing slips, the rest of the structure follows: until all that is left of reality's baseline to excavate are mysterious artifacts, and all of the rituals are twisted or lost.

Diane's image told a story. It simply wasn't hers.

They saw each other across the parking lot and waved slowly. Diane blinked at the vision of Helen in a tailored black tunic, navy leggings and chunky boots. As the other woman drew closer, Helen's chin-length silver bob, exuberant brush of mascara and sparkling eyeshadow sprung into view, and her armful of copper bracelets sang. Diane forgot to exhale. *Gorgeous.* She bit the inside of her cheek, slapping down the urge to tug at her faded shirt tails and hide one scuffed sneaker behind a threadbare knee.

Helen suppressed a grin at the welcome sight of the woman she hoped would not be a stranger long. *When you don't know much, you know what you know.* She scratched her palm with a determined nail and shook out her shoulders. Diane moved like a marionette with one short string, her limp half-dragging one leg. But Diane's eyes did not waver, meeting Helen's with more challenge than she had intended, and more feeling than either dared hope.

After the obligatory awkward hug and mumbled hellos, they found a spot at the window. The storm had settled, plastering the horizon with slate monotony. Whitecaps jiggered in the foreground, slapping the restaurant's pylons below. The windows, triple-glazed against the months to come, fogged in a little more with their breath across the small table.

Their conversation began as most do, at their chance intersection. Helen led off. "You were right, that is the cheapest gas for miles."

Diane wrenched herself away from the fascination of Helen's peacock feather earrings and pressed both damp palms on her legs. "Their sandwiches are always stale, but the price is right."

Helen wrapped up that topic with an easy reply, and over drinks they borrowed the obvious—weather, how empty the town was after the tourists were gone, favorite beaches. Conversation bounced but did not flow, and they ordered their sandwiches with a chaser of silence that threatened the end before it had begun.

Mistake. Diane tried to smile across the table as she took another bite of her turkey and stuffing on sourdough. *Nothing to say. Who did I think I was, anyway? Total waste of...*

"You know, I wouldn't pay a thousand bucks." Helen's words interrupted Diane's self-deprecating internal monologue.

"I mean," Helen continued, crunching a potato chip and swallowing it whole, "They say 'a penny for your thoughts,' but with the way you're plowing through your lunch, I'll be damned if I'm going to give you a chance to call this whole thing quits before you've given it a minute. Bad enough you're thinking it inside your head."

Diane stared at the other woman. "How did you—?"

Holding up one hand, Helen cocked her head. "Please! A little credit. Who are you, my grandson trying to figure out whether he's good enough to hang with the cool kids?"

Mockery can be an end in itself. Sometimes it is a bludgeon, meant to lessen or lower. And sometimes, like when Helen wedged it under Diane's hesitation, mockery is a precision instrument, sharpened by the target's own strength of will and willingness, designed to help shed a constricting skin.

In her other lives, before this early November lunch

in a whitewashed diner in Broadwell on the castaway side of Cape Cod, Diane had faced mockery that sought without quarter to wound. She had known it in childhood from both her parents and in a misguided marriage that she still hoped to forget. There had been a time in there, after, where mockery disappeared in a flurry of solidarity, of gentle humor, and of the need for old injuries to heal. No one else had known the scars of what had come before, and no one new had heard what came after.

No one had ever used mocking words with as soft a smile, with a hand that reached across the two feet of wood to touch her elbow, with a sly grin that wanted her in on the joke. Instead of tossing her overboard as ballast, Helen's voice raced for shared victory, and she listened. "What I mean is, Diane Howard, I'm here. So are you, and I think there might be something, and I'm not in the habit of letting a good chance slide by. Tell me you're in for the ride, and let's talk."

She nodded, her smile tightening. "I mean talk."

"It's been a long—" Diane half-muttered her reply.

Helen's excitement bubbled over into impatience. "Time, I know! Jeez, I'm sixty-two years old, think I don't know about time?" She sighed loudly. "But I don't have another conference call until three o'clock this afternoon, and the hell with wasting any more..."

Diane chimed in, cracking her own grin. "Time. I get it, I get it. Old woman like you..."

Pretending to throw her napkin, Helen laughed. The

sound filled the room. At the same time, they reached across to pick up the napkin and their fingers stumbled past one another. Intent on eliciting another magnificent gurgle from her date, Diane pulled back and skittered her finger shadows on the wall under the window. "Can't catch me."

Inches away in the air, Helen's hands chased her opposite pair. In the deceptive reflection on the wall, their hands entwined and tumbled. Helen breathed and said quietly, "You're fast. I'm faster."

Insults unexpectedly turned to insight. "Of course," Helen said, dropping her hands into her lap and trading her smile for a gentle nod, "Depends what you're running from, right?"

Lunch plates cleared, and over shared dessert Diane said something she'd been holding on to since late September. *Nothing from before that. Not that there was anything before.* But something in this life, something real. "You should know, Helen. About me."

Helen dipped her spoon into the peach cobbler and carried it, dripping, into her open mouth. "Only as much as you want, Annie."

Seeing the other woman's confusion, she held her hands. "Okay, okay, sue me. Trying it out for size. You don't seem like a Diane is all."

Thrown off by the unintended truth of Helen's retort, Diane pressed herself back in her chair, using two hands to steady her swaying body against the edge of the table. Sensing the need for a more sincere retraction, Helen reached out. "My fault. Don't even know why I said that, Diane's a beautiful—"

Start in the middle. Not in the beginning, where nothing made sense. Closing her eyes for a second, Diane scanned her options like ticker tape inside her head. *Laugh it off. Call it off. Tell Helen some of it. Tell her all.*

The sound of heavy boots snapped Diane back into place. Brendan stood over her, his hands on his hips. "Been two months, Ms. Howard. Not a speck of nothing come through on what you think you saw. Been up through Portland and down to New Jersey on the wire. All this time, we're going to call it closed."

Without waiting for Diane to respond, he added, "Easiest. Case. Ever." His smug grin trailed in the air as he swiveled, and his lunch buddies nodded and chattered like jackdaws. The tone in the diner shifted, and every resident present in the room quieted themselves, straining to hear Brendan Calloway's recitation of his triumph to the waiting table.

Helen pointed to the retreating man. "You know I have to ask. What was that about?"

Diane fumbled with her napkin. "Nothing."

"Nuh-uh." Helen gathered her eyebrows and tapped a glossy nail on the wood. "There's nothing that's nothing, and there's nothing that's something."

"An incident, at the end of the summer. No." Diane settled into her choice and fumbled the lie. "I made a mistake, nothing more."

"Don't sound like a person who thinks she made a mistake." Helen dipped her voice even more, until the buzz of feigned conversation around them forced Diane to move closer to hear. "More like a person who hasn't found the right audience for what needs telling."

She reached for Diane's hand and cupped it in her own. "Might be me."

In Helen's persistent grace, Diane found a pivot point. She did not swing back four decades, or even two. Diane Howard, eccentric artist, perpetual unknown quantity newcomer in this small town, used the fulcrum of the other woman's tenacious curiosity and tender insistence to tell the latest chapter in her shrouded story.

Ignoring the stares that gathered now from the previously disinterested crowd, Diane spilled the outline of her experience on the dunes. As she talked, the picture of the possibly-there-possibly-not fluttered in her mind's eye. "There was someone, but nobody believes me. Half the town thinks I brew up potions in a cauldron in the attic, and the other half figures that the nutty artist lady dreamed up some stranger in distress to pass the time."

She dropped her chin and spoke more softly. "But I've been starting out at that water for a third of my entire life, and all I've ever seen before that day after the summer crowds is ocean, boats, and gulls. There was someone out there that day. Waving. Drowning."

Helen leaned forward. Her belief gathered energy, pulling back like a slingshot. She picked up the thread of

Diane's story, adding color and arched eyebrows. "And here's these local yokels, hellbent on making it your problem, when you can't sleep every night since thinking somebody went under and never came back up."

Reaching under the table, Dianne fumbled the zipper on her khaki messenger bag. "I keep one of them with me," she said, "Just in case I remember a detail."

The paper perched on the table. Diane smoothed open its creases and pushed it across to the woman who had suddenly become much more than a first date.

Helen took it as though handling a fragmented scroll. She picked up her reading glasses and squinted at the penciled lines. "How long was it there? A minute or more?"

"Doesn't matter." When she shook her head, Diane's ponytail loosened and her limp hair framed her thin cheeks. "Can't ever see the face."

Her companion caught the sleepless months of frustration. Although she couldn't name it, Helen caught something else, too. Something more. She coughed to clear her head and focused on the drawing. "Of course you can't. Too far. No chance."

Diane shook her head and snorted, the annoyance splitting her expression. "That's my point! Face. Name. Reputation. That's how we know each other, right?"

Frowning, Helen reached over to pat her hand. Diane pulled away. "All these and more." She counted on her fingers. "Association. Position. Actions, good or bad or even indifferent."

"But what does this have to do with——?" Helen's warm voice held its tone, even though her eyes flicked with confusion.

Diane stood, scraping her chair. The rest of the customers in the diner obligingly hunkered down into their chowders and salads, pretending not to notice that the loony woman was about to go off again. In tourist season, all outsider eyes would have been on Diane's scattered ponytail and stabbing hands. After years of not having a clear who or what or why Diane was, the locals figured that at least pretending to ignore her was best for everyone.

Helen glanced around, hoping for a gawker she could at least swat away. Any interjection would have been welcome to break Diane's rapid-fire tirade. Helen had only been in Broadwell a week, but small towns know what small towns know. There's a time to listen at the door, and a time to mind your own damn business. Whatever you need to know, you will know soon enough—and whatever was not yours to fret over in the first place would slide away under the next neighborhood gossip. The rest of the people in the restaurant clattered their spoons into thick ceramic bowls, swirled the ice cubes their glasses, asked for more water, and carried on their conversations more loudly to compensate for the rising racket next to the row of windows along the far wall.

"But the unknown are all unknown in the same way: fuzzy, fanciful concoctions out of our own heads. No faces, no features. With these two—how do I even know they were real, Helen?"

This time Helen heard it. "Two? I thought you said—"

Diane slammed her hand on the table, breathing hard. Her half-truth combined with that slip threatened to tear the cover off everything that had come before. She went on the offence, growling out the words. "What are you talking about? Haven't you been listening? Someone was drowning and I was the only one to see him, and no one knows who it was, for God's sake!"

Helen let the words crash against her and ebb away. Diane sank back into her chair, out of air and anger and energy. "I'm sorry." She felt the tears warm her eyes and blinked them away. "No one ever seems to know what I mean by..." Her eyes scoured the room as her mind searched for the right word. "Missing."

Before Helen could reply, Diane doubled down on her single-stranger deceit and confession. "He's missing."

"I do." Helen squeaked out the words. A few tables around them changed tack, risking a listen as Diane's attention pointed to the woman across the table and seeped away from the rest of the people in the diner. "Know what you mean by missing. Or at least missed opportunities."

She took Diane's hand. "Not tonight, though. It's a story for another time." Helen rediscovered a smile reflected in Diane's relief that the outburst had passed.

"I'm thinking dirty martinis on Friday night, if you're up for it." Diane surprised herself by not rejecting the offer.

Helen winked. "There's line dancing after 10."

"I'm sorry," Diane said as they left cash on the table and headed out the door.

Helen led the way. She felt the eyes of the whole place watching every move. Helen had spent her life being the center of attention: her bright makeup, her unapologetic flair for the sheer and the shimmering. As she had since she was fourteen, Helen made the most of it. She paused, turned around, and tucked a hair behind Diane's ear, letting her hand brush the other woman's.

"No contrition required. Seems to me we've got a lot more to talk about, that's all." Helen's smile widened as she took Diane's hand and mock-bowed her through the door. "Besides, I think the sentiment you're clutching for is 'thank you.'"

The sound of the rising surf in the parking lot was louder than either one of them expected. Diane hunched her shoulders, curling inward, the pressure threatening to crush her like bleached coral. *Thank you. Whoever you are, thank you.*

Helen thrilled at the sound, still new after her lifetime of rumble from the city. She laughed into the wind, her trill sparkling and uncomplicated, daring a life of darkness in the details to undermine her deliberate joy. The wind returned it to her, calling her bluff.

"Hey, Annie—" This time, Diane didn't flinch, and Helen didn't back down. They held hands, sharing the restorative warmth of an inside joke. It had only been an hour, but the advent of that unlikely nickname seemed an hour and a day.

"I think you and I had our first fight."

Fumbling for her front door key, Diane blinked as the motion sensor flashed a light in her face. She kicked off her shoes and walked down the hall. She was halfway up the stars in the dark before her obsession returned her to the kitchen, to her table that was covered in dozens of sheets of paper, all marked in pencil, all of waves and clouds and something. "Someone,' Diane said, leaning across to gather her mind's-eye witnesses. "Somebody's someone."

At two o'clock in the morning, the fifty-six-year-old woman awoke in her oversized Tudor house in a tucked away town in Cape Cod. She felt the dripping sweat on her neck and arms and heard the whistle of a window gap under the onslaught of rough weather. She walked across the floor in barefoot, slammed and latched the window, and ducked into the bathroom for a glass of water. As she turned to go back to bed, she unthinkingly tried to slick her hair back and was jarred by how her fingers tangled in the long strands. Half-asleep, Diane Howard felt like someone else. She stood six inches from the bathroom mirror, examining her reflection that played like a daguerreotype in the streetlight's sodium glow. *Someone old? Someone new?*

She shivered as her skin dried in the cool air, thermostat low enough to sometimes fool the night sweats into letting her sleep through. *Someone else.*

She stuck out her tongue and said the name. It was louder than she had intended and she blinked hard. "Annie."

Maybe someday. She pressed her palms into the bathroom counter, grateful for gravity. Her skin prickled as the syllables tapped the roof of her mouth. She was suddenly hyperaware of the tip of her tongue, the 'n' becoming a soft click as she revved up speed. She repeated the word, whispering it over and over like a blessing. *Or a curse.*

Cape Cod (November 2018)

Diane dug out her third choice of plaid shirt from her closet and squinted in the mirror. Grumbling, she retrieved her glasses from the bathroom and returned to the decision at hand. "Red and green—too Christmassy, ugh. Red and blue? Lumberjack, jeez."

By the time she climbed into her car for the forty-minute drive to the country bar three towns over, Diane Howard already regretted her choice. The blue/green checked shirt was already secondhand when she'd bought it, and the safety pin that held the left sleeve closed scraped along her arm every time she moved. *Too bad it's not Irish dancing tonight—arms at your sides, no moving.* She sighed, looped her wilted hair behind her ear for the hundredth time, and checked the time.

Even with unseasonal traffic, she was early. The parking lot began to fill up by 8:45, and right on nine o'clock Diane saw Helen's car swoop into a space near the door.

Knowing she would not like what she saw but unable to stop herself, Diane looked in the rearview mirror one last time before she shoved her wallet into her back pocket, picked up the straw hat on the front seat, and got out.

For the second time in a row, Diane felt wildly

underdressed when she saw her date. Helen wore country the way she wore any style she chose: all out. Diane could see everything in the Venn diagram patches of bright light from the streetlamps. Helen had on a midnight blue tank top under a narrow-waisted, black and blue checked shirt, with buttons undone all the way down. The shirt was artfully half-tucked on one side, her jeans brand new, her belt buckle quartz inlaid silver with two mustangs running side-by-side, and she wore oval drop turquoise earrings with matching bangles and hoop necklace. Her beige boots, spit-shined and well-worn by someone else, had scuffs at the heel as though she'd been riding and dark saddle climbing vines stitching up the outside.

At least I can say my boots are well-used. Diane glanced at her feet. The size-and-a-half-too-tight footwear that she'd scored at a garage sale by sheer fluke the weekend before, water-stained and missing their toecaps, like someone might have dragged them off a cowboy while he was still twitching.

Helen gave her a kiss on the cheek, a hug that lasted a second longer than it should have and a day shorter than Diane would have liked. She twirled Diane in a circle and smiled. "Authentic. I like it."

Frowning, she craned to see the farmer's haphazard headpiece that Diane was diligently trying to crunch up and make disappear. Helen snatched it with a laugh, twisting it in both hands. "Though you might as well stick a stalk of hay between your teeth and sooey the hogs to the dinner trough in that thing, hon."

She linked her arm through Diane's. "That is not a hat. Come with me." At her car, Helen reached in the back seat, dropped Diane's feeble attempt at fashion onto the floor, and held up a white sequined cowboy hat big enough to take a bath in. "This, my dear, is a hat."

Diane shrugged an apology. "Best I could dredge up on short notice. Better without it, you think?"

Helen put her hand to her mouth in mock horror. "First you tell me you've lived on Cape Cod for nearly twenty years and not once set a toe-tapping foot in this fine establishment for cold beers and hot dancing, and now you're suggesting no hat? That will not do!"

With a flourish, holding her hat in one hand, Helen reached into the car again and produced its twin. The costume jewelry studs sparkled under the streetlight, and for a moment Diane remembered shards of rainbows in a room long ago and far away.

She shook her head to clear her head in time to hear Helen's triumphant explanation. "Thought you might be able to use it, Diane—I bought the matching set!"

Diane touched the brim of the offered hat. "I'm afraid to ask."

Helen was fast. She plopped the white monstrosity on Diane's head and nodded decisively. "Doesn't even matter what the question is, babe. All that matters is that we're going to walk in there and kick ass."

She scoffed at Diane's hesitation. "Dress the part, be the part, Diane. One thing you need to know about me right now is that I'm never going to be any more or any less than exactly who I am."

Misconstruing Diane's guilty conscience for simple nervousness, Helen propelled them towards the doorway. They followed a large group of young women into the bar. "I concede we're not exactly the target audience for this place," Helen intoned, her mock-seriousness making Diane laugh in spite of herself. "But wait until you see me dance."

Three hours later, Helen and Diane stood at Helen's car. "You were right," Diane said, pulling Helen towards her by the beltloop of her jeans. "You can dance."

"Damn straight, babe." Helen put both hands on Diane's hips and kissed her. "I've got an early conference call in the morning. Dinner sometime?"

Diane couldn't hide her disappointment. It had been a long time since she had felt like this. A long time since she'd given up ever feeling like this again. She returned the kiss, hoping to change Helen's plan for the rest of the night.

Helen pushed her away softly and spoke to Diane's thoughts. "Me, too. But I do still have a few clients I can't say no to, and this one likes to do business before breakfast."

She hugged Diane and opend the door. "My place, dinner? Wait until you taste my *osso buco*. You bring wine?"

Mollified, Diane nodded. Before she could ask, Helen added with a wink. "Lava cake for dessert, unless we think of something better. "Tomorrow. Unless you're busy."

Cape Cod (January 2019)

"That thing's a disaster." Helen slammed her palm against the rattling vent of her window combined heating and air conditioning unit. "I'm too cheap to install a whole new system, and I don't know what the hell that racket is, but this dinosaur has got to go."

Diane glanced up from the dining room table, where the New York Times lay sprawled in haphazard sections. She returned to reading the science pages, nodding absently.

Helen slumped. "Going to the store. Need anything?"

Diane mumbled to herself and turned her full attention to Helen. She stood up and kissed her wife. "I think bananas—those are mushy, going in banana bread this afternoon. And that yogurt you like, cherry? Out."

Returning Diane's kiss with a sweeping arm around her waist and a lingering hug, Helen's eyes were misty as she spoke. "It's this stuff, you know? Stuff that you notice." "I'll pick us up a couple of those almond croissants from the bakery across from the bank—what's that place called again?"

Diane tapped Helen on the forehead and laughed again. "Salvatore's. Don't forget to ask for cranberry jam on the side. He keeps it in the refrigerator behind the counter."

Helen had barely backed out of the driveway when Diane caught herself staring at the noisy machine. Loosening the two wingnuts that anchored the unit to the internal bracket, she lifted it up six inches and set it down again. The metal felt cool and comfortable in her hands. "Too easy."

She ducked out to her car, retrieved a large metal box from the trunk, and hurried back inside, whistling.

"Out of parsley, can you believe it?" Helen called out from the garage as she arrived home from the organic grocery chain that had recently made Broadwell its new home. She blew a kiss across the kitchen to where Diane knelt on the living room floor and continued her complaint. "I mean, give me a break—eight different kinds of pesto and an aisle full of detox teas, but no parsley?"

Irritated by Diane's silence, Helen walked through the doorway and stared at her girlfriend. "What the hell?"

"Figured you'd be awhile, so I took a stab."

"Hon? Hate to break it to you, but this is more than 'took a stab.'" Helen's sense of humor returned, resurrected by the absurdity of her rattling unit now in pieces on the floor. "Wasn't even technically dead yet, and this? This practically qualifies as vivisection."

She plopped on the sofa, tucked her feet underneath her, and patted the next cushion. "Anyway, forget about it. We'll drag a bookcase across the window and head out now. Home Depot doesn't close until eight."

Diane's face argued before her words scurried out. "Yes to Home Depot, but it'll be a cheap trip."

She continued, ticking off items on her fingers as though talking to herself. "WD40, felt pads, clips…"

She picked up a slatted front plate that still had four screws half secured. "This one's fine—a little rewiring, a little grease, and I'll get it going again quiet as a whisper before you know it." Her eyes glimmered with excitement.

Enthusiasm is the enemy of subterfuge. It is impossible to both convincingly carry off deceit and express open admiration for something that reveals the true nature of a situation. Diane's delight in the mechanical chaos that covered Helen's hand knotted Persian rug was like a third person in the room: it took up all the space between them, and more than half the air.

Diane realized too late that Helen knew something was up. She tried to backtrack with a shrug. "You know, probably something like that. I'm sure I—we—can figure it out from YouTube."

"At the risk of sounding like a bad stereotype of some no-nothing woman, Diane, my skills lie elsewhere." She scrunched up her nose. "But you might have some hidden talents I hadn't discovered yet."

"Must have picked it up somewhere." Diane felt her attempt at understatement collide with an outright lie. Her chest constricted and she counted her breaths.

Helen pointed at the web of wire on the rug. She nudged a pile of screws and bolts with her foot as though she were poking a dead rat. "Picked it up somewhere my ass, Diane. What are you, some mechanical whiz kid turned mediocre miniaturist?"

Diane hoped her fake pout would be enough misdirection. For someone else, it might have been. Diane had plenty of practice skirting the obvious in Broadwell. It was easy. Everyone wanted to know about her, but no one ever asked the right questions. Easy enough to slide into a gray story of office admin turned wannabe artist, with a wealthy relative on the side

For Helen, it paved the way for more pointed questions. She dismissed Diane's false indignation with a casual wave. "Please. Don't give me that. We both know that you didn't make the massive pile of cash you must be sitting on by painting those kitschy squares for twenty years."

Helen flicked imaginary lint off her blouse. "Don't think for a minute I assumed you were living a pauper's life in an artist's commune in the city before you ran up here."

She tousled Diane's spiky hair and thumbed the twin silver bracelets on Diane's arm. "Doesn't take a genius to notice that you're more yourself with this cut and color and bling, babe. Or to wonder where you got the money for that developer's dream you call a house."

Diane's hope that the conversation would fade into flirting and bed died with Helen's tightening glare. "Thing is, whatever it is, whoever you were, tell me or don't tell me, fine. For now, for what this is, fine. Don't ask for more than you're willing to give, and don't wait too long. I'm too damn old and cranky for half-truths and layers of bullshit."

Diane stared at her, wondering when Helen would

careen into some version of the truth. *Already has.*

"Mechanical engineer, doctorate from CalTech." Diane nodded ruefully. "A thousand years ago."

Helen saw that Diane could not dive any deeper, and that the next conversation would have to wait. She squeezed her curiosity and kept it to herself. Leaning into the problem at hand, Helen pointed to the scattered heap of metal and plastic. She offered an open smile and carried them over the abyss that threatened. "So I'm guessing that means you see something different than I do? Not a pile of junk?"

Diane exhaled and returned Helen's smile. *Not yet. Not quite yet.* "This thing's got another three years in it. She tagged the elements with her finger. "Compressor, evaporator, and motor all good. Or your money back."

"Who said anything about payment?" Helen spread jam on her pastry. "I'm obviously the one doing you the favor, right? You couldn't keep your hands off her!"

Giggling, she wiped up some crumbs. "I'm guessing this is going to occupy you the whole weekend? Poor lonely me, I'll have to find something else to do."

"Give me until dinner." Diane pressed her palms against her eyes and stretched her arms over her head. Her hip cracked and she winced. "Please."

Helen turned, still holding her half-eaten croissant. "Or what?"

"I'll pick up what I need, and this'll take—" Diane did all the calculations in her head, and her mind sang at the return to visions of numbers dancing—"three hours tops."

Helen more than liked Diane. She thought, against all expectations, that she might love the tall, thin, blunt-haired woman standing in her living room with a socket wrench dangling from a well-worn toolbelt. Her focus softened. "I'm going to hold you to that drink. Besides, from where I'm standing, you broke it, you buy it. My new heater-slash-AC is going to be fine."

"Ha!" Diane snorted so hard with laughter that she had to mop snot from her chin with her sleeve.

"Nice one," Helen said, tearing off a paper towel and handing it across the counter. "You've got the sexy drool thing going."

Diane pulled the wrench from her toolbelt and twirled it like a baton. "I've got it all going on, babe."

Home Depot was closed, the sun had set, and the two women were starving by the time they ventured down to the kitchen to make omelets for dinner. Diane could feel her hands buzz at the sight of the machine stripped to nothing on the rug, but she followed Helen willingly back up the stairs.

Early the next morning, Diane shut the bedroom door and eased her car down the driveway. The drive to her house only took ten minutes, and she scrounged up supplies from her own garage.

Pulling Helen's front door shut behind her when she got back, Diane worked as quietly as a nun living out a vow of silence. The only noises were the delicate *tink* of silicone nozzle to blade and bearing, the rubbery *swish* of soft caulk in the window frame, and the intermittent whirr of a wrench being put to good use.

It had been awhile since Diane had had the chance to pry apart a machine and put it back together.

Helen came down the stairs two hours later. "I thought I heard a noise down here. You been awake lo—" She stopped, arms prickling with goose bumps. "It's so cozy in here, what the—oh."

"Been up since five. Wanted to surprise you." Diane grinned with all of her teeth. "Surprised?"

Diane was like a child showing off her latest Lego creation. She pointed to a half-inch strip of oddly-recognizable brown mesh running between the air condition and the windowsill. "Forgot to pick some up when I went out yesterday, so I rigged up anti-vibration pads from two extra kitchen sponges you had under the sink. I'll keep an eye out and replace them if need be."

She continued as Helen tipped loose-leaf tea into a cat-shaped tea ball and filled a mug with hot water. "All I had to do was adjust the expansion valve, loosen the compressor bolts, clean and level the fan blades, replace the insulation foam with a strip I had lying around at my place, and caulk the window pane to decrease the transfer of vibrations to those additional contact points."

"That's all?" Helen's laugh sounded far away.

Diane shook herself free of the details. "Sorry, I haven't talked even the tiniest bit of shop in so long. Didn't even realize how much I missed it, even the little stuff."

Helen joined her in the living room. "Thank you. That's the first thing." She hugged her girlfriend and stood in front of the warm airflow. "And I'm going to be even more grateful by lunchtime. Weather channel says Artic mass moving down from Canada by dinnertime."

Diane frowned at her girlfriend's drink. "Still don't know how you can drink that stuff."

"Ginger, fennel, rosemary, turmeric. Best detox concoction on the planet. You should try it sometime." Helen played along. Only three months in, she and Diane already had their old jokes.

The familiar is easy. There were questions Helen had not asked the day they met, or the first night they spent together, or the night before. She needed to ask them now, but she saw that Diane had more to say about her work in New York before she braved disclosure of her whole old life.

"Okay, I'll bite." Helen put down her mug on the coffee table and stood behind the sofa. She pressed her fists into Diane's shoulders and padded softly. "What exactly does a mechanical engineer do?"

Exhaling, Diane closed her eyes and rattled off her job description. She charted her career path and told a few anecdotes of near disaster with mismatched units of measurement, hydraulic conversion, and power surges. Helen listened. After a few minutes, Diane's voice slowed.

"There's another story here," Diane said, pulling Helen down beside her. "Not today, but there's a whole other story."

Cape Cod (February 2019)

For their fifth date, Helen booked a French bistro in Boston. Sitting on the couch on a Sunday morning in February, she nudged Diane with a smile. "You might have to break out something a little fancier than plaid and denim for this one, babe. Up for it?"

Diane's smile was wider than either of them expected. Helen spoke first. "Cheese and crackers, I should fancy wine and dine you more often, hon! Someone ask you to the Prom?"

Giggling, Diane stood and performed a stiff-legged curtsy. She held out her wrist with her grin still in place. "I believe a corsage is customary for these special occasions, lovely lady?"

"Not quite ballgown and tails. But this place is pretty nice. I'm thinking at a minimum, socks without holes and a bra. Bet you gussy up pretty good."

Diane kissed Helen. "I didn't get this gorgeous for nothing, babe. You wait."

Despite her relative pariah status in Broadwell, Diane had been invited to the occasional celebration in her adopted town. She half-climbed into her closet, pulling out a garment bag with enough dust to make her sneeze as she unzipped it. Inside was a gray, soft-knit cowlneck dress that she had purchased for the dubious celebration of a baby shower for the high school aged daughter of the friendly-enough town librarian. Even with Diane's late addition to the guest list, attendance had been sparse, and she had not worn the dress since.

She mined deeper and came up with an even dustier shoebox. Inside, two absurdly comfortable taupe low-heeled pumps sulked in tissue paper, their insides lined with instep cushions and heel pads. Diane sighed, examining them closely as though scrutiny would make it better. It did not.

The problem with disguises is that they wear off. Not necessarily that they become less effective on the outside—people wear lifelong masks that suffice to divert attention from what is not there, leaving an audience of family and friends who may be quite sure about who they are (and completely wrong). No. The problem with a masquerade is that eventually, in an hour or a day or half a century, the veil begins to flay from the inside out. Diane's had slipped the day at the dunes, and again at the gas station. It had been pared away with cowboy hats and rhinestones and the kind of kiss she did not know how much she had missed.

After Diane pulled the dress over her head, she shoved in earrings she had scrounged from the costume jewelry tray at a thrift store two towns over. The nylons felt like fish scales on her skin, but she tried the outfit without them and her feet bulged out of the despicable vessels of torture that matched the clutch purse she held in her hand.

She pulled her hair back with a twinset of secondhand tortoiseshell combs and dug out an unopened tube of lip gloss.

Diane avoided the mirror until five minutes before she had to leave. Steeling herself, she confronted a vision that felt at once ludicrous and pathetic. *If she can like me like this, maybe we're on to something.* She sighed and rubbed her hip. Her winter jacket, an overstuffed navy down number that was too short in the sleeves and too loose everywhere else, mocked her from the coatrack. She tore it down and sat in the dark in the living room, waiting.

Ten minutes later, Helen knocked on the front door. Without comment on Diane's appearance, she kissed her longer than either one of them presumed likely. "You have no idea how much I've been looking forward to this. Tell me you're up for oysters and escargots!"

Diane's last foray into fancy had been Tucson's high-end Southwestern chic a week before Christmas, two days before the end of the world. She swatted away the vision and kissed Helen again. The contact anchored Diane and she laughed. "I'll race you through the first dozen as long as there's champagne."

The restaurant only had six tables, and all but one was full by the time the two women arrived. Cone-shaped Art Deco sconces in dull brass lined the walls at uneven intervals, casting butterscotch light across the creamy papyrus wallpaper. The high-backed, amply padded mahogany and satin chairs served as natural privacy screens in the small space, shielding diners from one another and mitigating the rumble of lively conversation to feathery static.

Helen shrugged herself out of her wrap and they sat across from one another in the corner in the subdued light. The oysters were fresh and plentiful, the lamb cutlets and grilled snapper seared and succulent, and the minted carrot mash with grilled asparagus understated but delicious. They had each had two glasses of champagne when Helen's face flushed, and she stopped in mid-laugh.

Diane held her hand without a word.

"We need to talk."

And here it is. Diane pulled away and picked at the skin of her fingers under the table. She lied to herself, waiting. *Didn't even think it would last this long.*

Helen slapped the table and they both jumped. No one else in the restaurant reacted, but a waiter swiveled and was at her side before either woman could say another word. "Is there something that Madam desires? Perhaps the menu for dessert?"

"Go away." Helen waved her palm at him. The man sniffed loudly, tossed his head, and swished into the kitchen.

"Not you." Helen's face reddened further, the color leaching into her hairline and dribbling down her throat. "I mean, it's not you."

This gets better. Head down, Diane scowled to herself. *Never should have said yes to lunch. To any of it.* She braced herself for the complete cliché.

"It's my daughter." Helen spoke slowly, as though

the words were burnt sugar in her mouth, her jaw working from side to side. "I think it's time to tell you about my daughter."

Diane pulled her head back and narrowed her eyes. "You don't have kids."

Helen sighed, head on her elbows. Her voice was foggy against the wood. "Yes."

With her back to the rest of the room, Helen was invisible to all but Diane and the manager, who stood watching them on the diagonal from her perch adjacent to the front door. The manager was no stranger to drama; Chez Julien had a reputation for being the kind of hyper-romantic spot that could harbor tearily accepted, down-on-one-knee proposals on the same night it hosted exasperated spouses flinging sheaves of divorce papers across delicate platters of *foie gras* and Melba toast. Still, the restaurant's most senior employee felt her heart sting at the rough night for both the old ladies in the corner.

Diane opted for linguistic confusion to stall for time in whatever this conversation had suddenly become. "Yes, no, or yes, yes?"

Without moving her head, Helen mumbled a single word. When Diane did not respond, Helen gingerly raised her face and found Diane's wide eyes. "Marissa. She's—" the elegant woman sagged, searching for the word that would condense the years into coherence— "problematic."

It had been a solid run: months of planned dates interspersed with impromptu winter walks along the boardwalk and wandering phone calls later than either one of them were usually up. Diane gawked at her date—her girlfriend, though neither had used the word—as though they had crossed paths at a bus stop and happened to share a seat on the way to their separate lives.

Diane called out the lie as directly as she could, still chasing alternatives. "You said no kids." The words felt like an accusation and tasted like dandelion leaves, fresh and bitter.

"She has a son." Helen drip fed more facts into the air between them. "Nathan's fourteen."

The name drilled into Diane's ears and she felt sick. Helen's voice buzzed without meaning. Diane squeezed her eyes shut against the vertigo that swished against her eardrums, the revelation of a living child named Nathan sloshing up against another long dead. Two distant galaxies collided, spiraling lazily toward one another, overlapping maelstroms of deception.

Secrets are not lies by nature; they are lies by nurture. Secrets without relevance to another are a single consciousness' prerogative, the lucky happenstance of evolved communication mediated by sound waves, not brain waves. But those other secrets, with consequence or concern to another overwrought biped stuck in their own heads? Secrets sown in fear of discovery, fertilized by selective disclosure, and harvested by accident or guilty admission are lies. The sequelae of secrets may be accidental or malicious, but they are always harmful and sometimes fatal to the relationship at hand.

Diane stared at Helen and heard a new voice. *No. An old voice.* Fidgeting in her seat, pretending to herself that it was grating nylon against her calves and the near-constant flutter of pain in her hip, Diane tried to return to cozy room and to Helen's revelation.

"'I should have told you' doesn't exactly cover it, does it?" Helen scrutinized Diane's face, finding only a disquieting void. "I'll understand if you...I'll drive you home." Abruptly decisive, Helen motioned to the waiter with an air signature and pulled out her credit card.

This is it. Diane watched the words scroll through her brain like a stock ticker. *She's going to leave without knowing. Any of it. All of it.* For the first time, Diane Howard discovered that she was more afraid of someone not finding out who she was than knowing everything.

"I was someone else." Diane covered her mouth with both hands, took a deep breath, and exhaled the rest. "In New York, for close to forty years, I was someone else."

Helen was a pragmatist, with a pragmatist's focus on the tiny steps of any task. The dinner was meant to be a joyous distraction—not casual, because Helen already thought of her Annie as much more than casual. Something both apart from and better than the relentless demands of a damaged, bewildered adult and the collateral damage of a blameless child.

When Diane stopped speaking, Helen shook her head in confusion. She jumped the tracks from her narrative to the other. "I already know. You had a different job. Left someone behind. I told you, you don't have to share any of that until you're ready."

Cackling without dropping her glare, Diane mirrored Helen's head twist. "Sounds to me like tonight's the night."

She stopped laughing, lugging her hands halfway across the table and shoving the snuffed candle and champagne flutes of her path. "We're doing this together or we're not doing it at all, Ms. Gilbert-Jones."

Helen inched her fingers over the open space, willing her body to keep them moving. "I can't feel my hands." She risked a flamboyant grin. "Might be having a stroke, all this excitement at my ripe old age. You let me know if I slur my words?"

Playing along, Diane felt frantically thankful for the grapple hook of humor her girlfriend had secured to the roof of their burning building. "As long as you're CPR's up to date, because I'm damn near certain I'm having a massive coronary event right this second, and there's probably no time for paddles."

Helen scoffed. "You know me, hon. Paddles are always an option."

Frivolity exhausted, both women focused on the space between their hands. Diane's nails were clipped and rounded, scrubbed but not polished; Helen's manicure was a shimmer of emerald and gold to match her ensemble. The gap closed to two inches without perceptible movement. Helen's fingers grew tired and she curled one of her fists;

Diane reflexively reached forward, palm up, and cradled Helen's hand.

The manager intercepted the check as it whizzed past on a silver tray. She shook her head at the waiter. "They need a minute."

The two women sat without speaking. Around them the tables disgorged their passengers, all satisfied with their meals, although each set either more or less content with their companions. The manager saw the parties out the door with a smile and the standard invitation to return, but she kept her eyes on the corner table. At eleven fifteen, she dismissed the kitchen staff with a quiet word through the slatted swinging doors and discreetly clicked off the 'OPEN' sign at the front of the restaurant.

Eyes on their intertwined hands, Diane and Helen busied themselves in their heads with tasks usually set aside for the monotony of waiting in line at the post office or grocery store. Helen made lists of the project deadlines she had promised her few remaining clients in her consulting business, mapping dates and deliverables on the calendar in her head. Diane nagged at the problem of a recently discovered electrical fault in her dishwasher, tracing the circuitry diagram and wondering if she could fix it herself.

While they pretended that their minds were occupied with essential minutiae of quotidian existence, the two women ran parallel scenarios to navigate the maze of the night's revelations. Neither dared hope for reconciliation, despite the warmth that occupied the nest of their hands.

Helen's ebullience held the line at mutual disclosure and a civil parting, with the half-imagined possibility of indifferent sex to end this bizarre night and close the loop on the whole (mis)adventure. Diane, the perpetual pessimist whose life stories merged to demonstrate how right she had been all along to doubt the glint of hope, drew an oddly surprisingly blank after the certainty of a stiff ride back to Broadwell punctuated with music that would either be too loud or not loud enough.

The manager watched them waiting. The manager watched them until she could wait no more. She tapped over to them in her patent leather heels and sensible black dress, the cuffs pulled down low enough to hide her shaggy gryphon tattoo on one wrist and Pegasus wings wrapped around the other. She left the folder with the night's tally on her pedestal with a note neatly printed across the top for her boss. He would be furious, but he might come around. She'd remind him what he jackhammered into everyone who worked here, that word of mouth was everything in this business.

"We don't need anything except the check." Helen twisted her mouth.

The manager had student loans from an ill-advised jaunt at a private four-year college that landed her with a joint philosophy/political science degree and a job market that left her breathless and even more broke. She was on a payment plan with her parents, a pair of trauma surgeons in Atlanta. She rode the T in from a crowded house share in

Framingham and sometimes crashed on friends' sofas in the city after work, and she stayed with the restaurant in large part because although rent might be tight, she would not go hungry.

The manager gave dollars to the homeless on payday, complimented people on the train, had watched *The Princess Bride* eighteen times, and sent small checks each month to support her adopted narwhal and cottontop tamarin. She was used to gratitude and surprise, and she was philosophically, quasi-monogamously, committed to kindness.

The manager also recognized love signs in other people, though she had yet to find it herself. She saw it in diamond rings that paled in comparison to wet smiles, and in fiftieth anniversary parties that went on long past closing with waltzes to music only the couple could hear. She saw it now, in the forlorn, forced disinterest of two women who had so much more to say.

If the boss did not come around, the manager would make it work. If he was moved neither by the story of his most overqualified employee or that of two women—*two people*, she corrected herself, so her boss' homophobia could not sabotage compassion's only advantage, which is seeing oneself in the other—the manager knew that a two-hundred-dollar debt would mean no indulgent Tuesday-night-single-fancy-drink with friends for eleven weeks, if she played it close.

The manager knew above all else something that

most people triple age her age had to experience over and over and over again before their sealed hearts and aporetic heads conceded: that the dull prospect of Netflix on the sofa with her roommates blanched in comparison to what might not happen next. *All in.*

"But you do." The manager's cleared her throat. Her voice sounded as though it had been mashed through a sieve. She crouched beside the table, her gaze alternating between the drab woman who belonged in a vintage detergent ad and the one whose flamboyance oozed from every saturated, mineral-glossed, cosmetically-concealed pore. Neither turned her way.

Diane counted electrical junctions in her head, watching the scene from outside the self she had sculpted to fit circumstances too perplexing for chains of logic and too grievous for sentimentality.

"You need each other." With that, the manager stood up and placed her palms on the table. "Dinner tonight? On me." *On us, fingers crossed.* "The rest? The rest is up to you." She skittered away.

Recovering first, Helen's bellowed protest sailed over the now-vacant tables to the manager's customary station as gatekeeper by the entrance. "You can't do that!"

Diane's initial flinch at the volume of the other woman's voice recovered mid-shudder and mutated into visceral indignation. "Don't tell that young woman what to do!"

The shouted retort shocked Helen for a moment,

but she lurched ahead. Louder. "Don't you tell me what the hell I can and cannot do, for God's sake! What's she playing at, eavesdropping on our private conversation and thinking she can come over here and dribble some sort of saccharine dross like she has the power to make this all go away!"

Helen had hit her combative stride, the tone she used for fee negotiations with independent contractors, unprepared merger-and-acquisition attorneys, and tardy clients. "None of this bullshit has anything to do with her!"

The manager sat on her stool with her back to the remaining occupied table and twirled a strand of blond hair. She soft-focused her eyes, until the headlights from the slow traffic on the street outside like rows of snow angels.

Diane had not yelled at anyone in longer than she could remember, if you didn't count rubbernecking summer tourist drivers and that one time two mostly-innocent missionaries had dared to knock for an optimist second go-around at her soul. She felt static charge of tension rising from her gut, until the potential energy of it threatened to rupture her throat.

"Of course, this has nothing to do with her!" Diane's fury crossed the boundary of civil convention. "She's nothing—nobody!"

The manager smiled. *Nothing. Nobody.*

Waving both hands in the air, her whole body riding the release, Diane was still shouting. "This is between you and me and your daughter and whoever I used to be and it's about us, for God's sake! Why can't you see that?"

Helen tapped the edge of the table. Her voice was frozen. "Us? How can there still be an us?"

Risk shuns company and sacrifices everything to save whatever might be waiting at the bottom of the well. Diane's whole recreated life—and her whole life before that night at the gallery in Brooklyn—were altars to the alter ego of risk: risk management. Everything in her engineer's mind and fractured heart spurred her to run the calculations three times over, to mitigate and control each known variable and a hundred other unknowns besides.

Diane measured twice. She ran the simulation, yes and no and maybe. When she dared, she peeked at Helen, who was staring at a point across the room with narrowed eyes and hunched shoulders.

"Can't call it even." Diane set out her argument like a geometrical proof, analytical and precedent-dependent. "Can't call it anything, if we don't know what it is."

She took a deep breath and willed Helen to meet her stare. "Don't you want to know what this might be? Or at least what might have been?"

When her flat eyes found Diane's, Helen flinched and swiped her bright hand across her face. "It's late."

They both heard the unspoken word. Diane forced herself to think the question, through her aching chest and adrenalin-soaked muscles. *Too late?* She laid her hands out in supplication.

The manager watched. *All in.*

Helen's hands wandered blindly across the table like

cave beetles, her spread fingers sliding across the smooth wood. Diane sucked in her breath as Helen's claws pressed tightly enough against Diane's upturned palms to leave a flutter of scarlet arrowheads across the second joint all four fingers. She let go with a flushed apology, which Diane shook off. They stood in synch and walked out, ten feet between them.

After they left, the manager poured herself a glass of leftover champagne, clicked off every flickering false candle in the holders on the wall, and locked the door. She hummed to herself, words falling like Morse code behind tired eyes. *Outcome unknown. Odds upped. Right thing done.*

The two women rode home in silence. Diane turned on the radio and killed it as the twang of a heartsick country song filled the car. Helen flipped stations and landed on the dark layers of Mahler before sighing in exasperation and prodded the power button.

At the last turn into Diane's street, Helen slowed until the car was imitating the half-life of some exotic isotope. A hundred feet the first few seconds, fifty the next, twenty-five.

The passenger rolled her eyes in the dark. "Let's get this over with. Flip a coin, let me out at the curb, whatever." Diane added darkly, "I'll call it if you won't."

"Can't." Helen drove with one hand on the wheel and the other elbow wedged against the window. The car crept forward, prowling up to the entrance of Diane's driveway. Twelve feet. Six.

Diane felt the exhaustion over her like an avalanche. She held her breath for a moment. "Far enough." She reached for the door handle and put one leg out as the car stopped.

Fear is a formidable dictator of prohibition and an inveterate foe of grit. Fighting her terror, Helen tensed her jaw and spat out a whisper. "Too far. You're already too far away."

Crying was not Diane's thing, but Helen's voice burst something. Diane was sobbing without words before she could even pull her leg back in and close the door, hunched over against the side. Helen unclicked her seatbelt, shoved the car into park, and stroked Diane's unresisting head. Her own eyes filling with tears, Helen joined Diane in quiet, persistent weeping as the idle engine growled.

After ten minutes, the only sound was the car's reassuring whirr and rumble. Diane leaned across over her hip's objection and put arms around Helen. She spoke into the other woman's shoulder. "Walk a girl to the front door?"

They pulled away and shared a fragile smile. Helen dug for sarcasm, came up empty-handed, and settled for sincerity. "I'd like nothing better."

She walked behind Diane up the narrow front path, their hands locked together. "Never did ask," Helen said without breaking stride, her voice rough. "About what I called you on our first date. Need to know if you like it well enough to keep it."

"I like Annie," the other woman said, tugging at a

loose strand of hair and turning to face her girlfriend. "Annie's…us."

Standing in the doorway, Helen put her arms around Annie and kissed her neck. "I know there's a lot more to talk about, after tonight. But I like the sound of us."

Cape Cod (March 2019)

The morning of the last day of winter, Annie woke up with the sun despite only managing three hours sleep. She stood in her sweatpants and t-shirt in front of her narrow closet, staring at the dozen hangers that constituted her entire wardrobe. She pulled out her least worn-out pair of jeans and her only non-plaid button up shirt and laid them on the bed. Nodding, she pulled everything else off their wire perches and dumped them into the waiting garbage bag.

The mall was only a half hour drive away. Annie fiddled with the radio until she landed on a rustling country station, opened the windows despite the chill, and hummed along.

Two hours later, with her donations dropped off and her three huge Macy's shopping bags crammed on the back seat, Annie drove past Broadwell to a hair salon two towns over. She parked right in front, pulled the rubber band out of her hair, frowned at herself in the mirror, and nodded.

Cape Cod (March 2019)

Annie did not like surprises, and she did not know Helen well enough to guess how the other woman felt about the shock value of a drastic change. An hour before she was due at Helen's house, Annie slumped into her only comfortable armchair in the living room she hardly ever used and picked up the landline. The phone rang twice, and a corporate voice answered, the sound sharp and sure.

"Helen Gilbert-Jones."

She knows exactly who the hell she is. Annie's mind stampeded with the rush of the other woman's certainty.

"Hello? Who is this?" The voice sliced open and hope fell out. Annie heard the warmth and tenderness as Helen said one more word. "Marissa?"

Stammering, the caller said, "No, it's…me."

Idiot.

"It's Annie, sorry, I…"

On the other end of the line, Helen squeezed the handset and suppressed a sigh. She dropped her shoulders and forced the corners of her mouth upwards. "Sure, Annie, hi!"

There was silence as both women tried to plot an altered course. Annie pushed aside the obvious question and tried to hold to her version of true north. "Still on for dinner?"

Helen's laugh found its feet and she exhaled. "I hope so, babe, or I'm going to have to invite the neighbors over, and I am pretty sure they don't want to hang out with an old lady on a Saturday night."

She paused and her smile softened. "Hope you still do."

Annie swallowed her giggle. "That's a firm yes, Helen Gilbert-Jones."

"Come over whenever you're ready." Helen finished up her end of the conversation.

"There's one thing." Annie was furious at herself that her voice trembled as she spoke. "You might notice a little something…different."

"Okay." Helen let the word fall into the space. She waited. "Did something happen? Are you hurt?"

This is ridiculous. What are you, fifteen? Annie could feel the reprimand press against the inside of her head. "I got my hair cut."

Helen's laugh started in her tight throat and jitterbugged through the phone. She laughed for half a minute. "You are a piece of work, Annie Howard. Here I'm thinking you're going to show up mummy wrapped from some horrible accident. Or worse—not show up at all."

Annie allowed the half-truth of her new moniker to sting briefly. *One step at a time.* She reached for an easy retort, the unanswered questions on both sides forgotten in the shared moment of generosity and acknowledgement. "Takes one to know one, Helen-I-don't-even-know-your-middle-name-or-the-source-of-the-hyphen-Gilber-Jones. See you in twenty."

After she hung up, Annie walked back to her bedroom and surveyed her refilled closet. She pulled on a pair of jade leggings, a knee-length black suede skirt and a three-quarter length white button up shirt. Digging into the plastic storage tub under her bed, Annie grinned as she dredged up her black leather jacket and a puddle of silver jewelry that had been stashed hurriedly in the top pocket.

In the bathroom, she surveyed her reflection with a buzz of nostalgia, excitement, and, terror. The woman who stared back at her was every person she had ever been, and simultaneously an alien she had never seen in her life. The frosted tips of her spiky hair stood two inches from her head in dark purple brushstrokes. Her eyes beamed through the lenses of her old glasses in a peacock display of penciled brows and shimmering make-up. Annie glanced at the three shades of lipstick that were still in their plastic sleeves and picked the claret.

She stepped out of the car to Helen's open front door and wide smile. Annie ducked her head back in to retrieve the wine and tried to steady her jelly legs. When she turned around, Helen was already halfway down the walkway, arms open for a welcoming hug.

"It's—"

Too much. Annie took a step backward, her arms at her sides.

"Gorgeous!" Helen's face caught up with her confusion. "I never would have pegged you for this." She took Annie's hand and pirouetted her appreciatively. "Love it."

Annie shifted her wait again. Her lips brushed the other woman's ear. "It's a whole new world."

Despite Helen's invitation to stay the night, Annie made her excuses and headed home by eleven. She walked into the house and turned on all the lights, from the kitchen through to the front door. The house was dusty with indifference. The hardwood floors had been swept without enthusiasm every few weeks for twenty years. The kitchen was clean enough—Annie could never stand dirty dishes sitting around—but the floor hadn't been mopped in months. Annie's squares of paper from that day in September were still everywhere—on the table, along the floor in the hallway, trailing like breadcrumbs up the stairs. By now, there were at least a hundred tiny portraits of what Annie still could not see clearly. She picked one up off the floor, hesitating. She held it in her hand like a sheet of origami paper, wondering what it might turn in to. Instead of a futile attempt at folding it into a crane or a lantern, Annie crumpled it in her dry palm. Without dropping the first crimped nest of her failure, Annie picked up another, and another. In a few minutes, her fist bulged with lump of paper that scraped at her skin. She held it to her chest and hop-marched to the trash can under the kitchen sink, shoving it in violently and slamming the cabinet shut.

When she stood up, the rest of the paper butterflies mocked her from the hall. She gathered each one, wrinkled them up together, and repeated her disposal, to the soundtrack of the squat heels of her black mules *skid-thumping* against the worn wooden floors.

She was done. She could hear the invisible voice of whoever was or was not in her drawings, and she tied up the garbage bag and pressed it down on top of the other bags in the trash next to the garage.

No photos, no pictures on the walls, no ornaments on side tables or cushions on occasional chairs. No side tables. No occasional chairs. A place where someone once landed because she had lost her wings, a place that did its best to shield its reluctant occupant from anything that happened outside its four unchanging walls. In the blaze of every incandescent lightbulb from top to bottom and front to back, Annie felt the house turn her out, abruptly hostile. Each bright spot of light was an accusation of what had and had not been there. She stared at the blank spaces on floors, counters, and walls.

"Right." Annie peeled a pair of waffled thermals and stained sweatshirt out of the dryer, pulled on a pair of woolen socks against the inevitable chill, and opened her utility closet with more hope than confidence. She dragged out every cleaning product she had bought since arriving in Cape Cod and spent the first half hour tossing out half bottles of dried up gunk.

She inspected what was left: surface spray, floor

cleaner, bleach. The rubber gloves that she had found crackled a little when she yanked them up to her wrists, and she had to wash the broom in the laundry sink before being sure it would sweep up more dirt than it ground in, but by a quarter to one she had an army of supplies and a mission.

Loading up with a full roll of paper towel and a bucket of rags—three tee shirts that went straight from dryer to the guillotine as she sliced them into strips—Annie started in her studio and worked until four-thirty. She fed her grumbling hip with anti-inflammatories and periodic stretches, ignoring the nagging concern that the noise of the vacuum cleaner would have the neighbor banging on her front door.

She left the baseboards, walls, light switches, light fixtures, and window sills. She did not bother with the pantry or the corners of…everywhere. This was a first pass, or at least the first passing attempt she had made to make the space hers. The cleaning was a meditation on all she had and had not been for so long she could hardly remember, a life that seemed translucent in its distance from her and closer than she dared recall.

Annie scrubbed the shower and tub, rubbed foamy circles on and off all the mirrors, vacuumed and swept and mopped. She pulled the slim pickings out of her refrigerator, salvaged what could still be eaten, and soaped every drawer and rack. She set her old oven to self-cleaning mode and banged the smoke alarm so hard when the fumes set it off that the plastic battery cap shattered in pieces on the floor.

Against the odds, she found a single shriveled lemon and an ancient bottle of vanilla essence as she tossed out old lettuce and past-date cheese. She sliced the lemon and a capful of vanilla into a pot of simmering water, inhaling the fresh scent as it spiraled to the ceiling. It had been someone else's trick a long time ago; Annie was ready to make it hers. *Home.*

Helen called on the day after she had made dinner for Annie. "Missed you."

Annie smiled into the phone, sitting on the floor surrounded by the detritus of her manic night's work and a half-crossed off list of people she needed to call before ten. "You weren't kidding when you said you could cook."

The next day was Wednesday. By Friday, Broadwell's gossip train steamed with all of the stories of everyone who had been invited to the crazy lady's house: plumber, gutter repair team, roof inspection, insulation installer, window cleaner (with scaffold to reach the turret glass), air duct technician, spring cleaning service, driveway sealer, garage door mechanic, furniture delivery, landscaper designer, interior and exterior painters. Everyone except the last group had been locals—rumor had it that old lady Howard had hired painters from a suburb of Boston to come last minute and spruce up the whole house with a team of nine in less than a week.

Annie had kept all of those things from falling apart for years, but Helen's arrival in her life sparked something willful. *Something about wanting to be in the world again.* The town wondered, as they had always wondered, where the money for any of it came from. When Annie appeared at the bagel shop or grocery store or library in the weeks that followed, as she always had, no one asked.

By the following weekend, the drab Tudor no longer hunched on the overgrown lot: it glowed. With expert application and a lucky run of dry days, the house mirrored Annie's metamorphosis. The broken fence had been replaced with a low boulder wall that was left curved and roughly mortared in foamy waves across the top. The stucco had color-shifted from dirty white to silvery frost, the crisscross trim and matching shutters had transformed from traditional chocolate brown to a whimsical teal, and the cranberry door sprouted a white-berry wreath. One dead oak and a rotting dogwood had been supplanted by a single proud white spruce, and three broken lead-lined windows had been replaced by replicas flown in from an artisan in North Carolina.

After everyone was gone, and the house was quiet again, Annie stepped through her front door, trailed her fingers across the puzzle bark of her new evergreen tree, and exhaled into the sharp air. She was still getting used to jangling as she walked, and she had mostly stopped brushing invisible strands of straggly hair off her forehead. *Might not know who I am, exactly. Sure of who I'm not.*

Cape Cod (April 2019)

"Neutral territory." Helen sighed, glancing at her phone. It was late April, and they had spent another weekend at Annie's house. By unspoken agreement, Annie's huge renovated (and incrementally redecorated) Tudor house on the corner had become their nest. They agreed more than they disagreed, and the first rush of finding one another had subsided into a growing sense of gratitude and calm deliberation about what might come next.

Over homemade almond biscotti and mutually exclusive sludge coffee and aromatherapy tea the night before, Helen had accepted both closet space in the master bedroom and an extra front door key on a lighthouse keychain.

Annie stepped out of the bathroom wrapped in a fuzzy lime bathrobe, her hair still dripping down her neck. "Missed that."

Helen pulled a taupe turtleneck sweater over her head and raked her hair with sunshine nails. She tapped the screen with an impatient thumb. "Haven't seen her or Nathan in over a year, and now she wants to change plans at the last minute. Something about taking the bus instead of driving."

Annie tugged a flowing dress over fleece leggings

and threaded on a half dozen silver bangles. "Still wants to see you, though, right? Probably anxious since it's been so long."

"Since when are you the optimist in this relationship?" Helen handed Annie a thin gold chain with a single bar pendant and turned her back. "Thanks."

Gently, Annie kissed her on the cheek. "Since you're the one freaking out about something in a way I've never seen you freak before, sweetheart. What's with the worry?"

"You don't know what she's like." Helen shrugged away and began to fold clothes from the floor. "Like her father, unreliable."

They were both ready with a half hour to spare. Helen triple-checked the address of the pancake place Marissa had texted her. She sat across the dining room table from Annie and clicked her fingernails together like a mosquito zapper.

"Nathan's probably a foot taller than last time I saw him. Called him on his birthday, but you know what teenagers are—" Helen stopped herself. "Sorry. No."

Annie stilled Helen's hands under the shelter of her own. "Ask her how she's doing like you think she's doing fine. Everything you've told me about her—Nathan's dad, the alcohol—is about what she's done wrong all these years. This time around eighteen months sober—new job, new place."

Helen listened to the catalog of vague successes, the missed opportunities with a daughter she had never understood. "What if it's not enough?"

Walking around to her side of the bed, Annie opened the bottom drawer of her nightstand and retrieved a dogeared book. She flipped to a blank page embossed with multicolored words in a narrow ribbon and held it up for Helen to see. "One of Amanda's art books. 'Fill the space that needs filling, leave the space that needs leaving, and you will see what you need to see.'"

Halfway through a derisive laugh, Helen stopped at the sight of Annie's somber face. "Wasn't expecting—"

The moment that had held Annie in a Brooklyn bubble passed. and she snapped her fingers with a grin. "Deep and meaningful? Don't know me as well as you think you do, babe? Full of surprises."

"That's her car." Pulling into the restaurant, Helen pointed to a green hatchback parked across two spaces. "Trying to impress me by not being late."

"You launch this whole reunion like that, Helen, and you'll be out on your ass as a mom and a grandmother before anyone's ordered iced tea."

Groaning, Helen turned her exasperated face towards Annie. "Should have sent you instead, Ambassador Howard. You ready to play diplomat?"

Annie shook her head and climbed out the driver's seat. "Hell, yeah. Even referee if that's what you need. That's why I'm here."

Marissa Williams had been sitting in the far booth with her teenage son hunched in the corner of one bench for twenty minutes when Helen and Annie walked in. Annie saw her first and would have recognized Helen's daughter anywhere as a fun house version of her mom—same color eyes, same height, but with skin pasted across protruding bones from wrist to collarbone and a nose that had been broken more than once. Marissa coughed nervously and half-rose. She was dressed in a pink cotton hoodie with rolled up sleeves and jeans with rips in the knees.

Annie shook herself loose from the collision of Helen's blunt descriptions and the animated stereotype that mumbled an unconvincing hello.

Helen ignored Marissa, using her long reach to tap Nathan on the shoulder and motion for him to take off his headphones. "High five for your grandma? It's been awhile."

Nathan tugged both buds out and grunted. "Who the hell's fault is that? Hers or yours?"

"Nathan!" *Even their voices are similar.* Annie took a step back as mother and grandmother agreed on at least one thing. *Younger one less certain, but the warning sounds the same.*

Smiling in malicious triumph, Nathan cocked one eyebrow at Annie. "Just as I thought. It's always my fault."

Trying to find a way not to be implicated in the adolescent's retaliatory conspiracy, Annie stepped past Helen and offered a firm hand. "Marissa? I'm Annie."

The introduction sounded new to both of them. Annie recovered first and slathered the situation with half-truth small talk. "Your mom tells me you and Nathan moved into a new place a few weeks ago. Don't know about you, but

I've lived in mine twenty years and I've still got unopened boxes! There's always more to do, am I right?"

Marissa blinked her eyes slowly. Before she responded, she glanced at Helen, her mouth tight. "Wasn't far from the old place. Friend with a pickup truck helped us move."

In the fluttering silence that followed, Nathan saw another opportunity. "Frankie's your sponsor, Mom. You're always telling me to stick to the facts. Facts matter."

Parents and children come by the lattice of their relationships through biology or circumstance, but there is nothing in the scaffold that knows pre-emptively how to hold up whatever comes in the moments after the first meeting. Fortune lashes together personalities, inclinations and characteristics that are more or less compatible from the beginning. When that rapport is natural and easy, parents and children navigate the rest of the world, and their rest of their shared lives, as a team; when dissonance is more pronounced, every moment of affinity is a rare intersection of luck and labor.

Helen Gilbert-Jones had spent more than thirty years trying to understand her daughter. She had researched and implemented parenting strategies to the best of her inherent talents, the way she had dug in and dug out of corporate deals, but she had been away. Despite Helen's intentions and Marissa's unheralded efforts to forge a different path for herself, the mother/daughter relationship was more war than peace from the time Marissa was three years old. The odd détente and long stretches of dogged reciprocal tolerance was tinged with mutual desperation for connection, driven by love. More than two people who might have fallen into well-worn tracks of empathy and congruity of temperament, Helen and Marissa loved each other with the traits they shared: stubbornness and resilience.

Where Helen's inclination had always been brash and forceful, Marissa's reticence left her vulnerable to pressures that her mother could neither tolerate nor understand. Combined with the addictive genes that swam in her veins from a father she had never met, Marissa's path was always going to be bouldered by challenges Helen could neither predict nor control.

That reluctance to fight back showed now. Marissa dropped her eyes at Nathan's cruelty and covered her face with chapped hands.

Helen's maternal instinct reasserted itself. "Nathan?" She pointed at the door. "With me. Now."

Nathan got up and followed her with a deeper scowl, but without a word.

The younger woman dropped her forehead softly on the table, sloshing over a steaming half cup of coffee. Annie sat down across from her.

"Marissa?" Without waiting for a reply, Annie continued. "If that's even ten percent as hard as it seems from the outside, parenting a teenager, I can't think what your life must be like."

The mother with an unruly adolescent glowered at

the mother who had never had the chance. "Nathan's a great kid. He's had a hard time is all."

Sensing the danger of her position, Annie backtracked. "Only meant that it seems to me he's a pretty normal kid—I'm guessing defying authority is pretty much standard procedure at his age. Helen and I are here to help in any way we can."

Another mine triggered. Annie saw it in Marissa's smirk. "My mother'd love nothing better than to have that boy all to herself, so that I couldn't screw him up any more than I already have. So he doesn't turn out like me."

Annie did not have the chance to defuse her mistake. Helen strode and Nathan slunk back in. The boy loomed over his mother, grinding out a single word. "Sorry."

Marissa wiped her eyes with the back of her hand and scooted over on the bench. "Apology accepted," she said, before turning her head towards Annie and mouthing, "See?"

Sliding in reluctantly next to his mother, Nathan pulled out his phone and slipped his earphones back in. Helen arched her eyebrows at his Marissa. "Seems to me that no device mealtimes are the least you could insist on."

Under the table, Annie nudged Helen's leg, adding a tight smile and a question with her eyes.

Marissa flinched and mumbled, "Could use a refill of this soupy excuse for coffee."

Helen took two deep breaths as though she was blowing up a balloon. "I'm sorry."

Her daughter added, "I remember what you thought of me at his age."

"Argh!" Helen's growl was much louder than she had intended. When the sound echoed off the grungy diner walls, she clapped one hand over her mouth and blushed uncharacteristically across her throat and up her cheeks. Several other customers' heads flicked over in Helen's direction, reacting with alarm to something that sounded both threatening and distraught.

The manager jogged over to their table. "Perhaps there is something I can help you with?"

Detaching herself from Helen's distress, Annie turned to the man. The manager was a bald, freckled man closing in on eighty, with three missing teeth and the four fingers of his left hand wrapped in stained, fraying tape. His voice whistled and he spoke with odd formality.

Helen nodded, but it was not enough for the man. He waited all day, every day for an opportunity to exert his fleck of authority. "If this is some difficult family situation, perhaps you would all prefer to continue this conversation outside?"

Annie knew she would not be able to swallow the laugh. She felt it as soon as the words 'family situation' tinkled out of his shadowed mouth; like a shaken seltzer bottle, Annie's insides fizzed and bubbled as she fought for control. In the half a second before she realized that she also had a mouthful of ice water, and that was only going one way, Annie tensed all of her muscles. Half of the water spurted from her nose; the rest dribbled down her chin, leaving her airway free to cackle and caw.

Helen's primary relief at not being the center of attention shifted to shock and shared hilarity. She joined her girlfriend, braying and slapping the table as her eyes streamed.

Marissa stared at the two of them. Her mouth twitched but she blew her nose instead, sitting primly with her hands in her lap.

Nathan had not heard the manager, but the twin attractions of two idiot adults and his mother trying to disappear were too good to miss. He tapped his phone to interrupt the stream of pop punk in both ears. His lips did not budge from their semi-permanent scowl.

The manager knew what to do about problematic customers. He had called 9-1-1 on a few fistfights and given away dozens of slices of free strawberry pie after complaints of chewy clam chowder or burned tuna melts. He had never seen anything like the two old ladies in the corner booth, hugging and crying and laughing while the scraggy mom and her cranky teenager gaped. Cutting his losses, he pirouetted on one heel and stomped back to the kitchen.

"What the hell was so funny?" Nathan nudged his boundaries. Helen glared but Marissa ignored her son.

Annie leaned over to Nathan, finally catching her breath. She held the pathways in her head, mapped out from here to there and back. She picked candor. "Relationships, Nathan. It's been awhile since you've all been together, and

I'm a new addition, right? The four of us, sitting here, not one of knowing what the other wants or needs or how to reach past the—"

Helen frowned, but did not interrupt. Annie took a beat and continued. "Past the past, I guess."

She gambled another move. Annie asked Nathan the question no one ever had. "What do you think about all of this?"

Nathan stared at her with the first artless expression he had shown all day: confusion. He glanced at his mother, who did not meet his eyes, and at Helen, whose sharply drawn eyebrows offered no safe harbor for his disorientation.

Annie knocked the knuckles of one hand against the table. "Yes. You."

The boy murmured. The three women at the table held their breath, their bodies turned to whatever he might choose to share, each primed to react in their own way.

Marissa's chest ached, the constant current of addiction's temptation buzzing below the threshold of her love for the child who was suddenly and unwillingly the center of attention.

Helen was more irked by her own failure to see what the boy needed than by her girlfriend's insight, but she let her anger waft in Annie's direction so that she did not have to confront her own demons about the other child at the table. Nonetheless, the thought bubbles persisted, appearing and popping inside her mind as she scraped both palms with her manicured nails. *My daughter. My responsibility. My fault.*

Annie was dizzy with daring, trying to shut out the inner voices that laughed at her arrogance. *Not a chance in hell you know what you're doing here. Before or after you asked that impossible question.* She spied on Helen from her peripheral vision; whatever she was searching for, Annie did not find it. Helen's face was an iceberg.

"Sucks." Nathan reached for his monosyllable of choice, without the profane qualifier he used when he had told his friends that he and his mother were moving forty-five minutes from school.

"And?" Annie's persistence shocked her, annoyed Helen, and made Marissa feel smaller than she already did.

Nathan stared at her. "Who the hell are you?"

On a thousand other days, the conversation would have ended with Annie's retreat and most likely an effusive apology to everyone at the table, starting with the teenager. On this cool, rainy day in April, there was no abort sequence in Annie's brain, no way to modify her course. Launched without a planned trajectory, the interplay between Annie's history and her possible future was lure enough to keep her talking.

"I'm the one asking you what this all means to you, Nathan." Annie's voice was a metronome. "Your mom staying sober, moving to a new place. What you've told your friends. What you wish you could tell them."

He stepped through. "No one knows anything. They all think we moved because she got laid off with everyone else in the office. Nothing new. Half the kids in my class have parents who have lost jobs and stuff."

Marissa's eyes softened. She reached for Nathan, who twisted away without conviction. When she reached for him again, he allowed her to rest her hand on his arm.

Helen's creased forehead stretched sideways, and the parenthesis of her lips yielded. She turned on the bench and nodded at Annie.

The boy felt the frail peace at the table and found more words than he had in the five years since finding his mother after her first morning passed out on the living room floor. Holding Annie's gaze, Nathan said, "My mom's strong, though, y'know? I hate that she's an alcoholic, I hate that it takes an hour to get to school every morning on the bus, but she's doing everything she can to make it right."

Helen's tears dripped down her nose and she sniffled. Marissa gripped her son with a single hand, not willing to risk rejection of the hugs and kisses she desperately wanted to pour over him. Annie bit her lip and blinked wet eyes. She held the responsibility of finishing what she had begun. "Seems to me your mom's not the only tough one in the family. I'm new to all of this—to all of you—but I'm already in awe of you, Nathan."

He cringed, but his eyes betrayed a deep pleasure at the compliment.

Annie doubled down. "You should know that every one of us at this table sees you. Appreciates you." The curveball surprised all of them, Annie included. "I can see how much your mom and grandmother love you, Nathan, and after today, I'm halfway there, too."

She pulled out her mobile. "In case you need another lame adult in your life?"

Nathan nodded and rattled off his digits. Annie's chirping laugh made him snort. "Slow down, kid! Old lady fingers here."

Texts exchanged, Nathan dropped his stare. "You're okay."

Marissa coughed into both hands, stunned at the revelation of the stranger across the table and her son's vulnerability. Nathan bent sideways, his shoulders brushing Marissa's. Helen curled her leg around Annie's, pressing their knees together. No one else said a word. The moment cracked like an egg.

Lunch was crispy burgers and soggy fries all around, served overcooked and underheated. Beyond Annie's intermittent slipstream of weather chatter and the other two women's shell-shocked participation, the only noises came from the rattle of plates in the open counter kitchen and the clatter of compression brakes from trucks outside.

Helen paid the check. Annie said goodbye, to everyone and for everyone. Helen's mouth fogged the passenger side window as she counted her breaths down the road.

"Tomatoes." Annie turned the classical station off as they drove into Broadwell. "And fresh bread for the soup I made yesterday." She glanced over and offered an alternative. "Or home?"

"How'd you know?" Helen gripped Annie's hand. She did not need to be more specific.

"Didn't come from me." Annie swallowed the tears that threatened. "His desperation was bleeding all over the place. Asking was the least of it."

They both knew this was not true. Asking was the whole of it, the wedge that opened whatever doors Nathan would be willing to walk through today.

Helen wiped her eyes. The words fell out of her mouth before she had a chance to think twice. "Five hundred days seems like a lot, until it isn't. She went near on a year when Nathan was twelve, after some New Year's party when she ended up in hospital for three days."

Annie sighed. "Once an addict, Helen. Cliché because it's true. Do you have reason not to trust her this time?"

Blowing her nose with a clump of tissues, Helen ignored the question. "Bet she hadn't slept in a week."

She pressed her palms on the dashboard. "Not as skinny as she was before, at least. Lot to be carrying for a kid, though."

Her voice trembled. "Drowning in 'shoulds,' Annie. Should have been there more when she was little, should have seen it all coming, should have made myself hard to ignore these past five years. Instead I haven't seen my grandson in a year, and I let two-word texts back and forth be enough. As if it were enough for me. As if it were enough for Marissa, or for Nathan."

She breathed like a winded horse. "Scared if I ask myself what comes next, I'm going to find out, and it can't possibly be good."

Annie slowed down and pulled into the grocery store parking lot. Reaching for her girlfriend, Annie pulled their joined hands to her heart. "Best you can at the time is always good enough. That's all there is. Two of us now. It's going to be fine. Nathan and Marissa both. They're going to be fine."

They let the impossible promise hover between them like a drowsy bee, stupefied by hope's smoke. Helen broke away first with a voice of quiet resignation. "It's going to be something, babe. Fine? Don't think we get that lucky."

Shaken to be the one keeping the faith, Annie gritted her teeth against Helen's uncharacteristic pessimism. She settled for a painfully cheerful march on the radio and a half dozen donuts with rainbow sprinkles at the drive-through. They skipped the shopping and ate leftover spaghetti together on Annie's couch, a single lamp casting worn shadows between them.

Cape Cod (May 2019)

"Annie!" Helen's voicemail bubbled and rose, the words rushed and wet with fear. "It's Marissa. She's been arrested, they're booking her over in Fremont. Call me. For God's sake, call me."

Pulling in to her driveway, Annie heard her unanswered phone beep a message. She retrieved the key lime and pecan pies from the passenger seat, mentally checking off everything on her list for Marissa and Nathan's upcoming Memorial Day visit to Broadwell.

Holding the door open with her weaker foot, Annie set dessert down on a crescent table as her phone rang again.

She tapped the screen. "Yes, I picked up the— what?"

Standing in the overflow parking section of the police station three towns over, Helen held her phone with shaking hands. "Goddamn DUI, Annie. With Nathan in the car, wouldn't pull over for a mile and a half. First offense, but—"

Annie propped herself up against the wall as Helen's voice dipped. Annie turned the volume to maximum and pressed the receiver against her ear. "Nathan's been taken by social services, somewhere in Trisham. Can't get the address until the lawyer gets here, something about transfer of *in loco parentis* rights."

"Twenty-five minutes. Fast as I can. I'm coming. Don't hang up." Annie snatched up her keys, slicing open the tip of one finger in the process. "Shit!" With her other hand, Annie locked the door, and got back in the car. She slid her phone into its hand-free cradle, swiped her oozing finger on the hem of her blouse, and switched to speaker.

"Helen?" Annie waited a moment, listening to her girlfriend's wet breathing. Her tires scattered gravel along the edges of the driveway, and she hunched over the steering wheel, driving on automatic. "Lawyer?"

Relieved to have a practical detail to hinge her response on, Helen rattled off the details. "Already put a call into my friend Justine, she'll have someone here from Boston within the next two hours."

Annie's eyes registered a cop car hunched on the shoulder of the road beyond the next stop sign and her foot rammed into the brake. "Find somewhere to sit. I'll call you when I get there."

The parking lot of the police station in Fremont was full; Annie parked around the corner, shoved a fistful of salvaged change into the meter, and skip-hopped as fast as her leg would allow to the police station.

Helen paced back and forth inside the revolving door. Annie gripped her by the shoulders before folding her into a hug.

Eyes red-rimmed but dry, Helen shook with anger and her voice boiled. "What the hell, Annie? With Nathan in the car? Thank God he's fifteen, any younger and she'd be facing child endangerment as well as the driving while impaired charge. Jesus Christ, of course she damn well endangered him!"

Without smiling, Annie squeezed her girlfriend's hand and spoke softly. "Google lawyering's no better than Google doctoring, love."

Unmollified, Helen spat out more angry words. "This is what I was afraid of."

They both allowed the lie to sift down into the substrate of conversations to come, knowing it was not the time.

"Ms. Gilbert-Jones?" A police officer approached them, a tablet tucked under one arm. "Marissa Williams' next of kin?"

Annie and Helen both stopped breathing. The cop shook his head. "Her mother?"

Still holding hands, they followed him through a set of double doors as he swiped them through with his security badge. "Can't see her until she has been processed and we figure out if she's going home today, but I've got one of our liaison officers here to discuss next steps."

He glanced at his computer and swiped left. "I understand there was a child in the vehicle at the time of her apprehension, is that correct?"

Helen nodded, her make-up smeared. "My grandson."

"Nathan," Annie added. *Names matter.*

"Right," the cop said, scribbling something on the screen with his finger while keeping one eye firmly skewered on the women's hold on each other. A herd of nasty comments stampeded through his brain and he sniffed loudly. "In here."

The windowless room swallowed Annie and Helen. They heard the door click locked as he left. The sat on a low, sagging two-seater that smelled as though it had been dragged backwards through a carwash made of cats.

Four minutes later, a middle-aged woman with chopsticks through her top bun, a long paisley skirt, and a small gold cross around her neck knocked and entered. Annie caught the transformation of her face as the empathy mask replaced ennui.

"Belinda." She pointed to her name badge. "I know this is a tough time for your family. She glanced at her notes. "Your daughter?"

Rolling desiccated eyes, Helen raised one hand. "Mine."

"Of course." Belinda's lips moved as she read the sheet in front of her. "Have you been able to secure legal representation for them yet?"

Helen nodded, but Annie questioned the pronoun. "Them?"

Belinda nodded vigorously, as though everything was obvious. "Your grandson may need separate representation, depending on the outcome of the social services investigation."

She crossed something off the page and pursed her lips. "You might, too. Depending."

Helen shrank in her chair. Annie folded forward across the table. "Depending on what?"

"Not up to me to say, at this juncture." Belinda balanced on her chair's back legs. "The determination of charges filed has not been fully established, but in due course the Commonwealth may need to establish alternative custody arrangements."

Tasting the words as she repeated them to herself, Helen flinched. Belinda ignored both women and continued. "No other children noted in the initial report, is that accurate? Guessing there's no father in the picture?"

"Yes." Helen paused. "No." She shook her head.

Annie stepped up. "You've got it right there, Belinda. Why don't you tell us what we need to do now?"

"Are you—" Belinda's mouth curled at the word. "—family? Because if you're not—" Annie watched her inner struggle again, glaring as Belinda's face landed smug. "—married or what have you, this matter does not concern anyone in this room but Ms. Gilbert-Jones."

"I'll tell you something, Bel—" Annie pushed away from the table.

"Annie, don't." Helen tapped her teeth. "Why don't you wait out front? Five, ten minutes tops."

Dropping her stance, Annie relented. "You need me, I'm right there." Without another word, she pointed to the door. Belinda rose, let her out, and returned to sit across from Helen.

A half hour later, Helen emerged. "No."

Annie pretended she had not thought any one of a dozen questions that the negative might answer. She held Helen's hand and waited.

"Justine's sending two attorneys. One will meet us where Nathan has been taken, the other's coming here directly. Bail likely, not sure about getting the charges dropped. Mitigating factors, maybe? She said something in there about a burned-out brake light being the reason Marissa was stopped in the first place."

Helen stopped, exhaling heavily. "I don't know about any of this crap, Annie. What am I supposed to do?"

"We." Annie hugged her. "We drive over to Trisham, we bring Nathan home." She did not say 'my place'—despite Helen still-rented apartment, they both knew that the Tudor on the corner in Broadwell was already home. "We let the lawyers figure it out for Marissa on their end, you talk to the other lawyer about what Nathan needs, and we take it from there."

"Six hundred dollars an hour." Helen grimaced. "Better tell my bank I'm going to need an overdraft."

"Bullshit." Annie shook her head. "Fifty-fifty." She held up one hand. "And if you argue, my offer's going to land on seventy-five/twenty-five, so I suggest you shut up about the damn money."

"Thank you." Helen left it at that.

"It's what families do." Annie's voice wavered as she

said the word. *Did not expect to find another. But here we are.*

They each drove their cars to the social services building in Trisham. Helen arrived a few minutes after Annie. "Three wrong turns, what the hell?"

Annie put her arm around Helen. "Let's do this."

The outside of the building was a smorgasbord of styles, with a mismatched array of weathered cedar shingles, faux stone, and robin's egg blue aluminum siding. The inside smelled like damp dog and was a 1970s time warp of green-and-orange curtains, stained velour sofas, and chipboard desks.

A woman who appeared barely old enough to drive met them with an overly-cheerful smile and an overbearing handshake. "I'm Teresa, Teresa Strathford. Welcome." They exchanged names and greetings standing in the narrow hallway. Annie frowned at the woman's friendliness. Helen's usually animated face remained set in cement.

"Nathan's through here," the social worker said. "I asked the front desk to grab him another sandwich." She tried on another fluorescent smile. "Teenagers, am I right?"

Finally stirred to reaction, Helen stared at Annie and mouthed in horror. *What the hell?* Annie nodded, using her hand and chest to mime deep breaths.

Sitting on a ratty beanbag in the corner of a small room, Nathan did not hear the three women come in.

Annie pushed Helen towards the boy before Teresa could announce their presence. Adding her own energy to Annie's encouragement, Helen blurred across the room and knelt beside Nathan.

Without touching him, Helen spoke loudly enough so that he could hear her through his earphones. Annie turned away, trying to give them some privacy, wishing the social worker would do the same. "You okay?"

Nathan glowered. Sluggishly, scanning Helen up and down, he pulled turned off his music and freed his ears.

"Stupid question." Without standing up, Helen backed away until she was five feet away from the still-seated boy. "I wouldn't answer me either."

"Stupid is right." Nathan craned his head around Helen. He waved casually, as though to a friend in the hallway at school. "Hey, Annie."

Annie whipped her head around at the sound of her name. Nathan nodded to her. "We were going to bring chips and salsa. To the party at your place this weekend. Guess that's off."

Sensing something happening beyond her control, feeling abandoned but focused on her grandson's well-being more than on her own discomfort, Helen edged out of the way. She watched and tried on a weak smile as Annie stepped in front of the social worker, blocking the doorway. *That's my girl.*

Annie met Nathan where he was and offered him reassurance he had neither word nor thought to ask for. "We've got pretzels and popcorn, two kinds of pie, four kinds of ice cream, and enough burgers to feed the entire town of Broadwell three times over. I think we're good on the food front."

She had misjudged the boy's intentions, but she had already banked enough credits with Nathan Williams to ride out a rough start. He persisted. "I'm guessing you're a hot salsa kind of person, Annie."

Idiot. Annie berated herself silently and offered him a grin. "Hotter the better. And don't even get me started on blue versus yellow or white corn chips, kid."

Nathan did not flinch at her term of endearment. On cue, they both said together, "Blue!"

As always, Helen's laugh raided the room and commanded everyone's attention. She watched in shock as her grandson stood and took two steps to where she leaned against the back wall.

Without touching her, he said softly, "It got bad this week, Grandma. Really bad, like before. I shouldn't have let her drive, I thought she'd be—"

Helen pulled him in as his voice cracked. He folded into her, losing four inches of height as his knees accordioned. She held him for a few minutes as he wept, keeping her own tears from falling. "None of this is on you, Nathan. None of this should ever have been on you."

Teresa interrupted their reunion with a whinny as she squeezed past Annie into the room. "Great to see everyone getting along so well. Helen, I've got some paperwork in the office. Routine stuff, signatures et cetera. Let's talk outside?"

Helen glanced at Annie. Taking her cue, Annie

crossed the room and opened her arms for the transfer. Nathan clutched her like a koala, his sobs getting louder as the other two women left and his grandmother shut the door behind her.

Annie Howard had never held her own child, though she had murmured to Theo through Amanda's swollen belly dozens of times. Two decades before this moment, she had mourned the loss without fully understanding it, because her grief for the baby was what she dreamed of, rather than what her body knew. *This is different.* She followed her thoughts, feeling her arms both as scaffold and bubble wrap for the boy between them. *He's here. He needs me. Now.*

The superintendent of Marissa's apartment met them on the doorstep with a key but without question. His sympathy bled through every pore, and Annie wondered how much he knew himself about the treachery of addiction. Helen and Annie waited in Marissa's peach-colored-everything living room while Nathan packed a duffel; they ignored the sound of objects colliding with walls as the teenager vented his anger in between shoving clean clothes and schoolbooks into the military surplus bag. The two women nodded in unison when the super appeared in the open doorway with a soft, "Is everything alright?" and exhaled together when he left with a sad smile.

The rides back to Broadwell were quiet. Helen drove too carefully and too slowly. Nathan retreated to his music, hovering behind her. Annie drove too blindly and too fast. She opened her window and felt the rough rain of a gathering stormfront on her face. She stopped for chips and salsa. She still beat the other two home. Time enough to stretch clean sheets across the guest sofa bed, ditch the lilac bedspread for a navy comforter, clear out half a chest of drawers, and appreciate the irony of a slugged-back double shot of bourbon from the kitchen cabinet before Helen's voice and Nathan's silence announced their arrival.

The holiday weekend passed with quiet meals and Nathan's unpredictable presence or absence in conversation. His comic timing was impeccable and his impersonations dead-on; alternated with hours of isolation in his makeshift room chatting to friends or playing video games, the two women relished their time together and fretted when he refused to come out.

Helen fielded conference calls with Marissa's lawyer and returned her daughter to the apartment after she was granted bail. The social worker suggested a week apart for mother and son, despite the lack of custody implications for a relatively unfettered path to dropped charges and expunged arrest record.

When he was in a connecting mood, Nathan cozied up to his grandmother on the couch and subjected her to hours of oddball British comedy. She held herself like a stone, afraid to scare him away, until he pulled a blanket over both of them and fell asleep on her shoulder much too early on Sunday night. Annie poured herself another cup of coffee in the kitchen and kissed them both goodnight before she headed upstairs.

At the boy's request, Annie took Nathan to within three blocks from school and picked him up at the same masked location every day of the short week after Memorial Day. The hour-long car ride was quiet on day one, until Nathan jacked in his music to the car's sound system.

"Pink Floyd?" Caught by surprise, Annie assumed a false intention. "Thanks for thinking of me, fossil that I am. Makes me feel right at home."

Nathan snorted good-naturedly. "You're kidding. This is a classic. You know most of these guys met in architecture school. Crazy, right?" After that, they cycled through '70s and '80s bands with Nathan's obscure commentary guiding them on the long trips back and forth.

Though he talked to his mom most days, Nathan was not in a hurry to return. In the end, he stayed through the week. On Sunday afternoon, he packed up his stuff, helped Helen clean the room, hugged her good-bye, and slumped into the back seat of Annie's car.

"What's it going to be?" Annie asked, turning around expectantly.

Nathan did not reply. Annie let him slide his earphones in and stare out the window while she hummed Led Zeppelin to herself.

Marissa's exhaustion was clear in her slumped posture as she met them in the apartment complex parking lot, but she smiled when Nathan got out. Her son submitted to his mother's zealous hug before turning to Annie and reaching out. "Thanks. For everything."

Annie glanced apologetically at Marissa, who shrugged with grim understanding of the work before her to repair the relationship with her son. "Anytime, kid."

Nathan pulled away and trudged towards the nearest building. Marissa nodded tearfully at Annie. "She didn't come."

Annie shrugged. "Mostly mad at herself, Marissa."

"And me."

Without blinking, Annie acknowledged the truth. "And you for things that are yours to control, and maybe even for the ones that aren't. And me, for everything else."

"But not—?"

Anticipating the conversation's angle, Annie interjected. "Never. Not Nathan."

Marissa's motherhood set itself square and nodded with relief and satisfaction. "Don't know if I'd even know where to start thanking you, Annie. You most of all."

"Like I told Nathan—nothing to—" Annie stopped, watching Marissa's lips move as she tried to find words for something she had not yet dared ask herself.

"Does she...does she say anything else?"

Annie considered an easy lie. She opted for the other. "Truth is always difficult. Your mother's feelings about all of this are complicated."

"Because she thinks I'm a waste of time." Marissa's short-lived joy at knowing her son was not the target of her mother's disappointment cascaded into self-pity. "Because that's how she has always seen me. Inconvenient, inconsiderate, incapable."

The last place Annie Howard wanted to be in that moment was playing defense on behalf of Helen's three and half decades of motherhood. *It's only been seven damn months. How the hell am I supposed to figure out this crap?*

She fell back on too many words. "Your mom knows it's a disease. We both do. As for what happened when you were a kid, whatever you feel about that—growing up not knowing your dad, your mom away for work half the week? Marissa, here's the thing—your mother did the best she could with what she had and who she was at the time."

When Marissa did not reply, Annie added, "We all did. Think of who you were five years ago, or five days. Can you honestly say you'd make the same choices?"

Must be love. Annie caught her breath at the thought, momentarily distracted from the situation at hand. *Because I believe with my whole heart that Helen Gilbert-Jones is the best person she knew how to be, every single day of her life.*

"Right." Annie answered for both of them. "She might not be ready to tell you how she'd do it differently, given a second chance, but believe me when I tell you she wants the chance to try."

Annie saw Marissa, her face more like a small child in need of a hug than a repentant, relapsed alcoholic with a teenage son and a crisis-pocked relationship with her imperfect mother. Annie did the only thing that made sense, which was embrace the younger woman and pat her ineffectually on the back.

Marissa pushed away with stiff arms and stiffer neck. "Wish there was a way to invest in apologies," she said with a wry smile. "I'd be a billionaire by now."

"I should go." Annie turned away. She climbed into the driver's seat, turned on the car and opened the window. "What I said to Nathan? Same goes for you. I am—we are— here. Not going anywhere. You miss a meeting, you can't reach your sponsor, you need to talk to someone outside that world, Nathan needs a ride anywhere—you call. Promise me you'll call."

The two women stared at each other, each waiting for the other to break or break away. Marissa was tired of making oaths she had no way of knowing whether or not she could keep. Annie relented without confirmation of her offer received or guaranteed, offered a two-fingered wave, and drove off. Marissa stood watching the car until it disappeared down the zigzag drive and beyond the trees.

Helen had left a note on the dining room table. Annie picked it up, reflexively checking her phone with her other hand to check texts and voicemail. The only thing she found were blanks and silence. The note spoke for itself: WENT HOME. I'LL CALL YOU.

That night, Annie ate half a tub of cherry yogurt and a handful of jalapeno potato chips, washed down with three shots of bourbon. She tamped down the guilt of a social drinker with an alcoholic family member, pulled off her clothes as she trudged up the stairs, and fell asleep on Helen's side of the bed. The next morning, she stayed upstairs in sweats and a t-shirt, sketching trees out her studio window, waiting. That night she ate canned soup and crackers, washed down with half a glass of red wine.

Love's power can be in connection, but it is strongest in the anti-matter of love denied. On the third day, Annie stayed in bed.

Four days after she left, having checked in with Nathan by text three times a day and having left two unanswered messages for her daughter, Helen returned to Annie's house without calling first. Late in the afternoon, as the sun dipped, Helen parked on the corner and trooped up the front path with the key in her hand. The sight of the closed door stopped her. She reached for the doorbell, thought better of it twice, and finally rang.

Annie pulled the blankets off her head and dragged herself downstairs. The path ahead stretched like a hall of mirrors. Leaning on one wall for support, Annie made her towards the sound and opened the front door.

Helen had crossed half of the three-foot distance between them before Annie mumbled, "Don't."

"I'm sorry." Helen took a step backwards. "I didn't know what else to do."

Annie stared out past Helen, curling her lip. "Newsflash: don't goddamn leave in the first place."

"I know, but it was all too much. Marissa and all her mess, Nathan choosing you." Helen wiped away a tear.

"You don't get to be the one to cry over this, Helen." Annie's voice was ice. "Marissa's got enough going on without you making this all her fault. And don't even think about bringing our grandson into this."

Helen stared. Annie took a beat and reddened, suddenly realizing what she had said. She crossed her arms. Annie flinched when Helen put out a hand.

"He is." Helen spoke at their shared threshold of hearing, her lips tight. She ran through a list as though reciting a recipe. "By any definition of family—shared resources, shared concerns, shared intentions—you're already family, Annie. And if you're mine, you're Nathan's—and Marissa's—too."

Nodding her head, Annie drew an invisible line. "Family stays and works it out, Helen. Here on out, that's the deal. Take it or—"

Annie heard a soft thump and glanced at Helen, who was balanced on one knee on the flagstones. Her mind tried to reconcile the image with her recent torment, but the cognitive dissonance hit her like an avalanche, and she froze.

"I take it." Helen wobbled on the uneven surface, widened her stance, and used one hand for support. "If you'll have a stupid, stubborn old woman who sometimes forgets that gratitude is life's greatest gift, Annie, I'll never leave again."

Annie put all of her weight on her good leg, reached down, and pulled Helen into the house. "Yes. Yes, to all of it, Helen Gilbert-Jones. Except another name change. Triple hyphens are a bitch."

Helen guffawed and kissed her fiancée. "Now let's

go to the kitchen and make engagement rings out of aluminum foil. For the moment that's as good as it gets."

"As good as it ever need be, love." Annie giggled. "From here to the flip side."

Cape Cod (June 2019)

"Honey?" Helen's voice was tight. "Did you see this?"

Annie trotted down the stairs. "Nathan texted and wanted to know if you found his other shin pad. Says it was in his backpack after soccer camp last week, but I did two loads of laundry and there was only one."

Laughing, Annie pulled open the refrigerator. "I swear, that kid! How is it that we're out of OJ again? You were at the grocery store stocking up before he left!"

She poured herself a glass and answered her own question. "Duh. Teenage boy. I love him to death, but sometimes he drives me..."

Helen sat at the kitchen counter with half a piece of toast in her hand, staring into the open screen of her laptop.

Annie reached across and touched her elbow, turned away, and picked up the coffee pot. "You okay?"

"Something scrolled by." Helen stood up, gently took the mug from Annie, and guided her to the computer. "Local news. Something about a DNA match from a body found on the dunes. Habersham."

Annie heard the last word and her fingers tapped on the keyboard. "That's only a couple of towns over." She typed in a blur and stopped, her hands shaking.

Nodding, Annie rested her wrists on the keyboard as she read through the local newsfeed.

"What if it isn't?" Annie voiced what she thought was her worst fear, the overlapping memories of skeptical authorities and helplessness making her feel nauseous.

Helen had never gone around when she could bulldoze through. "Sweetheart—what if it is?"

An hour later, Helen and Annie stood at the double glass doors of Broadwell police station.

Annie shook her head. "Maybe I should've called. Report said they're waiting to inform the family, we can do this next week, I can—"

"After how they refused to believe you?" Helen's voice was soft. No one would have ever returned your call."

"Okay. Okay." Annie took a deep breath and walked through.

Helen strode in behind her. "Let's find this guy and give him hell."

"Officer Calloway? Nope, not here. Might be back this afternoon." The desk sergeant, a skinny middle-aged man who cracked his gum while he talked, flipped through his roster and picked up a pen. "Leave a message?"

Annie started to speak, but Helen interrupted her. "Who's the officer in charge of the body discovered at Habersham? We'll talk to them instead."

"As I said, Officer Calloway is not—"

Raising the volume and grit in her voice, Helen broadcast her displeasure. "Not what I asked."

The man knew trouble when he heard it, and he had long since opted for the path of little resistance when trouble came calling. The older woman's voice signaled trouble. "Officer—" Helen pronounced ever letter of his name as she glared at his nametag— "Braskotovsky, we're here because my *fiancée*—"

The man reddened. It was one thing, all of them coming up from the city the last twenty years, buying up real estate and bringing all their ways with them. It was another rubbing his face in their sin. His indignation gave him a rare spurt of bravado. "No need to get hysterical. This is neither the time nor the place for—"

In thirty-five years in the software industry, Helen had crawled over acres of broken ceiling glass. She had fended off predatory bosses, staved off hostile takeovers, and stood up to dozens of men telling her, over and over again, that she needed to settle down and simmer down and act like a lady. Long after being a lesbian should not have been a disqualifying feature in an industry that promised everyone the future, Helen knew that she still carried the weight of other people's gossip and disgust. The name calling decreased, but the message that all she needed was a good man to set her straight never had.

As a successful professional woman, Helen was a lot of things: a gifted programmer, a skillful negotiator, a hell of a golfer. In her mind, she was not, and never had been, a lady. When she needed to be, she was brash, intimidating, and full of slow-surging righteous rage.

"—because my *fiancée* and I would like to talk to someone about a recently-opened investigation, because we think that some information from a previous missing persons report might be relevant, and because as taxpayers it is our government-sanctioned right to request access to police resources and public records." Her voice rose. "Isn't that right?"

"I'm betting you're a reasonable man." Helen was still speaking too loudly, and the half-dozen other people waited for where the noise might travel next. "Not like someone who's willing to have his whole day ruined over nothing."

The man tried to wheedle. "I can't make him appear, ma'am. I've told you, leave a message and—"

"Happy to talk to someone else who know about the case," Helen said, her voice dropping into a soothing monotone, which managed not to sound less dangerous than the rising shout. "And I am sure if you try a little bit harder, *sir*, you can find whoever it is that knows who the hell washed up in Habersham and whether it was the same person my wife saw drowning off Morgan Crescent."

He sighed. *Bitch.* "Wait over there." Picking up the receiver, he added, "I'll see who I can find."

"Thank you, officer." *Dipshit.*

Helen turned to Annie and gave a theatrical bow. "See, love? Ask, and ye shall receive. We're in. Won't have long to wait for your answers, and you can put it all behind you."

Ten minutes later, Officer Braskotovsky stood in front of them and pointed toward a fortified door next to the desk. "Over there. Officer Snyder will buzz you in. She's got the file."

Like the desk sergeant, Officer Snyder was unknown Annie. The cop nodded. "Follow me."

Annie got up slowly, her stomach roiling. Helen muttered, "At least you didn't keep us sitting around all morning. I'd expect better service from a small town. Not like you're busy."

"What the hell, Helen?" Annie whispered as they followed the uniform into a small conference room with six mismatched chairs around a square table. "You do know we're in a police station, right?"

Helen scrunched up her nose and batted her eyelashes. "Oh, darling, don't tell me you're embarrassed to be seen with me!" She kissed Annie full on the lips as Brendan Calloway walked in.

Annie stared. Hating herself for it, but unable to stop, she wiped her lips with the back of her hand. "They said you weren't here."

Brendan ignored her and waved at his colleague. "You can go. I've got this."

She scowled and dropped the manila folder on the table. "Be my guest. I'm out. At least one of these women is already a pain in my ass."

The young man sneered at Annie. "Guessing she meant you."

"Although," he added as he straddled a chair and surveyed Helen, "I can see how she might be as bad."

Helen opened her mouth to reply, but Annie cut in. "You know why we're here, Brendan. Shut up about the rest of this and tell us who they found in Habersham. Tell us who I saw in the water."

"Sit."

Once again, Helen thought to argue, but she followed Annie into the bucket chairs that somehow managed to be too big and painfully restrictive at the same time. Helen positioned herself on the diagonal, so she could watch the show and stay out of the way. This part was definitely Annie's fight.

Brendan flicked through the pages of the report. "Only got the full results this morning. Not supposed to release it to anyone until the next of kin has been notified, though."

He shrugged. "Out of respect, of course."

Annie stood up. "Let's go. He's not going to tell us anything. We'll talk to the press, file a freedom of information request in a week or two."

Helen glared at the police officer, but she stood with Annie and started to follow her out the door.

Brendan put up one hand. "You do that, Ms. Howard. Going to be Mrs. Something soon? Heard you got hitched, you and your...life partner here."

Before the door shut as the two women stalked into the hallway, he called out, "Of course, I *could* let you in on the coroner's report."

Annie felt herself pulled in. She paused. Helen had had enough. She stepped over the threshold. "You little—"

Brendan's rasping laugh took up the whole room. He slow-clapped her. "Ma'am, if I were you, I'd think about what you're about to say to a bona fide officer of the law. Be a real shame if you got yourself into any trouble, what with the honeymoon around the corner and all."

"You were nine." Annie closed the door, patted Helen on the shoulder, and took a seat across the table from Brendan. "First time you and your brothers egged my house."

She carried on. "We both know you weren't one of the worst kids on the block, but from what I've seen you've turned out to be a narrow-minded, self-centered, and emotionally insensitive son of a bitch."

His neck veins bulging, Brendan snorted. "You think you can talk to me like that, you stupid—"

"Nuh-uh." It was Annie's turn to hold up her hand. "Less said the better. You give us what we need, and maybe I can keep your whole dismissive, unprofessional attitude from making its way up the chain of command, or at least out into the world. Your boss probably doesn't not care how you treat an old lady, or at least this old lady. Papers might, a nice little letter to the editor, naming names."

Brendan appeared to surrender. He tried on a generous smile, which showed too much gum and too many spotted teeth. Annie returned his expression. Helen did not.

"You're right, you're right." Brendan's words came out slowly, as though through a tunnel. "After what happened on the dunes, you deserve to know. My bad."

Annie raised her eyebrows at Helen in premature triumph. Helen was not ready to concede victory, but she softened her eyes and gave in to the other woman's optimism.

Opening up the file, Brendan ran his index finger down a closely-typed form. "Let's see...says here the body's been in the water about six to fifteen months."

"That fits." Annie nodded again, squeezing Helen's hand under the table and smoothing her hair. She was sweating and was aware that she hadn't showered or put on clean clothes before they left the house. The tee shirt she had slept in was glued itself to her back; her armpits itched, and her tongue felt wooly.

Brendan mirrored Annie's head bob. "Yep. Likely drowning, few signs of other trauma, buried in high tidal sand."

"Wait." Brendan frowned. "Says here there was something unusual about the body." He muttered to himself, taking his time, paging through six or seven sheets before stabbing the page with his thumb.

Annie couldn't help herself. She stretched forward, as if to take the folder from him. He snapped it shut and grinned.

Over her career, Helen had been in a lot of boardrooms where the power lived inside whoever saw the train wreck coming and was first out of the way. She had abundant practice watching other people be caught off their feet, but her instincts were strong, and one of the things she never had to worry about was being the last one to know. Helen saw the expression first, saw how the tips of Brendan's ears brightened, how his pupils dilated, and the pace of his breath ramped up as he got ready. *He's enjoying himself. Something's wrong.*

She looked at Annie: bright, beautiful, Annie, desperate for something that Helen knew this man had no intention of giving her. *Peace.*

"Maybe we should wait." Helen butted in. "Come back later, after it's all been settled. Not right that we should know something the family hasn't been told."

Annie stared at her. "What are you talking about? You practically drag me down here, and now you want out?"

She gritted her teeth at Brendan. "Tell me."

When Brendan spoke, every consonant was dry and every vowel twice as long as it should have been. "You see the thing is, Ms. Howard—"

Brendan bowed his head, and Annie wondered if he was hiding tears. Helen knew he was not. He leered at them. "Thing is, this guy was military, multiple amputee."

Annie couldn't decipher Brendan's grin, but she latched on to his description and chased the narrative as far as it would go. "Got in trouble in the water. Maybe lost his leg prosthetics, overestimated his stamina. Possibly some mental health issues, likely far from home."

Helen wished with everything she had that her wife had the story right. It wasn't even close. She tried to take Annie's hand on the table, but Annie swatted her away with irritation.

Brendan licked his lips and shook his head. "What they've got over on the beach at Habersham, Ms. Howard, is the murder investigation of a decorated war vet. At least assisted suicide, they're investigating as we speak. Recent returnee, too. Only six weeks into rehab when he disappeared from Philadelphia. Coroner says there's no way in hell this guy—" Brendan tapped the open pages with disdain— "could have driven himself down to the beach yet. Let's not even get into the whole 'waving' thing that your bullshit story supposedly had going for it. This guy, arms blown off at the shoulders, plus half his leg. Metal plate in his head, stitches, infection, you name it. Poor bastard, they had him in the burn unit for a month until his brother got him discharged against medical advice."

"Did you read this now? While we've been sitting here talking?" Annie was still searching for a reason not to hate him, and Helen loved her for it. "Tell me you're surprised, Brendan. Tell me you called us in here thinking I was right."

"Oh, no. Read it cover to cover last night, knew everything that was in the report the whole damn time." He laughed in Annie's face as he jumped around in a victory dance like a demented gnome. "Wanted to string you along a little. See your face when I told you that the body we found was definitely, scientifically, beyond any reasonable doubt, the body of a..."

Annie's mind left the room. Her body stayed there, suspended, not sure what she was waiting for: confirmation or denial. Her mind dragged her to the dunes. All the sounds and sights and smells of the day fought for dominance: the scratch of pencil on paper, the nagging ache in her hip because she'd already been standing too long above the beach, the thick air in her nose and her mouth. The figure in the water, arms straight up. *Drowning. Waving.* Annie's chest tightened. *Drowned. Gone.*

Rage has no teeth. It may pose a threat to one or to many, it may even be a precursor to violence and destruction, but it is rooted in weakness and drenched in impotence. Helen was on good terms with her rage, in all its self-serving red glory, because she had succumbed to it once or twice when she should have known better. She much preferred righteous ire, the kind of anger that found its place in satisfaction of consequences congruent with the offense, rather than only being fulfilled by crushing eradication of the enemy at hand.

All she had as Brendan's laughed rolled over them was rage. Annie physically dragged and shoved Helen from the room, gripping her with the desperation of someone who had already lost too much on that day, and on so many others before. She did not plead or cajole—she pushed and hustled her seething partner out of the door.

"Mad old woman. Nothing there, I told you. I told

you so!" Brendan's last words echoed in Annie's ears down the corridor and down the stairs to the parking lot.

Annie adjusted the steering wheel and swiped her eyes with the back of her sweatshirt sleeve. "Not going home. Somewhere I've got to go first."

Helen sat still as Annie drove through town and parked in the empty lot at Morgan Crescent.

They sat in the car, staring across the top of the dunes. The wind had been threatening a fall blowout for three days, and the eddies of rough air had begun to dance with the sand. The thin lip of dull ocean they could see was grainy, like old film. Gray clouds gunned for the last few patches of blue sky and the temperature dropped ten degrees.

Annie got out first, swearing at the jolt of pain in her hip. She skip-hopped around the car and found the boardwalk, her loose boots flapping on the wood.

"Wait!" Helen was faster, and she easily overtook Annie before they'd gone ten steps. She held out a green duffel coat. "At least put your jacket on."

Ignoring her, Annie shoved her hands in the pockets of her jeans and walked to the end of the boardwalk. She clung to the rail next to the stairs that led down to the beach.

Helen shivered, pulled up her hood, and followed. "I'm sorry, I thought it'd be better to confront them, in case it was, in case no one ever told you it was—real."

Annie's laugh spat and gurgled. "You thought? Well, did you maybe stop to think that I'm not you, that I'm not going to be the one trampling around trying to make things better through sheer force of voice at top volume? That perhaps there's a time for putting your head in the sand and ignoring all of it and pretending it will all go away? Why the hell did I let you convince me to go down there, I could have waited, I could have…"

The other woman heard what Annie had not said, all the second guesses and should-haves that were trapped in the day of the incident last September. It was not what Annie might do now, going forward into even more brutal unpredictability, wondering if the next body that washed up might be the one. It was what Annie thought about what she had done (not enough), about who she was in the town (nobody) and who would act on her side of the story (no one). It was two decades of not being a part of something, of being studiously apart from it, in every unanswered doorbell the first weeks in Broadwell and with every letter from elsewhere returned (unopened) to sender.

"Besides, you think I need someone else to tell me it was real, Helen?" She narrowed her eyes. "Do *you* need someone else to tell you I'm not completely out of mind?"

Annie was quiet now, her shoulders heaving. "I did that after Amanda, after the accident. I threw my entire life away and came up here and pretended I was someone else for twenty years, because I couldn't face what was real. And because the one thing I knew for sure—the one damn thing that is clear as water to me about that night—is that—"

"Forget it." She rested on the fence and tried to stretch her cramped muscle. "But maybe I'm the one who's crazy."

Squinting, Annie tried to see the lull between the choppy waves below. Without realizing it, her hands danced out of her pockets, miming pencil and sketchpad, holding an invisible drawing at chest height. Amanda's introduction to drawing she had found on the shelf, a book she had relied on in the beginning, pounded in her head. *Don't look down. Never look down.* And with the words came the memories of those first days of darkness while she was still living alone in that permanently, absurdly, too-large apartment in Brooklyn.

Annie's cry came from outside herself. It came up from the earth, the loose particles of sand beneath her feet vibrating in concert with her pounding heart. It began as a scatter of grunts and expanded to a howl, pulsating out from her in sinus rhythm.

Helen sucked in as much air as she could before the sound from her wife hit her like a wind tunnel, before all they could both hear was the reedy keening that went on and on and on.

The ocean matched her pitch as the storm found its stride, kicking up sand and painting the water in scratchy whitecaps. Helen and Annie pressed their chins into their chests and closed their eyes against the grit.

At six o'clock that evening, the back door swung open and Helen called through the house. "Annie?" She bypassed the kitchen and kicked off her shoes before padding down the hall in search of her slippers. Noticing all the lights were off, she said again, "Annie?"

From the darkened living room, a voice breathed. "In here."

"You feeling okay?" Helen turned on the dragonfly desk lamp in one corner of the room. "Did you eat? Rest?"

"There was someone else." Annie writhed in the shabby olive recliner by the bay window, outside the circle of warm light cast by the lamp, hugging her knees.

Helen crossed the room and squatted down. Her voice was hollow as she parsed the words, settled on likely meaning, and braced herself for domestic rupture. "What are you telling me? Was, or is? Who?"

"What? No!" Annie reeled in her laugh when she saw Helen's carefully neutral face. "Not us, sweetheart. Me. Before."

"Who?" Helen's mind gathered possibilities like a squirrel scooping up nuts. She realized she'd asked the wrong question again. "What?"

"It's too terrible." Annie sounded like she was talking to herself. "There's no taking any of it back, Helen."

Helen tried to reclaim the blame for whatever Annie hadn't said. "I know I can be harsh, but the last thing I wanted was for you to be denied access to the information."

Her wife wasn't ready to contemplate anything more serious than a minor indiscretion or an embarrassing story. She kept her voice bright. "Bar's pretty low for regret or embarrassment, hon. You do remember that you've seen those photos of me at fraternity formals as an undergrad?"

Annie swam away from safe harbor. With shaky

hope that shame might transition to mere regret after confession, she met Helen's gaze and shook her head. "Not that sort of something."

Helen tried to throw her a lifeline. She crafted an easy out. "You want to spill more about your piece of crap husband, I'm all ears."

Her trademark, wide-open smile failed to dispel Amanda's dread. Helen tried a different angle. "And if it's something about Amanda, I'm here."

Leaving Annie where she was and breathing deeply, Helen dragged a low-slung chair over and sat in it so she could lean in and hold Annie's hands. Annie unfolded herself and tucked her feet under. She put her arms around her wife and muttered into the other woman's ear.

"I only told you...part of it. About Arizona. About why I'm here."

The story wound around them both like a snake, taking on breath and life of its own in Annie's strained confession. There is power in truth, but truth told out of order—truth told in light of something instead of as light for something—is more fragile than the deepest deceit. Annie's truth of how Lydia died and Diane was born, about how Amanda died and their son was never born, had always lived inside the premise of a need to start over. The whole of it was that stranger's voice behind Annie as she lay trapped and Amanda lay dying in the car, the cursory search, the disbelief. Everything set the stage and plot for how it could go again, on the dunes, two decades later.

Annie had told Helen the truth of losing herself when her family died. She had told her the truth of runaway heartbreak and Amanda's well-meaning-yet-suffocating friends, the truth of the ladybugs and tufts of grass and not-yet-drawn dragons on the walls of their baby's room. She had told her the truth about telling Roy she couldn't visit the following Christmas, or the Thanksgiving after that, and how the invitations stopped coming.

She had told Helen a separate truth about the September day from the shore, of the drowning and waving and nothing. But she had held on to the other half of that dreadful repetition, the curse of fate that once had left her wondering if she could have done more to save a stranger, and once whether a stranger could have possibly saved her.

Two hours later, Helen rose and went to the kitchen. On the way, she notched the thermostat up a few degrees and pulled a rose-trellised quilt from the closet in the hall. She poured two glasses of whiskey, grabbed a box of sesame rice crackers from the pantry, and shuffled back to the living room.

Anne had moved to the couch, where she sat cross-legged with her eyes closed and head back. She opened her eyes and took her glass from Helen with a nod. "Thank you."

Helen sat on the other end of the couch. She ate a handful of rice crackers, chewing them until the paste stuck to her teeth, and washed the gummy mouthful down with a bitter grimace. She doubled over, holding her drink in both hands. "All makes sense."

She was too tired and too shocked to be angry. The part of her that wanted to rail against deception, perceived as well as real, took a supporting role to the whole of her that wanted to love Annie through this fresh pain.

"It's all my fault." Annie gulped the liquor and coughed.

"No argument there." Helen tried on a half-smile, which Annie missed.

Hearing what she thought was confirmation of an unforgivable transgression, Annie sighed. "Don't even know if an apology is what you want. Don't know what I'd want if I were you."

Helen shook her head, sat up, deposited her drink on the side table, and put her arm around Annie. She spoke slowly. "Hell no, Annie. Even if I thought it would make me feel better, last thing I want is you saying sorry for something you thought you had every reason to hide. At my age the last thing I want is a fight that lasts long enough for us to die, so let's get through this and over it and call it a night."

Despite Helen's reassurance, Annie continued. "When I told you about the accident, it was the first time I'd talked about it to anyone who knew me since Amanda's dad in Tucson. You and I, it hadn't been that long, and I figured—"

Her tears returned, and she wept silently for a minute. Helen waited, willing herself not to dive in and try to smother Annie's fresh agony.

Annie cleared her throat, reached for another gulp of

whiskey, and steadied her voice. "Enough. I figured I was enough of a mess, enough of a basket case with my dead family and my huge dilapidated house and my being Broadwell's best candidate for town witch."

Helen chuckled, the laughter swelling. She sputtered, trying to regain control. "Jesus in a jumpsuit, Annie, you think I met you and thought *you* were the mess between us?

"Although," she said slyly, "Scout's honor, I did think that whole rat's nest hairstyle you had going on before you chopped it off was a catastrophic fashion choice, and no mistake." Helen ruffled Annie's silver-tipped crewcut.

Helen was serious again. "Don't think you're forgiven. It's not okay, what you did."

"I am so sorry." Annie's contrition spun out.

"But it is understandable. I get why it would have all seemed too weird, two separate situations of you seeing things that no one else thought were there. Like some sort of twisted Munchausen by proxy gimmick."

Annie felt her defensiveness return like an unwelcome rash. She stood up. "Now you? They were there, they were *both* there, this is exactly why I didn't want to—"

"Hush." Helen stood and stroked Annie's elbow. "Semantics are your friend. Said no one else thought you were right. I do. I do. Why do you think I practically sliced that desk cop in half this morning, trying to get an answer? Because I don't believe you were right, I know you were right."

"What kind of person am I, Helen?" Annie's face

was raw, and her lip trembled.

"What kind of person sits in a windowless room that smells like stale French fries in a police station in the middle of the day wishing the next thing she'd hear was confirmation that she'd watched someone drown?"

Helen swigged the last of her drink and pulled a Kleenex from the box on the coffee table. "The kind of person who cared enough to try to stop it from happening, sweetheart. Not your fault. Whether the person you saw ever finds their way back to shore, whether that woman walked towards something or away from something the night of the accident—not your fault."

"Those first few months, I thought about telling you a hundred times." The shame of her choice brought full circle. "But after a while, it didn't seem important, you know? It receded, became something that if I thought about slantwise I could half-convince myself that maybe I had conjured that woman up from nothing after all. Maybe I dreamed up a heroine that night because Amanda and Theo needed one, and I couldn't be the one.

Minor details of a person's life—a bad day at work, an argument at a stoplight—are only minor in retrospect. A misplaced decimal point here, a drawn weapon there, and the incidents that are filed under 'irrelevant' find themselves at the top of our minds for the rest of our lives.

"Half of our lives we live our lives in real time, in the minutes giving over one to the next." Annie picked up the tiny square sketch she'd been clutching half the night. "The other half we live in the papered over haze of years gone by or the gamble of years to come. I wanted to live in the future with you, Helen. Not in my past."

"Both are important."

"I know that! I have run the scenarios, both of them, a thousand times. But there's only so much fog, so much not knowing, that a person can take." She let the tears fall through her hands, sniffling and mumbling. "A heart can take."

"Besides," Annie added, reaching over to hug her wife. "After everything with Marissa and Nathan—"

Helen stood and turned her back. "Speaking of that boy, I'm going upstairs. Cleaned in there already, bound to be something growing under his bed, and I don't want to smell it for three days."

Annie hugged herself after Helen walked out. She half-rose off the sofa to follow her, crushed the thought, and sat back. Annie picked up the glass and held it with both hands as though she were conjuring fire.

Cape Cod (July 2019)

On the first Saturday in July, Marissa and Nathan Williams drove the hour from their place to what was now affectionately known as 'Grandmas'.' It was their first visit since Helen's proposal, although the two older women had shared the news on as soon as it seemed real enough to both of them.

Over a few mumbled phone conversations and rapid-fire chat sessions, Nathan had tried on nicknames for Annie, ranging from the oddly traditional to the downright ridiculous, but after all the congratulations and surprise subsided, he had settled on something simple.

"Nan!" Nathan hopped out of the car hit the ground running and threw himself at Annie. "That's awesome news, I can't believe you said yes!"

Helen stepped towards her grandson and graciously waited her turn for a long hug. Marissa beeped the key fob and smiled into the family reunion.

"Congratulations, Mom." She stepped forward, shocked at the open smile and genuine welcome in her mother's eyes. Marissa beamed over Helen's shoulder and winked at Annie, thumb and forefinger miming OK as she soaked in the warmth. Reluctant to peel away, Marissa kept her arm around her mother's waist as they walked side-by-side into the house.

Behind them, Nathan nodded his approval. "Guess all those e-mails back and forth between those two must have been something." He read Annie's question in her glance. "Not that I dug around hoping to find them or anything, but there *may* have been a time or two my mom's laptop was open when I walked by."

Annie was too happy with the prospect of the four of them in the house together for three whole days to scold the boy or burrow in for further confession. Curiosity can be an enemy of trust, but it is also a shield against repeated betrayal, and Annie knew that the teenager beside her had dealt with more than his share of that in his young life already. His excitement at the relationship's U-turn was sweet, eager, and long overdue.

She smiled indulgently and pretend-punched him on the shoulder. "Let's call it a good guess, kid, and leave it at that. Inquiring minds and all."

Watching the other two laughing easily with one another and faltering into the house, Annie nodded with satisfaction. "Besides, I have it on good authority from your mom that you're an online word games whiz. With those two keeping each other company this weekend, let's see if you're anywhere near as good at old-fashioned analog Scrabble."

The adolescent groaned, but his gurgling laugh told a different story. "Least I can still beat you up the stairs, Nan."

Annie watched him scoop up both suitcases off the sidewalk and sprint into the house. "No contest there, kid."

Her eyes glistened and her smile quivered as she felt her hip proclaim its ever-present reminder of what had gone before. She took a deep breath, thinking of Amanda and Theo, and followed her grandson into the home she shared with her soon-to-be lawfully-wedded wife.

Although she had lived in Broadwell for twenty years, Annie had never walked the twelve blocks to the nearest beach, a wretched shred of sand too small for weekend tourists and too forgettable for locals to name. She had always driven the mile and a half to Morgan Crescent— first because it was stunning and parking was comparatively easy, and later because she made it her desire and design to reclaim the horizon from the vision of a drowning man.

On Sunday morning, the air already chewy with humidity, heat, and salt, Nathan announced his plan over bagels and chive-and-onion cream cheese. "Beach day. All of us together. Thunderstorms later so let's head out as soon as we're done." He examined each woman in turn, gauging their reaction.

Marissa and Helen, sitting close enough so that their elbows brushed every time either one reached for the orange juice, both nodded with their mouths full. Annie grimaced and tapped her leg. "How about I meet you there?"

"No way." Nathan's eyes were wide and insistent. "You keep talking about wanting to get out there and get more active, so you're coming with. Grab some snacks and drinks, load up on the Advil and we're out of here, Nan."

Annie faked a huge sigh and rolled her eyes. "Kid,

you're impossible. But I love you and yes, I'll walk to the beach. As long as I get a promise you'll run back here for my chariot for the return trip. Don't think even fairy dust and magic wishes could get a loop back from the beach in this heat today."

"Ditto." Helen nodded, brushing crumbs from her chin. She turned to her daughter. "Okay by you to walk back with Nathan when we're done and pick us up?"

Marissa put her arm around her mom's shoulders and squeezed hard. "You need me to, Mom, I'll carry you all the way home myself."

Nathan mocked his mother. "Blah-blah-lovey-dovey-blah. Are we done? Let's go!"

The band of fine white grains was only eighty feet long. To Annie's miffed surprise and Nathan's fierce delight, there was already a group of teenagers clustered on the end of the beach with two picnic tables on a short cement pier.

"Yes." Marissa replied to Nathan's unspoken question after they had all set up their beach chairs and opened a bag of kettle corn. "No rides in anyone else's car, and text me if you're going further than the clam shack or ice cream shop." She glanced at the two older women, who nodded their shared assent. "Two o'clock okay to wrap it up?"

Grinning, her son glanced around to make sure no one was watching before kissing Marissa on the cheek. Nathan sauntered over to the other kids and inserted himself without apparent effort. It only took a minute or two to hear the echo of the big laugh he had inherited from Helen echoing around the group as he told jokes and made fast friends.

Helen admired her daughter. "You're getting good at that, honey."

With all the time in the world to practice by crafting replies to her mother's e-mails, Marissa's repeated nods of appreciation for recognition had become automatic. Nonetheless, she sounded sincere and reassured, though still too self-effacing for Annie's comfort. "Thanks, Mom. Nathan's a rock star, but thanks."

Helen pushed, as she always did, but this time it was on the newly-discovered connector between them of nurturing and support. "He's lucky to have you, Marissa. I mean it."

Annie watched mother and daughter navigate the black waters of past injury and distrust with the studied ease of breaching whales. *Long time coming.* She felt a flicker of annoyance in Helen's tightening posture as Marissa squirmed under too many compliments, but the moment passed and their poured lemonade into collapsible cups.

Lunch was aromatic cheeses, fruit salad and parmesan crackers on Chinette plates for the adults and ten dollars tossed to Nathan as he whizzed past in a huddle on their way to pizza and banana splits. The three women sat close under their sun umbrella, lacquering themselves with sunscreen and swapping Nathan stories with focused joy. The conversation hedged around sensitive topics with detours into Helen's dwindling list of consulting clients, Annie's latest miniatures, and Marissa's new boss at work, but it held the line on generosity, reciprocity, and love. Helen and Annie sprawled in folding chairs; Marissa sat cross-legged on the sand, tracing mandalas in an ever-widening circle until she was sweeping her arm low and long across the ground.

After they had packed the food away in Tupperware and reusable zip bags, Annie hobbled to the edge of the water and waded in. She faced the beach, watching Helen and Marissa laugh at something she could not decode over the slosh of waves. Hearing the first warning shot of thunder, she glanced at a looming horizon and hurried out.

"I'll text Nathan to come back to the house with you." Helen reached for her phone.

"Mom." Marissa's tone was gentle, but a warning nonetheless. "*I'll* text Nathan and tell him I'll pick him up from town, or he can walk back when he's done."

Chastened, Helen slid her phone back into her red canvas sling bag. "Course, honey. Sorry."

Appreciation. Apologies. Grace. Annie ticked off the virtues of this new relationship dynamic in her head, set in parallel with potential side effects of all this sweetness and light. *Resentment. Imbalance. Grudges. Ill-will.* She shook her head to clear the half-imagined negativity. *Right now is right enough.*

"Be back in twenty-five." Marissa half-jogged off the beach, her flowery tank top bunched up over fuchsia capris.

Helen took a deep breath. "So?"

Annie feigned confusion. "So we'll sit here like starfish until she brings the car, and we'll spend the next three days digging sound out of everywhere."

Helen let a single bray of laughter loose before setting her face into serious mode. "Thoughts?"

Annie stood up and began to massage Helen's shoulders. "Can't think of how this weekend could be going any better, love. They're here, we've found things to laugh about, the food is good, the weather's cursed us with enough sunshine to force us pretend that you and I like the beach to make our grandson happy."

"But." A statement, not a question.

"Not this again." Annie stopped her massage and pulled her chair up close to Helen so that their knees knocked. "How is it that in every other aspect of your life you're one of the most optimistic people I've ever met, but when it comes to your daughter, you're constantly waiting for the other lead balloon to drop?"

Shaking her head, Helen spoke softly. "You already know the answer to that, Annie. But sure, I'll say it, since no one else is saying it. There's always another lead balloon. With the crap Marissa's dealing with, her history and all that writhing genetic predisposition to addiction, in all the weeks and months and years to come, how could there not be?"

"Did you know that there's a one in three chance you won't live another twenty years?" Annie licked her lips. "Oh, yeah, I looked it up once. More than once. Actuarial tables. Actual odds of when you're going to die, man or woman, birth to age one hundred and nineteen."

Helen snorted at that last number, but Annie nodded fast. "Oh, yeah. Turns out there's a ninety percent chance of you dying within a year if you make it that damn long."

More concerned than amused, Helen put up her hand. "And you know this how?"

"I'm an engineer, babe. Engineers like to know how things work, and when Amanda died and Theo died, after I moved up here, I wanted to know how death worked. Should have seen the horror on the librarian's face when I asked for the death tables."

"Okay." Helen felt even less sure than she sounded as her voice wrinkled. "But what does that have to do with anything? With Marissa? With reality?"

"Everything," Annie whispered. "It has to do with the inscrutable, terrifying, immutable fact that we have no idea when we're going to see the people we love for the last time. Ten minutes? Thirty years?"

Helen growled and stood up. "Annie, if you're doing this to try to make me feel better, it's not working. Let's leave it. Marissa will be back any minute and I don't want our fight to ruin the rest of their time."

"No. I need to say this, and you need to hear it." Annie stood as well, her face four inches from Helen's. Both women blazed. "Because you know what makes it worthwhile? We don't know when we're going to see any of people we love for the first time, either. You and me? It's not cosmic or karma, love. It's roulette, hormones, chance. It's possibility. There's nothing in the stars or in the alignment of the planets or in some inherent wheel of balance of good and evil, ecstasy and pain."

Feeling her lover's words begin to dance in her head, Helen gripped Annie's elbows and breathed with her.

"So that's what humans mean when we talk about love. It's not the absence of fear—it's the omnipresence of the worst fear imaginable, the absolutely intolerable. And I know, because I have lived it."

Annie pressed her fingertips into Helen's upper arms. "Do you hear me? I had two people who meant more to me than my own life, and they died, Helen! They died, right in front of me, and I did not. For a long time, I thought of my survival as penance for not having done enough. I know now that my survival was as much an accident as their deaths. It has no deeper attachment, no special significance. Their don't mean anything; the single fact of my not dying in that car crash with them doesn't mean anything, either."

Helen gawked at her in horrified fascination as Annie's story wove its tendrils around both of their minds. "It's not supposed to."

"But I watch you with your daughter, how you skim the edge of full immersion in the feelings you have for her, holding back a tiny piece because you think it will somehow protect you against the unfathomable. It won't. Nothing can prepare or insulate you from whatever hellfire is coming, love."

"Do I hold back from you?" Helen puffed out her

cheeks and held her breath.

The other woman's laugh was so brittle and bright that it forced them both to blink, shifting the ground of Annie's plea. "We're too new for that kind of fear, Helen. Not unloved, or under-loved. You might think that those four days without each other were plenty, but there's not enough history for the terror of loss to have taken root. Time will come, I promise you. If we're lucky, time will come one day this year or five or ten years from now when the worst conceivable thing to happen might happen, and we'll know."

"So with Marissa?" Helen stared at Annie in wonder.

"With Marissa you treat every moment as a gift, not because it's gauche, but because you know that the likelihood she might die before you is something as real as the seagulls and the sky. But that doesn't make her any less precious. It makes the miracle all the shinier, her still being here at all, with you, taking a chance. I miss Amanda every day, Helen. But the loss of Theo? That's something else, something more primordial. His absence oozes through everything I am and everything I do because as his mother, I had one important job. One."

Helen found her purpose in the conversation. "You couldn't protect him. After all this time, Annie, holding on to any sort of blame, it doesn't make sense."

"Doesn't matter if it doesn't make sense. Doesn't matter if I couldn't protect him, if in a million different universes, Theo dies on that road. Only matters that I didn't."

"Same." Helen's combativeness subsided into a nauseous blend of surrender, acceptance, and horrified understanding. "Same."

Annie put more words around Helen's awakening. "You already know that you would never heal from that broken heart. There is no roundtrip from losing a child, whether or not you first held them in your arms, whether they're still waiting to take their first breath, or they've been walking around on this pale blue dot for more than thirty years."

Annie had no will to stop. "The one thing you need to know, Helen, is that this is your moonshot with Marissa. She's suited up and ready to go, and you're wandering around on the launching pad wondering if there's going to be enough air. Let me tell you something. That woman's been through hell and she's ready to fly. She'll fly without you if you don't deal with the fact that whether or not the oxygen tanks are full this is the only chance you'll ever have to share that with a child. Your child."

Annie's loss pooled with her frustration and leached anger. "Don't screw it up. She's still with you, do you hear me?" Her fists clenched and her body shook, threatening to topple over on her injured side. "Marissa needs you to get this right."

"Yes." Helen words were a vise on her doubt. She crossed her arms, hugging herself.

"She's here." Annie twisted her neck over her left shoulder. Marissa had double-parked and her car's hazard lights were flashing orange against the sand. The young woman waved.

Helen glanced at Annie. "There's a way to thank you for this, babe. I have to figure out what it is."

Annie dismissed the offer with a quick thrust of her chin in Marissa's direction. "Go kick some motherhood ass."

Without bothering to retrieve her sandals and ignoring her grass green silk scarf as it flowed out behind her and onto the beach, Helen Gilbert-Jones ran. Her long, strong legs struggled for traction on the fine granules of eroded rock and crushed exoskeletons.

Only thirty feet away, Annie heard Marissa's cry of concern when she saw her mother flying towards her. Helen went from pumping her arms to waving them high above her head, and that's when the laughter began. Helen Gilbert-Jones' trademark clown-honking laugh caught the wind and raced across the beach. Marissa's face cracked into a foreign smile that Annie had never seen: as high as it was wide, all teeth and wrinkles-in-training. That's when Annie heard a second harmonic in the cackling, as Marissa held out her hands to Helen with a shriek, and the two women collapsed into each other. Their song was drawn with best intentions, their duet written in the key of missed opportunities and with lyrics culled from second, third, or thirtieth chances.

All good. Annie herded their belongings like sheep. She opened the trunk of the car and shoved everything in before Marissa or Helen even noticed she was there.

Boston (September 2019)

The wedding was in mid-September—just the four of them in a courthouse in Boston. As part of the gift to her wife-to-be, Annie let Helen order the outfits sight unseen: rustling royal blue and white dresses, knee-high white boots, and the matching rhinestone cowboy hats they had worn for their date at the country bar what seemed like half a dozen lifetimes ago. They danced through the doors to music only they could hear and converged with Nathan and Marissa in the high domed entry.

"You. Did. Not." Marissa stepped into Annie's place and twirled with her mom. "Annie, you're a saint. You should have seen what my mom picked out for me on the first day of kindergarten."

Helen winced. *No chance she remembers me doing anything that day. She slept next door and the neighbor—what the hell was her name?—put Marissa on the bus.*

Reconstituted memory tastes like ginger and lime: fresh, sharp. It can blend with the base of what was already there, or remake itself entirely, depending on the flavors of the relationships around the recollection. In the overflowing, chiseled glass of rapprochement, Marissa's vision of her first day of school was inaccurate but exactly right. Helen closed her eyes for a second, and when she opened them, she remembered it the same way.

The whole family's shared laughter whizzed around their heads, gathering speed, intention, and consequence. The ceremony in front of the official was irrelevant. Everything that already needed sorting out among these four had already happened in their shared resolution to walk into tomorrow.

"Lunch is on me." Marissa led them out of the building. Annie and Helen glanced at each other in confusion. A platter of cold cuts and blueberry cheesecake were chilling in the refrigerator at home, alongside a bottle of carbonated grape juice.

"This is going to be good." Nathan smiled like a little kid on a snow day. He even half-clapped his hands, thought better of it midway through, and stuffed them into the diagonal pockets of his hoodie.

"What are we—" Helen caught up with her daughter, who shook her head mysteriously.

"Ten minutes." Marissa grinned and unlocked the car. "Fifteen tops. Shut up and get in."

Marissa knew exactly where she was headed, but she wanted the newlyweds held in suspense as long as possible. Following the route she had carefully mapped out in her mind ahead of time, the daughter (and now daughter-in-law) doubled back around long city blocks, meandered through neighborhoods, and sidled into a narrow street full of upscale boutiques and tiny restaurants.

Annie figured out first that their route was circuitous. She could feel the turns in her joints, and her engineer's sense of distance and direction kept failing to latch on to intended landmarks or destinations. After Marissa's third 'wrong' turn, she called forward from where she sat in the back seat with Nathan. "Want me to pull up the map on my phone? I can easily pull it up by name, wherever we're going."

Whistling along to the radio, Marissa shook her head and waved one hand as though swatting a mosquito. "I got this."

Nathan laughed again, that classic familial laugh that filled whatever space it found itself in. "You guys have no idea."

Annie had the math and the calculations and the design instinct; Helen knew people. As her daughter maneuvered aptly into an ample parallel space, Helen powered down the window and stared at the sign behind them.

"How in the hell?" Helen touched Marissa gently on the arm as the she slid the car into park.

Knowing precisely where they were geographically did not translate to Annie understanding exactly where they were. She followed the others out and stared up at Chez Julien's placard swinging on an ornate wrought iron pole.

"How did you—?" Annie's question went unanswered.

Nathan slipped his arm into Annie's while Marissa guided her mother through the door.

A voice on autopilot greeted them. "Welcome to

Chez—oh." The manager realized who it was and grinned like a pixie. She dropped the menus she held ready in her hand, dug under the lectern, pulled out a leather folder, and added, "Please follow me."

It was already two o'clock. The late lunch crowd had dwindled to three tables of suits lingering over *digestifs* and espresso. The light was brighter than it had been on that other night back, with javelins of sunlight piercing deep into the corners of the small space.

Helen reached behind her for Annie's hand and squeezed hard. Annie skitter-stepped until she was close enough to drape her arm around Helen's neck.

The manager seated them, her mischievous smile intact. She kept her voice steady and formal, knowing her job was to stay out of the way. *Already did what needed doing.* "Thank you for choosing us to celebrate this special occasion."

She pulled crisp, cursive-printed sheets of paper from the folder, offered them to each of the four people seated in turn, and waved to a waiter in the corner.

"Gotcha, Grandma." Nathan wiggled his eyebrows across the table. "You had no idea!"

Marissa came clean. "We were talking a few weeks ago. Annie mentioned you had tried a little French restaurant in this neighborhood way back when. Sounded romantic, figured it was worth a shot to ask if they kept records of reservations, so I called around."

Helen gawked. "There are a lot of little French

restaurants in the neighborhood, honey."

Enjoying the glow of her mother's approval and her triumph at having pulled off the surprise, Marissa snorted. "Fourteen. This was lucky number nine."

Turning to Annie, she added with wide eyes. "Weird thing, though. Got the manager on the phone here, and she remembered you and my mom clear as crystal. Didn't even put me on hold to check, said she'd be happy to put something special together for you two."

I bet she didn't say anything about what happened. Helen pushed away the pivot point and focused on the sheet of paper in her hands.

Annie spoke for both of them. "Thank you, Marissa. And well done Nathan for keeping this under wraps. It is a wonderful surprise."

As they read through the menu, Annie and Helen exchanged guilty glances. Annie tucked her hand close to her chest and pointed to the manager's perch. Neither was proud of their behavior on that earlier night, but a post-mortem of the cognitive dissonance would have to wait.

"All my favorites!" Helen tapped the menu. "Lobster bisque, lamb, lemon chiffon mousse."

Annie joined in the praise, licking her lips. "And mine, babe! French onion, grilled salmon, chocolate kirsch torte."

Nathan nodded with pride. "That was all me—turns out people don't even notice what they're giving away if you spread the interrogation over weeks."

Marissa made sure he saw her glance around to check that nobody else was watching before she reached over and hugged him tight without a word. Annie and Helen held hands under the table. The manager watched them through her mascara.

Lunch lasted three hours and was finished off with champagne flutes of ginger ale and a diminutive, four-tier wedding cake capped with a pair of Wonder Woman figures. The brides' first names and an elegant 'CONGRATULATIONS' with the date were scrolled in purple icing, one each side of the serving platter.

The manager held her hand palm to the ceiling. "Top to bottom, we've got salted caramel, cookies and cream, hazelnut vanilla, and mocha crunch."

Raising her glass for the toast, Marissa pointed to the statues on the cake and said softly, "How I see both of you. Who you are to Nathan and me. Family is all there is." Her voice thickened. "To Annie and Helen!"

The jokes and reciprocal appreciation flowed as easily as melting ice. Helen and Annie ate one-handed, their fingers clasped between them. Nathan had three servings of mashed potatoes and two fat wedges of the three desserts.

When they finally left, Annie deliberately left her phone under a napkin and feigned forgetfulness as everyone else got in the car. She felt her stomach froth as she put her hand on the door. Taking a deep breath, she stepped inside.

The manager stood up. "How can I help?"

Annie stared at her without speaking. She took in the

young woman's studied invisibility: long-sleeved black knit dress, black nylons, low-key make-up, sensible hair. Their eyes met, and Annie saw something else, a striking combination of satisfaction and humility. *Happy. Not smug.*

"You know what you did." Not knowing where to go next, Annie retrieved her phone from the table and returned to the front. The manager stood quietly waiting.

"You're the reason—what you said—helped us put the pieces back together." Annie ran out of words. Embarrassed by the revelation, she quashed the defensive instinct to reach into her pocket for a bloat of twenties. *This is not that.*

"I did what needed doing." The timbre of the manager's voice stretched and deepened. "You and your wife had two ways forward that night, apart or together. Obvious to anyone with eyes and heart that only one of those made sense."

Annie nodded, letting a single tear fall across her smile. She coughed and straightened her shoulders. "I hope you know how sorry we both are with how we treated you— and how grateful we will always be."

The manager took the apology and appreciation with mute grace, her smile soft.

"You know so much about us—about our family. I never even got your name." Annie tossed out the query as the other woman stepped forward to open the door.

The manager's voice swallowed the moment. "Amanda, Annie. My name's Amanda."

Cape Cod (October 2019)

Three weeks after the wedding, mid-morning on a Tuesday, Annie pulled into the Marissa's apartment block with a bungee cord securing the trunk of the car. Scratched rattan protruded like teeth. She texted her daughter-in-law. She called. No reply.

Annie left a message, her phone tucked under her chin. "Marissa? Annie—I'm coming in, hope you're decent—lucky I brought my key. Got that furniture from the garage sale over the weekend for you—you owe me coffee and a donut if you forgot we said eleven. Where are you?"

"Dammit!" Annie swore as a splinter slit the skin under her thumbnail. She wrestled out the circular, cracked glass-topped table and limped across the parking lot. Leaving the table in the hallway, she shoved her key into the lock and walked in.

The curtains were drawn, and the open living space was camouflaged in peachy-gray shadows. Annie dragged the table in and called out "Just me!" before turning to grab the matching chairs from the car.

As she swiveled, Annie's eye stuttered on an incongruous glare on the kitchen tile. Stepping closer, she took in a dozen large chunks of glass, globs of canned pineapple, and the smell of—*what?* Annie's brain listed apple juice, watermelon, and the unmistakable scents of blood and vomit.

Marissa was in a tank top and boxer shorts, folded in half at the waist around the iceberg remnants of the Waterford bowl Annie and her mother had re-gifted to her from one of Helen's clients after the wedding announcement. The young woman had cut her foot as she fell, and the gash on her heel bled richly into the grout in crisscrossing channels.

"God, no!" Annie knelt at Marissa's side as she dialed 9-1-1. Marissa's face was clammy, and she was clutching her stomach. Annie jabbered circumstances and the address at the operator, pressed the wound with a dishtowel, and cradled Marissa into a rescue position. The prone woman's eyes drifted open and closed, her pupils pulsing, and Annie parroted the dispatch's instructions into Marissa's ear. "Stay the hell awake, Marissa! Do you hear me?"

The ambulance took a year. Annie rode with them, met a sobbing Helen at the hospital, and called the school to talk to the counselor.

"Marissa's in with the doctors now. Nathan's at school, I asked them to pull him from class so he could call me. He's got someone with him."

Annie saw Helen's broken face. "I know. She has to be okay."

Helen chewed the rim of one opalescent nail. "This can't be how it ends."

A doctor strode towards them, her ponytail swishing.

She nodded seriously and double-checked the chart in her hand. "Acetaminophen overdose. Possible liver damage, but we've given her the first round of acetylcysteine and she seems to be tolerating that okay. She's also got a scopolamine patch for the nausea. She'll need doses every four hours for the next three days, so you can plan on her being here for about a week."

Mother and mother-in-law hugged each other hip to hip. Helen barked out the only important question. "So she's going to be okay?"

The doctor knew when to answer and when to let the moment pass. The only way to know in cases like this was to wait, watch, and hope. She offered support for something else instead. "Lucky you found her when you did." The doctor chewed the inside of her cheek. "People treat something as strong as Tylenol like Skittles. We see this more often than you'd think."

An hour later, during visiting hours that the nurse manager had offered to extend to as long as the patient would have them, Helen and Annie each picked a side and hovered.

Opening her eyes at the sound of them entering the room, Marissa sighed and dropped her head. "I hurt my back last week, stacking boxes at work. Doctor wanted to prescribe something for the pain."

Seeing Helen's glare, Marissa held up her hands. "Mom, I didn't fill the prescription! You can check with the office. Told the doctor I'm in recovery, and she said ice and heat and Tylenol would be enough."

Her voice crumbled. "Which it was until yesterday. Took two at lunch, two at dinner, two last night before bed, woke up at three a.m. and could barely move, took two more. Felt kind of crappy when I got up this morning, stomach ache, but figured it was nothing. My back was still in spasms, so I dropped Nathan at school and took two more when I got home."

Gratefully, Marissa added, "Next thing I remember is the sound of the bowl hitting the floor and you screaming in my face."

The younger woman let the tears gather and drip. "I'm such a moron, I should have realized. Seemed harmless though, right?"

Marissa wiped her eyes. "After everything."

Helen and Annie sighed with her. Annie nodded. "Thought it was something else until the paramedic found the bottle in the sink."

"Could have been." Marissa acknowledged the truth that would always be with her. "I need you both to know that it wasn't."

Helen reached down to hug her daughter. "We believe you, sweetheart. We believe in you."

Calmed by assurances that his mother was fine and an hour by her bedside that afternoon, Nathan got them all to agree that he would spend the next few nights at a friend's house instead of with Helen and Annie.

The three women were together in Marissa's room

the next morning when someone knocked on the door and came in without waiting for an invitation.

Dressed in khaki pants and a rumpled collared shirt, a twenty-something man introduced himself. "I'm Martin Anderson." He bulldozed through their confusion. "Someone flagged an overdose for a Ms. Williams?"

Marissa sucked in her breath and grabbed Annie's hand. Helen squared off with the intruder. "Our family has no need of your...services, Mr. Anderson. My daughter's recovering from an accidental situation that has nothing to do with what happened before."

"Nothing I can about that, ma'am." The man used the honorific as an insult. "You've got a file with us, you've got a file. Period."

His eyes narrowed above a hyena smile. "And where is the minor child—Nathan, is that right—now?"

Jutting out her chin and looming over the much shorter man, Helen barked. "None of your goddamn business. Our grandson Nathan is fine."

The man shook his head. "Right, right. Got it in one." He turned towards the door. "You'll be hearing from us before close of business this afternoon." He sneered at Marissa. "You get better soon."

Before Helen could say another word, Annie limped out of the room. She caught up with the social worker at the elevator. "Mr. Anderson, wait."

He turned and smiled superciliously. "You have something else to add to what your wife said in there? I can put it all in my report."

"This could have been something else." Even as she said it, Annie knew that there was no appealing to the vacuum in the space where another person might have cached their better nature. She said the words aloud for herself. "The woman in the bed in there fights every single day for the life she is building with her son, and her mother? My wife? She found a way to fight alongside."

Annie spat the last words at him as she stomped back down the hall. "Put that in your report."

None of the three women spoke of the encounter again during the hours that followed. They were all too afraid to give the worst-case scenario life by giving it breath.

"Hello?" Helen answered Marissa's phone from across the room as her daughter slept. Annie glanced at her watch. *Four forty-five.*

Helen gestured to Annie and they headed into a quiet corner of the waiting area before Helen spoke again. "We're both here, Teresa." She put the phone on low-volume speaker as she and Annie leaned in.

"Annie, hi." Teresa's tone was high and thin. She launched in. "Here's the thing—between you and me, Martin's a son of a bitch who has no business in our business."

Helen cracked a smile and flicked a tentative okay sign at Annie. Teresa was still talking. "Or yours."

"Couldn't agree more." Helen could not keep the disdain from her voice. Annie laid a warning hand on her wife's free arm and Helen nodded grudgingly.

"I can't do anything about Martin, but when I saw your names on the allocation file this morning, I brought our supervisor in on the whole story. She has agreed to a time-limited, low-parameters arrangement that I hope you'll see your way towards accepting."

Helen grunted. Annie filled in. "Meaning?" She tried to keep the statement neutral, but there was no hiding the froth of fear and irritation.

"Meaning—" Annie and Helen heard Teresa take a deep breath— "Nathan spends tomorrow at our offices under the care of our family therapist, you two take Nathan for three months, and we will consider this matter closed pending any additional disclosures."

"And Marissa?" Helen's heart broke again for her only child. Her voice rattled with indignation.

"Supervised visitation on site at Trisham for the first two weeks once she is released from hospital, unsupervised after that, bi-weekly meetings with a substance abuse counselor through the probation period, and a re-assessment every six months for the next twenty-four."

"No. No goddamn way." Helen mumbled, riding the rise of her temper. Annie clenched her jaw.

Across the line, Teresa's chagrin sounded genuine. "It's the best I can do. I'm sorry, I know your family should be focused on Marissa's medical recovery right now, and there is nothing fair about this. We are in a situation where an abundance of caution is indicated, given her history. But if you give me the verbal go-ahead over the phone, I can e-mail you the papers to sign. You can bring Nathan by in the morning. His appointment's at 8:30." She stopped talking and waited.

By the time her mind had caught up with the details of the social worker's proposal, Helen was irate. Annie grabbed the phone before her wife exploded and shot back. "Thanks, Teresa. Give me five minutes to call you back."

Helen roared and paced, trying to snatch her phone. Following the feints, Annie kept eye contact, her voice cool and detached. "Not the time, babe. Be angry later. Is what it is. If the alternative is whatever that bastard Anderson recommends, we don't want to know."

Annie confirmed with Teresa. The newlyweds talked to Marissa, waking her from a deep sleep. She called Nathan, who raged and swore and got his mother to ask the social worker for permission to take a taxi from his friend's house to the office in Trisham the following morning.

Exhausted, Marissa waved them away. "Call me after you pick him up tomorrow. Damn sure he won't want to talk to me again for a while, at least until I get the hell out of here."

No one slept that night. Helen was shuffling around downstairs by four; Annie headed down soon after. They drank tea and coffee in silence, pottering around the house in search of chores or projects, scowling each time they intersected. Finally, after a silent, late lunch, they got the house ready for their unexpected guest. Everything was harder than it should have been, which is a direct and unavoidable consequence of life's demands being unpredictable and factious.

Annie thawed first. Without filling the space with words, she projected how she thought they might get through this day and those to come. *Humor as a sledgehammer. Worth a try.*

"If you ask me again, I'm going to shove you down the stairs." Annie put her arm around Helen's waist and shuffled her out of the way in the hallway outside the guest bedroom. "Now give me five minutes to get this bed made up and we'll have plenty of time to get pick up Nathan from Trisham by three."

Keeping it as lighthearted as she dared under the circumstances, Annie raised her eyebrows and grinned. "Six loaves of bread in the freezer, jumbo jar of crunchy peanut butter, school schedule on the refrigerator, and a rolling password on the wi-fi. We've got this."

Annie stopped as her words rolled into the silence. She allowed her careful smile to drop and stepped back towards her wife.

Helen sagged against Annie and sighed deeply. "Right thing to do. Right?"

Annie hugged her wife hard and gripped Helen by both shoulders. She met Helen's fear with the relative objectivity that came with being the only one capable of seeing the puddle of the immediate future without drowning in the past's deep, blurred sea. One hand chopped into the other as she ran down the list of steps that had led them to this Tuesday in mid-May. "Paperwork that says so, babe. Best interests of the child and all that. More lawyers than God if need be to make it stick. It's sealed. It's sorted."

Seeing Helen's misery, Annie's compassion reasserted itself. She spoke in a low, steady voice. "We're family, love. Nathan and Marissa, they're our family. It's not only the right thing to do, it's the right now thing to do."

With a kiss on Helen's forehead, Annie ducked into the bedroom. "I grabbed two pillows out of the chest in the attic and the comforter from my stuff in a storage box. Think Nathan will mind if it all smells like moth balls?"

Helen had been in Nathan's bedroom at Marissa's house only a few months earlier, helping him excavate the indeterminate mounds that covered the floor for a lost science assignment while his mother worked a double shift. The thought of her teenage grandson even being able to distinguish the tang of mothballs from whatever combination of adolescent funk, high-powered anti-perspirant, and half-eaten snacks under the bed might soon be the odors *du jour* in their guest bedroom was enough to cement her sense of humor about the entire absurd situation.

"You might have noticed in the grocery cart, I bought three boxes of baking soda last night to stash in there before we even bring him home, Annie." She stood tall and picked up the laundry basket on the landing. "First things first, we teach that kid how to use the washing machine. Seriously."

As she tucked in the sheets and smoothed the covers, Annie caught sight of her wedding ring, a thick, sapphire-studded black titanium band. Only a few weeks out from their brief exchange of vows in front of Marissa, Nathan, an enthusiastic justice of the peace and two willing bystanders coopted as witnesses, Annie could still feel the heft of the metal and the cool frost against her skin. She tapped the flush stones with the ridge of her thumbnail and closed her eyes. *For better and for worse.*

The drive to child services the next afternoon was quiet. The building made Helen flinch and Annie want to run, but they walked in holding hands and signed the papers before the boy appeared carrying his overnight bag. Teresa talked nonstop, filling in all sides of the conversation and patting Nathan on the hand as he dodged a hug from his grandmother.

The drive back was quieter still. Fifteen-year-old Nathan sat against the window, wireless earbuds in place, knees pressing against the driver's seat.

Helen's restraint broke as they pulled into the driveway. "We've got your room ready, Nathan. Plenty of room in the closet for all of your stuff, and we can buy whatever else you need. We can do a road trip back to your house this afternoon or tomorrow to pick up more stuff, and—"

Nathan was already a half-inch taller than Helen. He raised his arms and stretched on the door jamb. "School tomorrow. I already missed a day and a half this week."

Helen nodded, matching his monotone. "School. Yes. We'll make it work."

Nathan's gaze swam from Annie to his grandmother and back again. "I've got lacrosse practice Tuesdays and Thursdays until 5:45. Can't miss another one or the coach will cut me from the team."

Daring us to fail him. Annie recognized the resignation and distrust in the boy's jutting jaw and raccoon eyes. *Daring us to let him down.* She pointed to his backpack and tethered the three of them to the next moment, so they could all make it to the one after that. "Homework?"

Annie held his stare and did not blink. The boy felt his clammed-up chest open a little and he risked a deep breath. He unzipped his backpack. "Chemistry—lab's due next week. Probably have to go in early to make it up. And English paper on some Shakespeare thing the week after."

He joined Annie in her laughter as she glanced at the title of the book in his hand. "I'm sure the Bard would be gratified to hear you call *Othello* 'some Shakespeare thing,' Nathan. One of my faves, though. You need help, ask."

Silence squeezed into the space between them again. Nathan repeated Annie's offer in his head, his mind spraying memories like graffiti and shutting him off.

Helen tried something else. *Anything else.* She strung her mouth into a forced smile. "Cookies? Fresh this morning."

"I'm not a little kid." Nathan frowned, but slid three pocked chocolate chip cookies onto his plate. "Not like you can make it all better with warm snacks and cold milk, Helen."

His grandmother nudged her beaded reading glasses down the bridge of her nose. Her sarcasm leaked all over the room. "Pray tell, child, since when are you and I on first name terms? Let's stick with Grandma. At least until you're old enough to vote and pay rent."

Slowly, watching Helen with wide eyes, Nathan crushed the cookie that was halfway to his mouth, spilling crumbs all over the kitchen floor. "No damn way I'll be here that long. She said three months." They all knew who 'she' was. Annie and Helen closed their eyes. Nathan picked up his glass of milk, sloshing it wildly, and stomped up the stairs.

"That went well." Leaning against the opposite wall, Annie stage whispered. Halfway up to the second floor, Nathan swore loudly enough for them to both hear. "All things considered."

Helen's eyes swished across the scene: spilled food, half-laced sneakers and filthy socks on the counter beside the toaster, a patched military surplus duffel bag wedged up against the pantry door. She started to wipe up the mess and lay her head on her arms. "Can't."

Annie smiled softly, picking up the dishtowel and pulling the broom from the utility closet. "We can. We will. You'll see."

Cape Cod (November 2019)

Nathan held the receiver as though it were an alien. "Why do we even still have this thing? A landline is so last century, Annie."

"Hang up." Annie stooped to pick up the last bag of groceries. "Bound to be another robo-call, this close to the election."

The teenager scoffed and put the phone to his ear. "What if it's a real live political campaign? I've still got three years before my voice counts on the ballot, damned if I'm going to pass up the chance to talk issues with someone who cares about what's going on in the world."

Annie shrugged and slid a gallon of milk across the shelf to make room for some sliced cheese. She resisted her standard retort of 'I promise you, politics gets old faster than people do, and people get old real fast' and heard him ask who it was on the other end of the line.

Nathan listened for a moment and held out the corded anachronism to Annie. "Says she's from the police."

Annie shook her head and mouthed, "Not here."

"I'm sorry, ma'am, she's not here. Would you like to leave a—" Nathan stopped and hung up.

"No message. Guess it must have been a scammer after all." The teenager pulled open the refrigerator door.

"Got any more of those drinkable cherry yogurts?"

"Haven't you got homework?" Annie reached passed him, pulled two small cylindrical cartons out from the back and handed them over. "You know your grandma's right about your history grade, right?"

Nathan took the snack and peeled the metal foil back before swigging the yogurt in a single gulp. He eyed Annie sideways. "I'm carrying As in everything else, what's the big deal?"

He basketball-tossed the container in to the sink and picked up the other one. Nathan tried on his sweetest smile. "Besides, I've already decided I'm going to apply early decision at UMass Amherst for mechanical engineering."

Annie's eyes lit up at the last word, her face softened. "Okay, buddy, got me there. You know I can't wait to have another engineer in the family. I love your grandmother, but she thinks 'live load' means a truck full of chickens, and her idea of 'added mass' is two slices of pie for dessert."

Nathan crossed the kitchen and gave her a side hug. "You're the best, Annie." He grabbed his backpack and took the stairs at a sprint.

Charmed his way out of trouble. Again. Annie grinned to herself as she wiped the counter and made herself a sandwich. *Where that kid's been, it's a miracle he's still standing.*

She had only taken one bite out of her brie and cranberry sauce on sourdough before she realized what Nathan needed from her. Annie sighed, practiced the words in her head a few times, and went up to his room.

Sitting cross-legged on the floor, his phone in one hand and the other hand mining deep inside a family-sized bag of corn chips, Nathan mumbled through a mouthful. "Yeah?"

Annie stepped across the threshold into a realm of ankle-deep dirty laundry, narrow unmade bed, and electronics covering every surface of the room. She ignored any pretense of preamble. "History. It's about your mom, isn't it?"

Nathan had known Annie for less than a year. It had been the worst year of his life for the obvious reasons, but Annie had been the one thing he could count on not to remind him. That and school, where all the equations made sense and the literature was easy and gym class meant being picked first or second for every team. This was new.

He stared at her. "What the hell, Annie?"

His step-grandmother absorbed the anger on his face, the lines across his nose both as legible as Helen's own expression and as foreign to her as though she were seeing him upset for the first time. *First time directed at me.*

Annie crouched down in the doorway so that they were at eye level. He didn't look away. "She's the one who took you to see all the monuments when you were little, right? Your grandma told me it was one of the things she loved to do with you, drive around all over the state reading historical markers and telling you all the stories that went along with the plaques and the gravestones."

"Out." Nathan's voice dropped into a growl, his gaze steady.

Holding up both hands, Annie said, "You don't have to talk to me, Nathan. But eventually you're going to have to talk to someone."

She left, holding her breath and tiptoeing down the stairs. The door slammed behind her.

An hour later, with Helen still out shopping and early sunset closing in, Annie heard the upstairs door creak open and heavy treads coming down. Nathan set the table in silence and without being asked, mopping up the water he spilled on the floor and remembering napkins and the salt.

"Thank you." Annie fished for civil conversation. "I appreciate that."

Nathan mumbled acknowledgement and reached up to take three pasta bowls from the glass-fronted cabinet above the desk alcove. As he set them down on the counter next to where Annie was adding angel hair to a cauldron of boiling water, he added softly, "She said knowing what came before makes the future possible. That history's a barometer of the best and worst in people, and if you understand history, you understand everything."

"Sounds about right." Keeping her eyes at chest level, she retrieved the tomato sauce and mushrooms from the refrigerator and tipped a capful of olive oil into a waiting pan.

Nathan held a tower of three water tumblers in his hands. He stood at the sink, filling them slowly from the filtered spout. Putting aside the first full glass, he said softly, "How can that be right? My mom knew everything there was to know about history, but she didn't understand anything about anything."

Annie had opened the door to Nathan's pain. She owed him at least the courage to walk through with him. "Best and worst in people, hon. Your mom was trying to show you that if you know where you've been, you'll have a better chance of figuring out where you need to go next."

Immobile, the teenager watched the glasses he held reflect light across the kitchen and down the hall. His step-grandmother put down the wooden spoon she had been using to stir the pot of pasta and stood next to him, their elbows almost touching.

"How come she's so messed up, Annie?" Nathan edged his arm closer, until their sleeves overlapped. Annie resisted the urge to put her arm around him. "How come her future plans don't include putting me first?"

The woman's eyes blurred, and she breathed deeply. "There are things we will never understand, sweetheart. Choices people make, things that happen. But I do know your mother still loves you. Even though she can't take care of you right now. This time was an accident, but I know you know the next time might not be. Even though she's a person with her own messed-up life and messed-up priorities and messed-up point of view."

Nathan's focus slipped, as did his hand. The bottom glass of his impromptu column sculpture slid sideways across the kitchen counter, bounced off the toaster, and hit the floor like a firecracker. They both jumped backward, colliding against the island and reaching out. The boy put his arms around Annie and his face against her shoulder without a word. She let his tears fall between them, rocking him back and forth, hoping she had done the right thing.

Three days later, Helen whistled at the piece of paper Nathan handed to her as he walked in the door after school. "Ninety-six percent on a history test? That's more like it!"

Nathan grinned and reached into the cabinet for the box of lemon cookies. "Figured I'd even it up there with my other grades. You know how it is, superstar's gotta be a superstar, right?"

Annie overpoured the lemonade, her back to the conversation. As Nathan walked past her to the stairs, he gave her a quick hug and whispered directly into her ear. "Best and worst, Annie." She caught his warm smile over his shoulder and nodded.

Helen could not decipher the words, but she saw the interaction. She kissed Annie on the cheek and mirrored her smile. "We're officially family, hon. How's it feel to be temporarily raising a teenage boy as a newlywed, with me, your lovely wife?"

"About as nuts as it sounds." Annie put away the lemonade and raised her glass. "Cheers to a future I never thought I'd have."

Cape Cod (December 2019)

In spite of herself, Annie glanced at the phone on the passenger seat as it rang. Five-twenty was a Tucson area code. Amanda ignored the beep of the left message until a red light offered her the chance to read the first few words. The transcription software wasn't perfect, but Annie could read it fine in the soft light: *Good afternoon. This is a message for Ms. Lydia McCray. I believe she is now known as Diane Howard? Ms. McCray, this is Officer Lewis, matter loses from too suns...*

The car behind her honked, startling Annie into a jerked acceleration. She drove the last mile home and only realized she had been holding her breath when she blew all the air out of her lungs and gasped as her arms caught her head on the steering wheel. Closing her eyes, she reached one hand over to the passenger seat and retrieved her phone. The metal box should have been cool, but it singed like a brand as she crushed it against her skin.

The phone double-beeped its voicemail reminder. Annie's knees shook as she climbed out of the car, steadied her key hand with the other as though she were holding a revolver, stumbled inside, and slid down the kitchen cabinet to the floor. She hugged her legs and stared at the quiet phone.

Twenty-one years. Now this.

Annie inventoried her options. She lingered on 'ignore' and its cousins, 'neglect' or 'deny.' She played with 'discredit' and scoffed at 'forget.'

An operator answered and transferred the call. Annie willed every global cataclysm to interrupt the moment, wishing for the epic destruction of fire or flood in the thirty seconds it took for a voice to respond. "Officer Lewis here. How can I help you?"

The voice was the same—warm and sincere—but Annie could hear the stretch of adulthood in Maddie Lewis' tone. *Things have happened to her, too.* The insight gave Annie courage, as only mutual acknowledgment of hardship can.

"You called a left a message." Annie gritted her teeth. "This is Lydia McCray."

"Ms. McCray." The cop's voice sounded rehearsed. "Not an easy woman to find."

Annie did not have the story in her. Mercifully, the officer did not inquire further.

"There's been a development in the case." Officer Lewis inhaled audibly. Nothing about this was straightforward. She remembered the broken woman on the phone the first time and could hear the fissures reopening as she offered up the impossible news. "This is Maddie— remember me? Without waiting for a reply, she continued, "Lydia—Diane—we've found her."

Too much. Too late. Annie clasped the phone with two hands and pressed it to her ear.

The cop was still talking. "Followed a hunch. There

was a case over in New Mexico, missing kid. Cops trailed a foul play case for years, and three weeks ago an excavator operator on a new construction development dug up bones."

"How can that—" Annie's half asked question died on her lips.

Maddie could not stop the landslide of her explanation. "I've got a colleague, transferred over there a few years back, and we saw each other at a regional training conference in Albuquerque. She mentioned the case over coffee. Got me thinking."

Annie counted her breaths. "Where?"

The cop sighed. "You were right. That hitchhiker was headed for the farmhouse behind you after the accident. So, I checked it out the possibility of construction projects near the site of the crash and got a lucky break. That stretch was scheduled for underground gas line maintenance."

Annie breathed in, trying to follow the police officer's twisting story. Maddie was still talking. "Turns out, three months ago one of the teams had a couple of machines out there digging trenches for new pipe, and report came in of human remains along the perimeter of the project. Would never have seen it because it got sent straight to forensics."

Maddie sounded excited. "I took a team out as soon as I realized it might be in the same spot."

Annie let out a strangled laugh that she disguised as a cough. Her mind slipped sideways into sarcasm, ditching listening for the protective veneer of snide internal commentary. *That's the definition of non-time sensitive—two decades too late.*

Maddie stopped. "Lydia—Ms. McCray—if this is too much for you, I can—"

Annie returned to herself and blushed with embarrassment. She risked a full sentence. "Please, no. I need to hear it. All of it."

Mollified, the officer picked up the narrative. "We walked every pace of the ground around the excavation. One of my rookies found an old flashlight at ground level, half buried, and another few feet took the four of us to the edge of a slip in the rock and dirt. A little nothing, by rights she should have missed it, it was down to plain old bad luck that she stumbled in and was hidden by the grass and shelf of debris. As far as tests can tell, she lost her footing and went down into a narrow rift in the terrain. Hit her head on a rock that they found down there, fragments still embedded in her skull. No other signs of trauma, though. Probably never even woke up."

When there was no more reply except the scrape of labored breath, Maddie continued. "Covered up so well, wouldn't have seen it on aerial surveillance. Gap's only eight feet by three, could have been missed even if they'd had a whole team out there doing a grid search."

Which they did not. Annie saved the caveat for inside her own head. She scrubbed her face with her sleeve, forcing herself to weep without a sound. "I'm here," she whispered finally. "What else?"

"No prints at this point. Age estimated in the mid-sixties but could have been as young as fifty." The officer galloped through the details, with little left to offer. "No match to any reports, and our data's a lot better these days."

"Family? Friends?" Annie skimmed the veins of the hardwood floor.

"We might never know who she is, but she tried, Lydia." Maddie's voice slowed down. "She tried to save you all."

Tucson (December 2019)

The air was the same: dense and cold, as though someone had squeezed it fresh that morning. Annie stepped out of the airport ahead of Helen and inhaled what felt like someone else's memories.

"Told the nurse we'd be there by ten," Annie said as she and Helen climbed into a waiting car.

"Nathan's happy to have us gone—I'm glad Teresa got us permission to leave him with Todd's family for a few days."

Helen nodded and held Annie's hand. Annie had not wanted to talk about any of this before they left the East Coast, and she obviously did not want to talk about it now.

The nursing home was outside of the city, past a long snake of strip malls and set in garishly irrigated gardens. Squinting through the tinted glass, Annie tried unsuccessfully to find any desert native plants among the mobs of lady fern and hibiscus. The buildings were extended hacienda, all archways and heavy timber trim with a terracotta roof. The driver dropped them off and they headed inside.

"Leave your bags with me, if you like," the receptionist said, pointing to a cleared space behind her. "I'll get the nurse to take you over to Roy in the Felicidad Room. It's where our guests usually receive visitors."

Helen made a face with her back turned and Annie sniggered nervously. They sat quietly in bucket chairs in the foyer for a few minutes and stood to greet the young nurse who was dressed in sunflower scrubs.

"I'm Benjamin. Roy's been talking about seeing you again. Lydia, is it?" He introduced himself and shook their hands.

Annie stammered a reply. "Y-yes. And this is my wife Helen."

"Nice to meet you both. Roy's finishing up physical therapy. Let me show you around for a few minutes while we wait." The walk across three courtyards, past the panopticon circular dining room, and into the next building over seemed to take forever. Annie felt her feet sink further into the ground and was grateful for Helen's easy chatter with their guide. Benjamin pointed out all the facilities as they went along, stopping to share a word and a smile with half a dozen other residents as they went.

Annie saw the top of Roy's head the moment she stepped under the looped cursive sign proclaiming this the room of happiness. The room itself was small, four sets of furniture arranged like a cloverleaf around a central indoor water feature that made Annie's ears strive for sound.

He was sitting in his wheelchair by the window, newspaper spread across his lap, one finger tracing the words across the page. At eighty-four, Roy Marquez still had a lot of hair, and the ginger persisted across the crown despite gray's incursions.

Helen stood back and watched as Annie—*Lydia!*—picked up her pace and strode over to the old man. Benjamin moved forward. "They don't need you," Helen said, her firm hand on his elbow. "Let them have this." She turned away from her wife and pulled Benjamin out behind her, gently closing the double doors. "Grief doesn't deserve the indignity of an audience."

"Roy?" Annie crouched at his side. He was much thinner than she remembered, but he sat straight up.

"You're here." His tone was more welcoming than Annie had thought possible. She had prepared herself for indifference and anger; she was not ready for acceptance or love. "I missed you. Both of you."

Annie felt her throat closing and she coughed, reaching behind her for a chair. She sat next to Roy, afraid to face him directly. Roy dropped his newspaper on the floor and gripped her hand, his words muffled from the effects of the mild stroke he had suffered two months before. "I know why you didn't come, Lydia. I would have run away if I could have, too."

When she could not answer, he added, "From all of it."

The Felicidad Room faced one of the inner courtyards of the facility. Annie focused on the fountain outside, a small pillar of irregular rocks and clay jugs set on a monolithic cube of polished granite. The water chased down through the vessels and over the stones, landing with an outsized splash in the shallow pool below. Annie's eyes stung as she tried to count the rings.

Still holding her hand, Roy maneuvered himself awkwardly until he blocked Annie's view. "What you need to see is right here, Lydia." His voice was a salve, spreading over what Annie had not realized would be open wounds. Twenty years had seemed like time enough, because she had done everything to keep her back to the storm. There would never be time enough.

Shouldn't have come. Annie frowned as Roy took her other hand, which had been absently scratching the inside of her elbow into red furrows. The old man had been a magnificent father to an incandescent daughter once, and he recognized the signs of despair. Roy pressed Annie's palms together inside his huge hands, forcing his dragging left appendage to comply. "Between the two of you, you and Amanda would have been the best mothers in the whole goddamn world, you know that?"

Annie gasped, her empty dream returned to her on someone else's sorrow. Her mind cartwheeled, desperate to cling to the ground but tugged away from the center by Roy's courage to say aloud what she had always believed in her heart.

Roy's eyes were half-closed as he spooled his memories into words that drew pictures in the air. "Smart as hooty owls and brave enough to shove your big toe down the gullet of an alligator, the pair of you. That kid of yours, that Theo, he would have been bright as a new penny and double-backboned, too."

Roy's story rolled on, giving life to the child no one had ever had the chance to meet. "Hellraiser to boot, that kid, like both his mamas. No doubt about it."

His eyes snapped open at Annie. "No sense you never got the chance. No sense at all."

Annie saw his face, mottled and sagging, carrying the weight of a sad smile that had been well worn over the years. She saw how his clothes hung off-kilter, as though his shoulders were a wire hanger bent out of shape. She smelled the antiseptic whiff of too much institution and tasted the end of everything on the tip of her tongue.

Letting go of her hands, Roy pressed his lips until they disappeared into his creviced face. Annie risked meeting his eyes. *Too much Amanda.* Two words pushed up roots in the center of her chest, finally bursting through as a hollow squawk. "I'm sorry."

"You left us. She didn't have a choice, Lydia. But you?" Roy paced his words carefully, joining Annie in the muck.

"I wasn't me anymore, Roy." Annie swallowed, her mouth like metal and cinders. "I couldn't be me anymore."

"Took us two years to open up that crate of Amanda's paintings you had shipped over." Roy's voice broke. He slowed down, marking each syllable with a tap on the arm of his wheelchair. "Never could bring myself to hang a single one until Evie was gone. She wanted to remember her baby girl before the world took her away. I wanted to remember what might have been. And don't even get me started on the photo albums. Evie wouldn't open the box."

In an abrupt shift of mood, Roy grinned widely. "Got them to change the damn by-laws in this place, special fire safety dispensation and everything, to make sure that my girl's art well-nigh covers the walls in my suite, now. Not an inch of the old beige paint visible. Showed them who's boss."

He clapped his right hand against the side of his wheelchair with a thump. "Want to see?"

Annie felt her mind shear down the middle. *We are talking about my dead girlfriend's art, the other mother of my only child, the last remnants of her creative spirit, jammed onto dry wall like insects on pins, and the man who is basically the father I never had is sitting here crowing about a bureaucratic victory in his last stop before...*

The word inked itself across her mind's eye. *Death.* That was what all of this was about, death and dying. Except maybe it was not about that at all. Death defines itself by absence, by the undoing of all that is known and knowable. Annie's pilgrimage to Arizona, from a dismissed phone call to her sitting here, belly clenched against an old man's good intentions, was not a journey to the dead. It was a journey for the living, a mission set in motion by kindness and perseverance, and faced now with the pox of cowardice and retreat.

Fingers steepled, legs aching from the too-short chair, tears imminent, in a room designed for impossible conversations between those still living about those soon to be or long dead, Annie felt a twinge of hope. She arched into Roy, wrapped her arms around his broad but now bony shoulders, and whispered. "Lead the way."

Helen and Benjamin were sitting on a bench in the hallway when Annie pushed Roy through the doors and made a sharp left. She caught Helen's eye and gave a diffident thumb's up. Helen nodded an encouraging smile but did not move to introduce herself.

"I'm not even here," Helen said to Benjamin. "Not in any way that matters, except for prep and recovery. Whatever she needs."

Benjamin stared at the woman beside him, dressed in a tailored pantsuit and mounds of matching jewelry, her hair coiffed to within a single strand. She had bubbled up in his estimation from 'reluctant tagalong' to 'essential element' in the space of twenty minutes. "Mostly around here we're always dealing with whatever everyone else needs. Residents are easy. It's the families, all the weight they drag in, fifty years or more of whatever went wrong."

Benjamin slumped in his chair, his glum face tempered by compassion. "From their faces though, and yours? Something's going right."

"Ta-da!" Roy swept his arms around the studio apartment, his eyes glittering with pride. "Pick a favorite, Lyds." He craned his neck and saw her face. "Lydia."

A single tear birthed itself at the corner of Annie's right eye and squirmed down her cheek. She refused to brush it away. "Lyds is fine, Roy. Lyds is...perfect."

Who I was. To both of them. Once.

The sofa was beige. The kitchenette was beige. The recliner was dark brown. The comforter on the bed she could see though a half-open interior door was white with an inobtrusive blue stripe. The rest of the apartment was...

"Amanda!" Annie reveled in the shock of her own loud voice.

Roy nodded, wheeling himself further into the space and spinning the chair. "Everywhere around me, every single day."

The canvasses were all at least a square yard in size, up to a narrow mural that occupied most of the ten-foot length of the living room. The colors and composition were exactly as Annie remembered: deep, overlapping brushstrokes in compelling combinations of unfettered primaries and complex tertiary hues. Amanda's subject matter had broadened over their eight years together, but the core of space and light and whitespace occupied repeated, harrowing patterns.

Annie's breath stuttered like a woodpecker. She pressed her hands against her chest, feeling the crush of the shocking exhibition.

"Management's not thrilled by fatal heart attacks around here, Lyds." Roy stuck with humor's defense and pointed to a rope with a round plastic knob hanging next to the closet. "There's an emergency bell pull for that. They thought of everything."

Giggling through her nose in spite of the fact that nothing was funny, Annie glanced at Roy. "What, so you don't end up dead in a—"

After that, both were quiet for a few minutes. Annie used a paper towel from the counter to wipe her eyes and nose. Roy heaved himself to his feet with the aid of a walker planted by the bathroom door and plodded over to her. She hugged him and they sat together on the sofa, heads swiveling as though the walls were the bright stars and heavy planets of a dark, lost sky.

"It's not my loss I mind so much," Roy said slowly. "It's hers. Hers and Theo's. No chance."

Annie nodded. "Took me years to understand that. Not sure if I did until now, Roy. I was so wrapped up in snuffing it all out, starting over."

"And you have. Beautifully, Lyds." Roy smiled and stroked Annie's chin with a raspy thumb.

She nodded, holding his hand to her cheek. "It's Annie these days. My wife Helen and I are taking care of our grandson while his mom figures some stuff out."

Sometimes part of the story is enough to know. Cruel curiosity might demand more, but Roy erred on the side of kindness and followed the line she hoped he would. "How old's the boy?"

"Sixteen. Junior." Annie smiled as her mind conjured a picture of Nathan, sassy and sharp like his grandmother, telling jokes over ice cream at the dinner table. "Smart kid. Tough couple of years, but he'll get there."

The not-quite-daughter put her arm around Roy. "We all will."

A few more minutes of silence fell to other unavoidable subjects.

"And Evie?" Annie had to know but did not want to ask.

Roy's face grew serious. "Nothing for her to latch on to, after. She left within a year." Seeing Amanda's mask of sympathy, Roy shook his head. "All for the best. Married a Catholic plastics tycoon with an ark full of grandkids. Last I heard they were living in Pelican Bay."

Annie made instant coffee from the clumpy granules in an old jar in the cabinet. She stirred in sugar for herself and handed Roy his, bitter and black. "Just like a certain someone used to take it," the abandoned father said, wincing at the liquid singed his tongue. "Never converted you though."

They drank their coffee, soaking up Amanda's kaleidoscopic stories. The sun inched higher, sparking rainbow reflections from a small, covered vase on the mantle above dinette set.

"It's called 'The Mermaid.'" Roya pointed. "In the catalogue. I sometimes pretend that they swam away because the world could not hold them."

Sputtering through the last sip of her coffee, Annie saw that the vase was both opaque and capped.

"Yes. Both. When Evie left." Roy answered all of Annie's unspoken questions. He added another mystery. "Wait here. Something for you."

Annie glared anywhere but back at the vessel while

she counted the minutes Roy was gone. She could hear rustling in the bedroom and the occasional grumbled 'Hell's bells' and 'Like putting socks on a rooster.' As she stood to see if she could help, Roy called her in.

He motioned to a duct-taped box on the bed. "Been waiting a fair while to give this to you, Lyds. No time like the present, since that's all we got."

She frowned and cocked her head. Roy exhaled deeply. "All that marital assets equitable distribution hoo-hah, y'know? When it came time to split the ashes, didn't seem right not to count you in. Scooped half of my half and packaged them up neat as can be."

When Annie did not respond, he added, "Got your own crystal mermaid in there, bubble wrapped and everything."

"Unless—" He matched Annie's puffed out cheeks and downturned mouth. "I thought you'd want…"

"Roy." Annie's voice was night-blooming jasmine and her finger were vines, caressing the box and its promise of remembrance. "All this time, you kept it for me for all this…"

Before she could finish, Roy pointed to two stuffed photo albums on his dresser. "Those I dragged out of storage last week."

Annie dared herself to squeeze into the narrow space between the bed and the nightstand. She remembered the weekend Amanda had stripped the bought covers to the cardboard shell, covered them in satin white paper, and doodled galaxies of interlocking shapes with every color fine-tipped Sharpie that she kept in a cookie tin in the bottom drawer of her studio desk. Unlike her paintings, which Amanda had always sketched in miniature before leaning into to the larger scale works, these album covers were evidence more of innate talent than careful composition.

Annie traced the whorls and ridges, feeling the smooth paper as her fingers slid across the surface. She closed her eyes, reliving Amanda's soft humming to herself as they kept each other company on the living room floor, Annie with a hard copy of the full schematics of her latest project and Amanda with the task of making their memories beautiful.

She could not force her hand to turn the pages. Roy ducked in next to her and stood close. "Can't tell you how often I dug those out. I missed Amanda, more than I could count on fingers or toes. She was gone for good. I never thought that you'd be, too."

"I couldn't be that person anymore." Annie navigated her regret. "Wasn't running away from you, Roy. I ran away so no one would know I'd lost everything."

It was past two o'clock by the time Annie hugged Roy good-bye. They had eaten lunch in the dining room with Helen, whose jokes were racier than Roy's and made the whole eight-person table rock with laughter. Annie watched Roy appreciatively, seeing how his natural extroversion and all-around aura of a good man who had led a good life made him the center of the extended friendship circle. She saw how the woman he introduced as his 'special friend Genevieve' joined in the loud laughter and told a few embellished stories of her own, with Southern slang that sounded more Alabama than Texas, and how she never once let go of his weaker hand.

As he said goodbye to Annie at the curbside with the cab waiting, he jerked his thumb at Helen and declared loudly, "She's a keeper, this one. Next time we'll all hang out."

"So's yours." Annie nodded slyly as Roy blushed. "Not bad for an old geezer."

She hugged him again, hard enough to make them both hold their breath. "Besides, that next visit's going to be sooner, not later," Annie said. "I'd forgotten how beautiful the Southwest is in winter, Roy."

The old man gave them a lopsided thumbs up. "You two should bring that grandson of yours." He winked at Annie. She blinked in confusion, and words settled into a hollow that she had been carrying in her chest all day. *My grandson. Our grandson. Yes.*

Annie tuned in to hear the rest of Roy's request. "Sounds like a neat kid. This place could always use a little more adolescent snark. It's only us oldies getting up to trouble in here. Or maybe I could rouse these old bones for a trip out East. Been a long time since I saw the ocean. Be nice to hear the waves."

With both promises offered and meant, Annie and Helen climbed into the back seat as the taxi driver hauled their two small suitcases into the trunk. Annie held the box and albums on her lap. *Another stop, another story.*

Helen felt Annie deflate beside her and stroked her arm. "We could call and postpone, it's been a long day."

Annie shook her head so hard that her teeth chattered. "I'll drop you off. Something I need to do by myself, anyway."

At the hotel, Annie refused the bellhop's offer to place the box on the luggage cart. She cradled it as though holding an injured bird and set it down on a cleared space on the desk in the room.

Unasked questions can be louder than the quietest inquiry. Helen busied herself, unpacking her stack of garment bags into the mirrored wardrobe and whistling a repetitious riff of something Nathan had insisted they listen to in the car on the way to lacrosse practice.

Annie adjusted the angle of the box, swore under hear breath and plopped on the bed. "Ashes. It's an urn. Another long story."

Helen joined Annie. "For another time or for now?"

"For now, it's enough that I want them with me. To take home and put somewhere I can see them every day." Annie inspected the side of Helen's head. "I missed a lot of days."

Meeting her worried gaze, Helen nodded. "Your family is my family, Annie. And mine is yours." She stood up, stroked the top of the box tenderly, and glanced back at Annie over her shoulder. "We'll take them back to Broadwell with us where they belong."

Fifteen minutes later, Annie was alone in the main downtown station of the Tucson Police Department. She had checked in with the obligatory ID confirmation and invitation to 'make herself comfortable.' She gave up sitting in the low-backed chairs after less than five minutes and was pacing in long strides across the entrance when a voice called out her old name.

"I'm Lydia McCray." Annie was not surprised at how much that felt like a lie. She had been a lot of things since the accident, but none of them was that Lydia McCray.

A young male officer used his finger to check something off on his tablet. "Follow me."

Maddie Lewis was at least seven months pregnant. She saw the other woman's gape and launched into apology without introduction. "I'm sorry. Should have mentioned it, I didn't think, it's absolutely my—"

Annie snapped her mouth shut, ignored the heat rising to her cheeks, and steadied her voice. She launched into her speech in a monotone that openly declared she had been rehearsing this moment for weeks. "Officer Lewis. Thank you for giving me an appointment. I won't take long. Wanted to—"

The cop held out a hand. "I'm Maddie. Helps to put a voice to face, Lydia. It has been a long time." She motioned to the folding chairs along the wall. "My feet are killing me, mind if we sit?"

Annie sat, trying not to stare at the other woman's

straining belly. After the accident, she had crossed the street every time a pregnant woman appeared on the sidewalk ahead of her; it had been a long time since she had been this close.

Maddie misread Annie's gaze for interest and thought she might have overestimated the other woman's initial discomfort. "Number four. Eight years younger than my last, but we'll make it work. At least I've got a few built-in babysitters."

A moment or two later, Maddie let out a low chuckle. "There she goes, kicking again. Orange juice for lunch, does it every time."

It had been a day of firsts. With the memory of the as-yet-unboxed remains of her lover and son in her fingertips, Annie asked the invasive question she knew most women dreaded. "Do you mind if I—"

Maddie Lewis heard the hesitation in Annie's voice and smiled. "Not a bit." She guided Annie's hand over the right side of her stomach. "Give it a sec."

Annie felt the jazz thumps and closed her eyes. There was no imagining another place or time, no possibility that fantasy could railroad reality, but she remembered. Remembered the dozens of moments in those precious months when Amanda would tell her to stop everything and crouch or stand or bend in and place her hand against the distended skin, listening with her hands to something that was at once reassurance and celebration.

When she opened her eyes and pulled away, Maddie

was watching her. "Nothing I could say, Lydia. Nothing to say now."

Annie appreciated Maddie's straightforward acknowledgement. Condolences are false apologies. They lack the singular element of sincere contrition that makes the whole interaction worthwhile: the ability to make something, at least a small part of something, better for the person who has been wronged. The language for expressions of solidarity for someone who is stranded in grief are weak imitations of the impotence of words without the power of restitution.

Maddie did not apologize for what she could not change. Annie nodded, allowing a grim smile. "I read the notes, obviously. But I need to hear it from you. Tell me exactly what you found. Where you found her."

Retrieving a manila folder from the table in the middle of the room, Maddie opened it to the third or fourth page in and began to read. Annie closed her eyes.

"Still a Jane Doe." Maddie stood up to indicate that the meeting was over. "Not sure we'll ever get any more than that, but her DNA's in the database."

She stood in the doorway and touched Annie's shoulder. "This room is empty for another forty-five minutes."

The kindness was more than Annie could take. She flew off her seat and hugged Maddie Lewis until she could feel the imprint the officer's hairclip left the side of her face.

Letting go, she said, "There's a whole lot of thank yous in that hug, Maddie. You'll never know how much it meant to me that you even tried to believe the story I had to tell of that night. The story was all I had left."

Annie made one more stop on her way back to the hotel. She took a hot bath, they ordered steak sandwiches and French fries with a gooey brownie sundae to share from room service, and they fell asleep to Laugh-In reruns with Lily Tomlin.

The following morning, Annie got up before sunrise and stopped by the concierge desk after ducking down the block for better coffee than they'd found in the room. "Is it here? They said they'd deliver by seven."

The concierge was working out his last few months before retirement.. He had laughed out loud when the surprise appeared in the hotel's circular drive, but when he saw the tall woman's excitement the mockery slunk away. He offered her a broad, open grin instead, nodding enthusiastically. "Yes, ma'am. Valet took care of it, they'll have the keys when you're ready. Everything else you ordered is in this bag."

He heaved a huge, see-through shopping bag from behind his desk. "I'd ask if you need help getting this up to your room, but something tells me you've got it covered."

Laughing, Annie pulled the package to her chest and wrapped an arm around it. "You get me in the elevator, I can take it from there."

He nodded approval at the chaps, boots, and jacket that showed through the plastic. "You're going to need all that out there, it's cold in the desert before the sun finds it feet."

Annie smiled as her eyes stung. "I know. It's been a long time, but I spent some time here. With family."

The concierge imagined what she didn't say. The details in his mind's eye were all wrong, but he got the feelings right. He steadied his voice for both of them. "I already checked, there's enough room to store lunch in the saddle bags. Had the kitchen pack it for you special, iced up and everything. Be ready when you are, out on the road."

Annie's thank you stumbled over itself as he graciously waved it away. "Mind if I check it out? It's been awhile."

Twenty minutes later, lattes in one hand and bag drooping over one shoulder, Annie returned to the room. She could hear Helen in the shower. After longer than Annie had yet to get used to, the water stopped, and her wife walked out of the bathroom, body and head wrapped in soft white towels.

"Ta-da!" Annie crowed. She whirled around, a black-clad dervish, boots stomping.

Helen shrieked with laughter and threw up both hands. "What in the hell?" She stepped closer, running her fingers over the studs on the jacket collar. Her voice was low. "Can't say I mind, though. You make one sexy biker babe."

"You said it." Annie kissed her, held her at arm's length. "And don't say I didn't warn you, love. Those words are coming back to bite you."

Her wife's eyes crinkled with a suspicious smile.

"What now?"

Annie pointed to the bed. "Now you get dressed, I've got bagels coming from room service in fifteen minutes, we grab a bite to eat, and we go."

Realization found Helen's face. She shook her head, her smile unsure. "Go?"

"Perfect day for a drive." Annie pulled her down on the bed so that they were both sitting on the pile of waiting clothes. "Or a ride, as it so happens."

If single words are hesitation's best friend, repetition is its annoying cousin. Repelling unwelcome information comes easier with a syllable than a sentence; cajoling takes a lot more sound and structure. Annie had all the arguments ready, lined up like tulips in precise rows in her head. She had been planning for weeks.

Putting her arm around Helen's shoulder, she used a steady tone to lay out the agenda for the day. "Out to the hills. I talked to the guy at the rental place, he mapped out a route for us with a panoramic view of the valley for lunch. Make a day of it."

When they found each other, Helen had been clear in her requests, and Annie equally so. Annie had bought more flowers and written more notes of rigged affection in the past two years than she had ever done in her life. The sentiments were real enough, but the manifestations were more about giving Helen what she needed and asked for when it came to articulating what had grown between them. In turn, Helen had grudgingly acquiesced to Annie's deep need for nature and tried to share the joy in trees and ocean and quiet sky. They both required and respected the reciprocal sacrifice. Annie made it work for her now.

"We came all the way out here, I need to feel the space. Cape Cod's got endless ocean, but you haven't seen the sky until it domes over you in the desert." She touched Helen's hand. "Bonus from you, I booked us into the spa later. Facials and everything."

Helen's surprise overtook her. "You? Beauty treatments, I thought you..."

"Hey, you're the one always talking compromise!" Annie smiled playfully. "Besides, I'm hoping for at least a little windburn from our adventure on the road."

"Anyway, one thing you can't use is the oldest excuse in the book, babe." Annie pointed to the outfit laid out on the comforter. "I knew you'd say you had nothing to wear."

"More likely to be road rash." Helen frowned. "You know this is completely nuts, right? When was the last time you—"

Her wife smiled, playing to Helen's curiosity. "Just come. You hate it, I'll go out by myself, we can take the picnic to the park instead." Annie rounded the corner of her argument, confident that the line of reasoning she had rigorously constructed had plenty of bait.

She reached in to the bag and pulled out two pairs of black leather gloves. "Now this is a real fashion statement. Said yourself it's fabulous. You don't want to say no without seeing what you're missing, right?"

Helen's skepticism showed a crack. "I'll try it on, take a picture with the motorcycle downstairs."

"But I'm serious, Annie." She snapped her teeth. "That's it. That's as far as this goes for me."

Annie's voice crackled with glee. "Absolutely. A couple of snaps to show Nathan when we get home, we've still got a story."

They ate their breakfast sitting on the sofa, chaps squeaking every time either one of them moved. Helen giggled. "This is not exactly what I envision when I think 'sexy leather,' babe."

"Oh, yeah?" Annie dropped her bagel on the plate and reached for Helen's zipper. "How's this instead?"

An hour later, the two women pulled on their new outfits for the second time that morning. Helen checked her makeup and sprayed her hair, twice. Annie came up behind her and kissed her neck. "Perfect."

As Helen opened the door, Annie held up one hand. "Press the button—forgot something."

Helen pulled the door shut behind her and Annie scoured the room for something sharp. *Damn.* She settled on the hotel pen from the desk and used the ballpoint to slice open one side of Roy's gift. Without giving herself time to think, Annie transferred a glassful of ashes to an extra plastic bag from the wastepaper basket under the desk. She double-knotted the container and shoved it forcibly into the pocket-within-a-pocket of her jacket. Without another breath, and with the detached practice of someone who had spent an entire fabricated lifetime ignoring what she did not want to acknowledge, Annie shut down every thought of what she had done. *Time will come. Whether I want it to or not.*

The elevator was empty on the way down, but the lobby was full of conference attendees and new vacationing arrivals. Robbed of her usual bluster by the novelty of biker gear, Helen blushed and put her head down; Annie grinned defiantly and met every staring eye.

In the garage, the valet attendant saw them coming. He'd already had a good riff with the other guys on duty when Annie had arrived earlier that morning; it was hilarious to see two old ladies getting ready to take out the restored vintage vehicle that squatted in the garage. He coughed a choked-off laugh into his hand.

Ignoring his open scorn, Annie sucked in the dry desert air and stroked the handlebars. The buffed chrome was cold and smooth. "More beautiful than you were an hour ago."

A few paces behind, Helen walked stiffly around the corner to where Annie stood triumphantly, keys in hand. She stopped abruptly, her eyes dancing. "It's a...it's got a..." Helen doubled over with rumbling laughter, slapping one hand into the other and trying to catch her breath.

"I think the word you're searching for is 'sidecar,' ma'am," the valet said, with a patronizing edge.

Yes. Annie watched Helen's meticulously penciled left eyebrow arch and the corners of her mouth turn down.

Nothing I say makes any difference now.

It is an axiom of the cult of youth that older people are invisible. The lesser-known corollary, known to anyone who has found him or herself on the receiving end of a sideways glance and an indulgent smile, is that whatever comes next will be a demonstration of strength. The war only ends one way.

"Did I ask you? Don't you have somewhere else to be?" Helen spat the words and turned her back on the valet, who swore under his breath but ducked back through the glass doors into the lobby.

Helen pointed at the sidecar. "In there?" Her fear fought with her pride, and for a moment fear won. She lowered her voice after glancing over to ensure that the valet had disappeared from view. "I don't think so, babe. I know you love it, and I love you, but I haven't even been on a bicycle in twenty years, let alone a flimsy attachment to hell on two wheels."

"The sidecar's more Gatsby than biker gang." Annie laughed, waving her hands close to Helen's face. "Besides, time for a little adventure. Think of me as your Zelda."

Helen clicked her tongue and puffed out her cheeks. "Fitzgerald? Now I know you're not playing fair."

Annie picked up a black helmet and slid it onto her head. She slid the visor into place. "It's got all the cool vibe of vintage with all the modern conveniences. Top of the line." Her voice was muffled. "Rental place upsold me. In-built speakers and microphone so we can talk on the way."

Helen picked up the other helmet, matching style in blazing hot pink. She followed her train of thought without a filter. "So we die in style, out in the desert, and some other poor, lost tourist finds us three days from now, dead in a proverbial ditch?"

It was too late to unsay it. There was no claiming ignorance, no retreat into apology. Too specific to unimagine. Too involved to avoid altogether with swift deflection by mutual consent.

Of course Helen knew all about the accident. Of course she knew how it had changed Annie's life. Of course she understood the entanglements of throwaway remarks and fresh pain. But like most people Helen knew did not live the chronic threat of losing a child to addiction, and the persistent terror that the next time a call came it would be the last, she hadn't survived a fatal car wreck and lost everything but her life to it. Nonetheless, the human mind survives through selective recall. In that moment, the neurons in Helen's brain that stored Annie's life took a momentary back seat to throwaway gallows humor, and the words split the earth between them.

A beat. Helen scrambled. "Sweetheart, I'm so sorry, that was obscene, I—"

Annie pulled the helmet off slowly, turning it over in her hands as if examining it for the smallest flaw. She was quiet, and she stepped away sharply when Helen touched her shoulder.

Without attempting to bridge the physical gap, Helen

tried again, rushing her words. "Jesus, I can't even ask myself the question, let alone come up with an answer that makes sense about why that came out of my mouth. Obviously no excuse, no explanation, no—"

"You're not me." Annie's voice was deflated hiss. She put the helmet down into the low bucket of the sidecar. Her eyes found a spot on the far wall of the garage, past Helen's ear.

Unable to barricade the legion of her regret, Helen kept talking. "—way in a million years I thought that something that...stupid...that sickening could come out of my mouth, I—"

"Stop." Annie clung to her refusal to acknowledge the tears that dotted her cheeks and made tiny, irregular splotches on the concrete floor. Her voice wheezed as she counted breaths, two-by-two. "Not. About. You."

Relieved by and afraid of the interruption, Helen inspected her nails. The glossy fuchsia arch on every tip matched her motorcycle helmet perfectly; her eyes bounced between the two accusations of argent color. *She was thinking of me.* Internal recrimination replaced spoken remorse. *She's always thinking of me. This past year, with Nathan, with Marissa, she...*

Love is not always patient, or kind. Love's power is not in its appeal to gentle abstractions, but in its concrete effects. Love is a skein of clashing strands, in an untidy flux of winding and unraveling. Every interaction among those wrapped up in its self-obsessed spring is a relentless battle.

Closer to one's beloved, or ever further away? The clichéd tender moment of complete entanglement, a nexus of total understanding, unravels in the reality of two or more separate bodies, hearts, and voices trying to find a place to stand together against the world.

"That life." Annie edged towards her thoughts, as though reaching to cup a baby bird that had fallen out of a nest. "That life I had before, it doesn't live in my past. Not to me."

Helen held her breath, wondering about the border between unforgiven and unforgivable. She had no idea which side she was on, or how porous the wall might be. Gulping the plea that threatened to spew into the silence, she waited.

Annie cleared her throat and scraped the rough leather of her sleeve across her flushed face. Standing with the motorcycle between them, the women risked eye contact. Helen broke away first, and Annie tracked her wife's wide jawline.

"I got this!" The sound of a hurried voice in the lobby and the arrival of another guest's car down the driveway intervened. Mercifully, the man who appeared to wrangle the keys from the driver with the usual exchange of small talk was not the same one whom Helen had intimidated into retreat.

Both the hotel employee and the young couple who poured out of their car with luggage enough to engulf the proffered trolley ignored the women. The woman stopped the string of chatter on her mobile long enough to dig out a five-dollar bill and hand it over with an empty smile before heading in first.

Grateful for the distraction, Helen risked another glance at her wife. Annie exhaled, walked around the motorcycle, and put her arms around Helen. "Could be worse." She stifled a half-sob. "What happened to me out there in the desert will never be over, Helen. But it could be worse. Now could be then."

Helen hugged Annie around the waist and pressed her face into the studs. She welcomed the insistent tingle of minor discomfort and held her position, fumbling with more useless (but necessary) words. "Never do anything to hurt you. Not in a million years."

Because it was her prerogative, Annie led them out of the dark. She tried on humor, shaking her whole body like a wet dog. "Anyway, the screw this. I'm calling it a win."

Helen's disbelief bled over both of them, and Annie's laugh rumbled. "Because you know, after this, you damn well owe me."

"Hell, yeah." Helen felt her hesitation drown in relief, but the nagging need for additional penance kept her mouth moving. "This and more, Annie. Anything you want, I promise I'll—"

Annie twisted her carbon fiber sphere onto her head, handed Helen the other helmet, and pointed to the sidecar with a tired smile. "Shut up and get in. I know where we're going."

It was only an hour after dawn when Annie swung

her leg over the bike and Helen double-checked the canvas lap belt that secured her in the low, three-wheeled accessory.

Grinning, Annie rocked the vehicle side-to-side and watched Helen brace her legs and grip the plastic handles mounted on the inside of her pod. Annie raised both arms above her head. "Steady as a rock, see? You're basically sitting in a giant tricycle. How scared could you possibly be?"

Helen, who had shut her eyes against the see-saw motion, risked a glance. "I'm not going to say you don't deserve to enjoy this, but give a girl a break, okay?"

The balance of their relationship restored, Annie conceded the point. She reached down to squeeze Helen's hand. "You're safe with me. Cross my heart."

She flipped down her visor, motioned to her wife to do the same, and eased the motorcycle into traffic. Through the headphones, Helen heard Annie's exultant, "Yes!" as they took the first corner at a green light and followed signs out of the city.

The dense blocks of urban development gave way to low adobe suburbs and strip malls before finally surrendering to what, under Helen's city scrutiny, was wilderness. Annie scanned the low brush and imposing saguaro. They passed half a dozen decaying farmhouses like the ones that had been offered as salvation a lifetime ago, and with every skeleton of decrepit habitation Annie sucked in her breath and forced her attention back to the road. Helen caught herself humming an old country song about beer and dirty dancing. She stopped when Annie didn't join in the chorus and listened instead to the dull wash of the wind in her ears. Glancing up, Helen felt the open sky press down on her whole body, and she breathed deeply, trying to welcome the weight.

Annie had mapped out this route in her mind in too many nightmares to count. As she turned left at the open rural crossroads, the rusty sky and slanted sunlight met in her memory, and she squeezed the handlebars until her wrists ached. The full span above her, still cold blue at the apex and banded by a rainbow of oranges and reds, competed for grandeur with open space ahead and the crest of Catalina State Park's hills to the east. There was no one else on the road on that early Thursday morning. The asphalt river wobbled over the horizon, and Annie counted the miles by markers along the verge. Forty-five minutes out of Tucson. Cape Cod felt like another planet, let alone another life.

"Let's take a break. Almost there." Annie's voice knocked.

Helen jumped at the unexpected noise. She half-nodded before remembering that Annie could not see her and tapped the microphone at her lips before speaking softly. "Whatever you need."

Annie's biting snarl caught them both by surprise. She slowed the bike, pulling in to a turn-around with a squeal and a low arc of crunching gravel. Helen held herself stiff against the jerk and was first to pry off her helmet. She put it in her lap and blinked cooling sweat out of her eyes as Annie turned off the motorcycle and flipped up her visor.

Neither made a move to get off or out. Annie nodded to herself and twisted her body to stretch out muscles that hadn't been used in twenty years. She breathed in the air that tasted like musk and sage even without rain and stared at the purple clusters of Gooding's verbena that grew along the side of the road. *Good and ready.* The words echoed in a dead voice inside Annie's thoughts. It was only half of one of Amanda's endless staple of botanical jokes, but the reminder was enough to set the survivor's teeth chattering with a sudden internal chill. Annie shook her head. She could not look at Helen. *Not yet.*

The better part of discretion is not valor, but practice. Helen Gilbert-Jones had never loved someone as self-contained as her Annie, never before had the opportunity to hone the skill of wait and wonder. If she wanted to know something, she asked outright. But even a year can be a lifetime of learning, done right, and Helen had had enough self-reflection and opportunity to moderate her extroversion when her mate needed it most. Annie needed it now. Helen sat, quiet but not still, tapping her boot lightly against the inside hull of the sidecar.

"Three, three-and-half miles max, that way." Tugging off her helmet and smoothing her rough-cut, blue-tipped hair, Annie pointed ahead as the road curved to the left. "There's a rusted out double-wide trailer off to the right. I remember."

She closed her eyes against the snapped image and settled back in the saddle. "Maddie says it's still there, says the owner of the land keeps promising to remodel it. Anyway. Landmark." Sighing, Annie climbed off the bike and stood facing the mountains.

Helen saw her opportunity. She clambered out, leaning heavily on the sidecar's frame and kicking up dust as she landed awkwardly. "This thing's made for short people," she said lightly. "Next time, you ride shotgun and see how you like your kneecaps under your chin."

When Annie didn't reply, her wife stood next to her and interlaced their fingers. The bulky gloves made the position uncomfortable, but they clung tightly to one another.

"Gorgeous doesn't cut it," Helen said as the sun breached the summit of the hills and sent crystals of light bouncing down the slope. She held the line on shallow conversation, trusting Annie to take it deeper when she was ready.

Without moving her body, Annie pivoted her head to face Helen. "I do, you know."

Helen bit her lip and nodded. "I know."

Neither padded the moment with more words. Neither had to. The two women standing in the new light of a desert day knew that Annie was talking about her need. She needed Helen's presence like a house needs a foundation, to hold up all that came afterwards between them, the careful construction of something new, plank by sandpapered plank. She needed Helen to steady her and to help her veer away from a sidewise slip into a past that might have been distant but would never be dim.

"I'm her here. Lydia." Annie's words sounded like confession. She tasted the name on her lips, and it felt like coming home to a house that had been ransacked. She put her hand to her throat.

"Of course you are, love." Helen kissed her cheek. "Lydia. Diane. You're both of those women, everywhere. All the time. And Lydia never loved or grieved more than out here, in the desert, on that awful night."

Annie's eyes carried the weight of doubt, cowardice, and loss. Helen held her gaze and nodded steadily. "The one that ran away, and the one you ran to become. Lydia to Diane and ...you."

"Lydia died here. She has to have died with them, or else what have I been doing all this time staring at the sea?"

Helen rubbed her sore eyes, knowing the tears that threatened were not hers to cry. "You tried to leave her out here. The way that Amanda and Theo left you. But you never left them, Annie. You carried Amanda and your baby with you. Through Diane. To me."

They hadn't seen another vehicle since the outskirts of Tucson, until a quarter mile from their first destination of the day. Even with their helmets on, they both heard the noise. Helen craned her neck to see over the plexiglass windshield of the sidecar. Annie squinted into the long shadows, trying to make out what was coming towards them. As they got closer, she saw a black Corvette convertible roar full throttle past an ambling truck loaded up with chickens.

Annie slowed down, and the driver of the Corvette ducked into his own lane before waving them a thanks and speeding by. The truck driver tipped his hat as he ambled past them, a thick wash of exhaust trailing behind.

A few minutes later, Annie slowed to twenty miles an hour. Her voice sounded as though she was a million miles instead of two feet away. "I think I—"

She pulled over without another word. This time, she leaped off the motorcycle, ripped off her helmet, and slammed it into the dirt. Annie let out a primal scream, her arms wrapped around her body, and felt to one knee.

Helen was at her wife's side before Annie toppled over and lay sobbing, her body sprawled halfway on the shoulder and halfway on the blacktop. Without a word, Helen pulled Annie to her feet and they lurched further off the road before she set down the weeping woman.

When Helen tried to move away, to give Annie whatever space she needed, Annie grabbed her hand. "Stay."

The sun found its legs and strutted over the hills, dragging relentless blue sky across the desert scrub. Annie wept for an hour or more, Helen cross-legged next to her, until the tears were more memory-soaked than fueled by impotence.

Seventy-three feet. After the phone call, after the blubbering and the disbelief and the quiet static of a conversation where neither party on the end of the line knew how to hang up or begin again, before their face-to-face meeting at the police station, Annie had read Officer Lewis' emailed notes. Three paragraphs of cop speak, with a red stamp 'CLOSED' over half a page, of where, how, and when the body had been found. She had spent a whole career estimating distances and calculating trajectories for a living: Annie didn't need a measuring tape to pinpoint the spot across the knee-high beige grass. *A hundred steps.*

She glanced at the ghost of the car wreck, invisible to everyone in the world but her, and imagined the woman stumbling, injured but determined, across the uneven ground of the brush. *Thank you. Thank you for trying to save my family.* Not a prayer. An acknowledgment of gratitude, and a surrender of the acrid rage that had consumed so many of Lydia's sleepless nights while she daydreamed Diane, until Helen came along and they both met Annie.

Annie wiped her nose on the sleeve of her leather jacket and stood up. "This part's me."

Helen nodded without a word.

She had marked the exact location with an absurdly jaunty blue flag on the map on her phone. Annie walked stiffly to the edge of the gravel. Within ten feet, the sparse tussocks overlaid on rough brown dirt gave way to snarls of clumped, knee-high grass. Even through her thick boots, Annie could feel the tentacles of the hummocks wrapping themselves around her feet and up her calves. Wishing she had thought to grab a stick to steady herself, Annie hop-stepped her way across the rough terrain.

Within thirty feet of the road, the air and the sound shifted. The sky overhead began to press down, until Annie felt as though her eyes were bulging from their sockets and her ears might pop. The rumble of rare traffic gave way to a silence that made her skin itch, and Annie twisted her neck over her left shoulder. A sudden breeze blew grit into her face and she shielded it with her free hand. She could see the chrome handlebars of the motorcycle and the monolith of her wife's quiet vigilance as Helen stood facing away, cut off at the waist by the slight slope of fibrous ground cover.

"Helen?" Her voice bled over the short distance, louder than Annie intended. The wind refused to carry the plea for reassurance; Helen stood motionless against the tawny dome of the hills beyond and the empty azure above.

Annie took a deep breath in through her nose and coughed as the cool air scraped her throat. She watched the still figure on the other side of the world, sending out an invisible line to tether her to a life as precious as it seemed ephemeral, but she did not call out again.

Dark. Cold. Danger. How far? How long? Annie clenched her eyes shut and bit the inside of her check until she tasted a trickle of rust. Holding both arms out crookedly like a fledgling's bent wings, Annie slid her good foot forward until her toe met the first obstacle. She allowed one eye to flutter open, snapping it shut at the glare. Wobbling on her weak leg, Annie transferred her weight and took a few hesitant steps, moving like an ice skater in a blizzard. The ground fought her, wrenching her gait off-kilter and sprouting hurdles and snares with every laborious stride. Her muscles screeched with the effort of keeping her torso upright without the benefit of sight, and her mind tapered its attention to the slow progress measured in stumbling inches instead of confident strides.

Annie thought she was ready for the fall. She was not. Betrayed by her lagging leg, her boot tangled in the coarse vegetation and a missed dip, she went down in a splayed lunge, hip to knee to ankle. *Helpless. Then and now.* Although she only held the pose for a moment before wrenching herself onto two hands and pressing into a mangled standing position, Annie felt the terror of emotional paralysis mutate into the horror of physical immobility.

Thirty feet forward, eight feet to the left. She heard Helen's proffered escape route from earlier in the day in her head. *Don't have to, Annie. Maybe you've come far enough.* Annie risked everything with another glance at safe harbor. The anchor of a reconstructed life had not moved from her position. Oblivious, Helen held steady. Grateful for the inattention and its provenance, Annie allowed three tears to wet the treacherous ground before shaking her head and reorienting herself to the western horizon.

After a moment, Annie returned her attention to the map. She focused on her feet, willing them along the invisible laser line. Another twenty paces found her at the edge of what had been the construction site, with upturned earth along a straight track running parallel to the road. Annie paused, allowing her eyes to pin down the disturbance until it disappeared to the north and south.

Her eyes jerked upward at the *kek-kek-kek* of a low-flying Cooper's hawk, it's salmon-colored underbelly a band of pink against the cobalt span. The smooth arc of the bird's flight slowed Annie's hammering heart. She granted herself an interval of delusion, allowing her mind to hear Amanda's bright enthusiasm for the sighting as a welcome replacement for Annie's darkening dread. She felt the seismic rumble of self-deception as real as though a tremor had rippled under her feet. Reality's juxtaposition of past revisited and cherished present ping-ponged between Lydia's devastation and Annie's earned optimism, with a blurred diversion through Diane's two decades of fugue.

Annie stepped over the bare mound. Another ten feet straight ahead found her at the rim of a crevice too narrow for a hand. She shoved her phone into her jacket pocket with her standard favor to the right hip, allowing her fingers to brush the rough stone. The sun caught glints of quartz and mica embedded in the dirt and shone into Annie's wet eyes, sparking diamond bands along the edge of the channel. She transferred more weight to her hands, wincing as the uneven surface scratched her skin.

Crab-crawling sideways along the widening gap, Annie approached ground zero. Her engineer's easy habit of calculating distance and trajectory offered no quarter from the alarm of proximity; she knew exactly how far she had come and how far still to go. The inevitable countdown surprised her anyway. *Six. Five. Four.*

With three feet until the coordinates of one stranger's unheralded compassion collided with Lydia's lived desolation and Diane's denial, Annie rose without shunting her eyes from the site of recent forensic investigation. The grass was trampled and two leftover stakes from the police tape marked the ten-foot diagonal tangent of the location. *The body. Her body.*

Annie counted her breaths. She peered into the gully, wondering if it was this boulder on the near lip or that one in the corner that had cradled the stranger's crushed skull. She telescoped her vision, trying to determine about angles and point of origin. She tasted more blood in her mouth, pressed her thumb into her hip, and glanced at Helen in the middle distance, two lifetimes away.

Since that phone call, in the repetitive days of early waking, in the hours of sitting alone in the olive wingback armchair in their living room, Annie had mapped out her emotions of this moment. Determined to control the uncontrollable, she had categorized them by intensity and source, the demarcations clearer than either necessary or possible. *Anger, disappointment, confusion, gratitude, disgust, guilt.* She had not anticipated the feeling that swamped her in the moment her gaze found and held the oval cocoon. The scooped earth was smooth and deep, its secret turned out, the absent stranger who had tried to do what Lydia could not released into a brave new world.

Relief. Adrenalin had locked Annie's arm, leg, jaw and back muscles into a rank imitation of rigor. The release of the unexpected turned her scaffold to mud: viscous, thick, unstable. The moment before she fell again, Annie willed her legs into rods as the rest of her body trembled and throbbed. *Relief.*

For the first time, with every neuron cleaving to every other inside her cluttered brain, Annie knew she had not imagined the woman at the window. Her knowledge was titanium, not kryptonite. Someone else had also done all she could to save Amanda and Theo; someone other than Lydia, whose memory of being trapped and helpless would always be a wildfire. Someone else had stepped in, stepped out and stepped through an irretrievable doorway for humanity and love, and still it had not been enough.

Annie rubbed her hands together and wedged a finger and thumb into her pocket, feeling around until she heard rather than felt the crinkle of a plastic bag. She cupped the package as though she might drink it, holding the opaque cargo of ash and bone up close to her face. *Love.*

The knot was impossible. *Shit.* Annie swore to herself and pushed a finger through the film, feeling the sandy texture of what had once been her future under one nail. She poured a palmful of Amanda and Theo and watched a few loose grains fly into the slight wind. Crouching with her good leg with the other at a right angle, the survivor turned her hand face down and patted off the dust against the side of the shallow gully. *Found them, see? You found them, and someone found you.*

At the edge of another world, Helen wanted to watch her wife high-tread through the treacherous grass. She wanted to hold her up. She wanted to go along. The hush of a cemetery overruled her curiosity and care. Helen was a part of everything now, and nothing then. She held the timeline in her hands like a cracked geode, willing it whole, and knowing it would never be. She kept her eyes on the road. She sang a lullaby. She visited her own demons in soft sepia tones, as neutrally as she could, fighting the urge to chase them into the light. She kept vigil for Annie.

Annie stayed by the stranger's grave, carefully brushing every kernel from her hand, for another fifteen minutes. She did not say goodbye to anyone as she left, leaving drifting particles like breadcrumbs by trailing one hand behind her in the breeze, letting her first family rest in the grass. By the roadside, a few breaths from Helen's own solitary observance, Annie drizzled the last of Amanda and Theo's remains directly on the spot where her girlfriend had bled to death, and her son had yet to take his first breath. She watched the slate-colored fragments land in the gravel and disappear without leaving a scar on the ground. She turned away.

"It's done." Annie stared at her receding path in the grass.

Helen pivoted to face her wife, limbs stiff from standing guard. She joined Annie, leaning in until their shoulders touched. She defended the silence. Annie swigged water from a bottle in the sidecar's front pocket. "Nothing more here for anyone, babe. Let's go."

The scene of the accident released them to the road. With the sun's warmth soaking into their leather gear and

Annie's jazzy soundtrack jittering through their helmets' speakers, Annie headed north east into Catalina State Park. The lone Cooper's hawk danced infinity symbols on currents unpredictable and scarce.

Cape Cod (September 2020)

"Still takes too damn long to get to school."

Marissa frowned. "Nathan, language!"

Her son growled. "Doesn't make it any less damn far. Seriously, an hour each way in the car? I'm wasting half my life in the back seat!"

Watching him with a concoction of pride and exasperation, Marissa handed him a paper bag. "You already know that our apartment in Broadwell makes sense despite the distance. No chance of being left stranded if you've got three chauffeurs instead of one—four when Jason's got the afternoon off."

Marissa added the last bit mostly to herself. "Your friends should be so lucky, having all of these adults who care."

Nathan stuck out his tongue, but a half-smile replaced the scowl.

She counted on her fingers. "Three sandwiches, apple, banana, potato chips, and five bucks in case you think you might starve to death between lunch and last period. Annie's got the usual pile of snacks in her car."

He rolled his eyes and stuffed the bag into his backpack. "Thanks."

Marissa buttered her English muffin, tore off a scrap

of paper towel and picked up an envelope wrapped in Christmas paper. "Besides—I've got something for you."

Nathan laughed at the gift. He was silent as he tore it open. The boy's eyes shone. "But you said—"

With a shrug, Marissa mimed capitulation. "*I* said you'd have to wait until you were seventeen, had a job, and could pay for half of driver's ed yourself."

Marissa smiled. "But we've been talking this week, and Jason convinced me that I was the worst mother on the planet—that holding this over your head pretty much defined 'cruel and unusual' in the scheme of teenage punishment."

Laughing at the mention of his mother's boyfriend, Nathan pumped one fist in the air. "Yes! I knew he was a keeper even before he moved in!"

His mom peered at him, eyebrows raised and teeth showing. "Funny you should say that, Nathan. There's a little something else I need to tell you. Something…wonderful."

Cape Cod (November 2020)

Annie and Nathan picked Roy up from Logan Airport. At his insistence, they did not park and wait for him in baggage claim, but drove around for half an hour until he shouted down the phone that he was curbside at Terminal A.

Annie saw his ginger frizz and giggled. "There he is! Crazy man!"

She parked as close as possible to the man who should have been her father, hobbled out of the car, and embraced him as hard as she was willing to risk. After squeezing her even more tightly, his eyes wet and his smile halfway up his creased cheeks, Roy coiled around his cane and waved away her offer of an arm.

Nathan got out of the car and put out a hand in greeting. Roy stared at it. "Young man, in our family, reunions mean hugs."

The boy hesitated. Roy laughed, a sound that made Annie think of Amanda. "You'll have to excuse an old man, Nathan." Roy shook his hand. "Put her there, and apologies if I come across one bubble off plumb. Don't know whether to blame age or this damn jet lag. Long day."

Nathan shot an eyebrow at Annie. She laughed. "Roy, meet Nathan, my grandson. Nathan, meet Roy—and don't mind all the slang, you'll get used Tucson via Texas."

Suitcase stored in the trunk, Nathan started to climb in the back seat. Annie shook her head. "You drive."

Nathan swallowed his fear. "Damn straight I'll drive!"

Roy's guffaw joined the boy's, and Annie nodded to herself as she sat alone in the back seat. *Mission accomplished.*

On Thanksgiving morning, with the turkey timed for four hours and the sides ready to go in both ovens, the clan met up for a project Annie had been planning for months.

"No, you can't climb the ladder." Jason Stahl—forty-seven, twenty-two years sober, high school geometry teacher and newly-minted stepfather—tugged Marissa off the first rung and appealed to Annie. "Seriously, you'd think my lovely wife had forgotten altogether that we're nineteen weeks pregnant!"

Helen scrutinized at her son-in-law with mock horror, but she drove her point in tight. "We, Jason? Pray tell, kind sir, how is it that her uterus is suddenly common property? I'm betting you won't be up five times a night to pee because baby girl's elbows on your bladder!"

Jason kissed Marissa on the nose and took a step back, bowing to Helen. "Touché, Mom." They both nodded at the sound of the label. Helen tasted the word in her head. *Sounds about right. Best son-in-law I could have asked for.*

Turning his full attention to his expectant wife, Jason added, "Sometimes I forget we're two people. But I know you're always going to be the better half."

Marissa kissed him back and blushed. "Now, won't

someone give me a paintbrush? Baby's going to be here before the nursery is finished if we don't get this done."

The nursery in the three-bedroom in a manicured townhouse complex five minutes from the Tudor on the corner faced west. Shafts of slanted, late-autumn sunlight crept across the room.

Settling for a broad brush at chest height, Marissa filled in the outline of a green-and-gold fairy perched on a toadstool while Jason held the can of paint for her to dip and scrape.

Nathan and Roy shared chatter and masking tape as they outlined the door jamb for its new coat of powder blue.

Helen and Annie stood in the corner, drying brushes in hand, taking in the silver-and-purple swoop and slide that covered the two far walls of the room.

"We're here, Helen." Annie fluttered her fingers across her wife's palm. Neither needed to hold on. "We're all here."

In a fractal pattern of wide-open wings and torpedo bodies, a descent of dragons waited to welcome the baby who would come early on the last day of winter, in a town on the ocean, at the edge of an uncertain world.